WICKED ASCENDING

Claimed by Gargoyles Book 4

Wicked Ascending
Claimed by Gargoyles, Book Four
Copyright © 2022 by Sarah Piper
SarahPiperBooks.com

Published by Two Gnomes Media

Cover design by Luminescence Covers

VI

E-book ISBN: 978-1-948455-89-3
Paperback ISBN: 978-1-948455-90-9
Audiobook ISBN: 978-1-948455-91-6

BOOK SERIES BY SARAH PIPER

Reverse Harem Romance Series

Claimed by Gargoyles

The Witch's Monsters

Tarot Academy

The Witch's Rebels

M/F Romance Series

Vampire Royals of New York

GET CONNECTED!

I love connecting with readers! There are a few different ways you can keep in touch:

Email: sarah@sarahpiperbooks.com

TikTok: @sarahpiperbooks

Facebook group: Sarah Piper's Sassy Witches

Twitter: @sarahpiperbooks

Newsletter: Never miss a new release or a sale! Sign up for the VIP Readers Club:
sarahpiperbooks.com/readers-club

CHAPTER ONE

WESTLYN

You, my moon, may call me Father...

Verrick's cold, cruel voice slithers along my spine, and everything inside me recoils.

I exhale so sharply the chains wrapped around my midsection rattle. "No. You're not my... *No!*"

Denials gather on the tip of my tongue. A hundred. A thousand. But every one of them dies just as quickly as it forms.

Deep down in the darkest places of my heart, I know he speaks the truth. I knew who he was the moment he stepped out of the sacristy in all his fae finery, that cruel golden crown glittering atop his head.

All the mysteries, the magic, the runes, the nightmares... It all comes back to this. To *him*.

My father isn't just some dark fae noble who manipulated my mother into sleeping with him in Faerie.

He's the Wintermoon king. The evil, sadistic dark fae monster who slaughtered the families of the men I love and cursed them to become the immortal guardians of his precious portals, fated to watch the rest of their friends and allies die, their souls forever trapped in stone.

And I brought this beast to our realm with a spell. With magic I didn't even realize I possessed until last night.

> *Blood of my blood, my magic, my fire*
> *I call unto you, my king and my sire*
> *Return to this realm to claim what is ours*
> *By flame and by force, so shall we devour...*

The words echo through my memory, making my stomach churn.

Was it him all along? Pulling the strings behind the scenes, urging me to tap into my power, to push myself harder and harder to open the Codex, to discover its secrets?

Goddess. I spent my whole life allowing Brian and Eloise to manipulate me because I thought I had no magic. Now, I *have* magic—a good deal of it, apparently—and history seems determined to repeat itself.

No. I refuse to let it. I'm not some meek little girl anymore. I'm a dark fae witch, for fuck's sake.

I close my eyes, take a deep breath, and try to find that spark of magic inside me...

The rune on the back of my neck burns, but I don't feel

anything else. I open my eyes and look for a sign of that precious indigo light crackling across my palms, but there's nothing.

Just two useless hands roped to a chair.

"The longer you refuse to accept your legacy," King Verrick of Wintermoon says, the voice of my nightmares brought to horrifying life, "the more painful it will be when destiny finally calls upon you."

I hiss at him through gritted teeth. "My destiny is my *own.*"

"Is it?" he taunts. "Tell me. How did you come to be bound to a chair in this cathedral? Did you bring yourself here? Tie the ropes with your own hands?"

"No, I... I must've..." I close my eyes, reaching for the memories of last night. There was the dream, the woman from the Tarot card... A dark cauldron. A spell. The fire, and then—

"Destiny whispered in your ear," he says, "and you walked out into the darkness beyond the wards, straight into my waiting arms."

I open my eyes and spear him with a deadly glare. "And then what? You just called us an Uber and we zipped down to the city for father-daughter day?"

No response. Nothing but that cold, terrible grin.

Magic, then. More dark magic.

"Once I've re-established my rule in the human realm," he continues, unbothered by the litany of curses I unleash, "things will begin falling into place. I'll need someone to rule Wintermoon in my stead, of course, and—"

"Great! Take out an ad on Craigslist."

"I am unfamiliar with Craig and uninterested in his list, but even if he stood here now with a scroll of candidates as long as the aisle before me, it wouldn't be possible."

"Tough break for you, I guess."

"Only a Queen with Wintermoon blood may assume the throne." He puts a hand on either side of my chair and leans in close, dark eyes glittering. "And the power that comes with it."

A hint of that power brushes over my rune and down my spine, settling deep in my gut. I feel the call of it, a warm and steady pulse. An invitation.

In the black depths of his eyes, I see my future, and a tendril of desire unwinds inside me.

His crown on my head, my black-and-silver locks woven through it.

Throngs of fae subjects, bowing as they throw roses at my feet.

A gleaming white castle nestled among the highest snowcapped peaks, every room filled with riches beyond imagining.

And an immortal life devoid of warmth and love.

I tear my gaze away and shake my head. He's trying to use his thrall on me, but I'm not my mother. I won't fall so easily under his spell.

Verrick takes my chin between his thumb and finger, his touch gentle as he turns my face toward his once more.

I brace myself, waiting for him to put me under or curse me or yank me right out of this realm and into the depths of those icy mountains.

But he only grins as if he's the one holding all the secrets, then releases me and backs away.

"You must be famished, my moon. Dine with me." Verrick waves a hand, and a table draped in wine-colored cloth appears between us, along with an ornately carved wooden chair at his back. He sits down, and with another casual wave, a feast shimmers to life on the table—grilled meats and roasted vegetables, tiny boiled eggs no bigger than grapes, poached pears dusted with cardamom and cinnamon, terrines filled to the brim with succulent, fragrant sauces.

The ropes binding my wrists fall away, revealing the watch Rook gave me. Verrick must not have realized what it is, or he would've taken it. A spark of hope ignites inside. Maybe I can call them. Send them a text... something. I rub my wrists and try to surreptitiously tap it to life, but the thing is toast. Cracked screen, no juice.

Damn it. It's ruined.

I lower my hands to my lap and wait for the chains around my midsection to vanish as well, wondering how quickly I can grab a knife off the table and stab him with it before he realizes what's happening.

But the chains remain firmly in place.

So much for trust.

"What is all this?" I don't bother couching the suspicion in my voice.

"Our first meal together, little moon." Verrick unfolds a cloth napkin and places it in his lap, then reaches for his wine goblet. A matching one appears at my place, along with a fully loaded plate. "I've so much to tell you. To show you. We've got some mundane business to wrap up here this evening, but then I can take you home and—"

"Home?"

"To court." He sips his wine, then gestures at me with his fork. "Eat, Westlyn. You need to recover your strength. We've a long night ahead, and it's barely noon yet."

Barely noon. Dread sinks like a stone in my gut. The guys won't be awake for hours yet. They don't even know I'm gone. They don't even know the library is—

"No need to stand on ceremony," Verrick says with a forced smile. "Please. Eat."

Rage simmers inside. "Okay, first of all? I'm not a toddler. You missed the part of my childhood where you get to tell me what to do."

"That was... an unfortunate circumstance beyond my control." Something that looks a hell of a lot like regret flickers in his eyes. "Please. Allow me to make it up to you. Break bread with me. A fresh start to—"

"Sorry, pops. I'm vegan, so that's a hard pass on whatever carcasses you've magicked into existence here. As for the rest?" I fold my arms across my chest and sneer. "I'm allergic to... everything."

"You're allergic to *human* everything. Synthetic foods, chemicals. Your fae blood requires pure nourishment, but you can't get that here. *Everything* about this realm makes us unwell—the water, the soil, the very air. It wasn't always the case, but humans being what they are, they can't help but destroy the very things that grant them life. You'll see when we get home. You'll take one breath of Wintermoon air and feel..." He closes his eyes and inhales deeply, a smile gracing his lips like he's imagining himself rolling around naked in a sun-dappled meadow with flowers woven into his hair. "... positively invigorated."

"Hate to break into your little vision quest, your highness, but *this* is my home. New York City, planet earth, human realm. The only thing that *positively invigorates* me now is the thought of watching you wither and die here."

He scowls and glares at me again. "*This* is how you treat your father? Your flesh and blood? A king, no less? One whose greatest wish is to provide you with wonders untold and power you can't even begin to fathom?"

"Oh, where *are* my manners?" I laugh. "After you went to all the trouble of magically manipulating me, kidnapping me, drugging me, and chaining me to a chair!" I shake my head and press a hand to my chest like I just can't believe my own rudeness. "Goddess, who even raised me? Wolves?"

His highness is less than amused. "I gave you a mild fae sedative and restrained you out of an abundance of caution.

Trust is earned, little moon. If you want mine, I suggest you begin by treating my arrival with the respect and deference it deserves."

This guy is something else. No wonder Draegan led an army against him. I've known him all of fifteen minutes and I'm already imagining how satisfying it would feel to shove a grenade launcher up his dark-fae ass.

"You're right, *Father*," I say, forcing out a beatific smile. "Welcome to the Big Apple." Then, through clenched teeth, "I hope you fucking *choke* on it."

He arches an unnaturally elegant eyebrow and opens his mouth. To scold me? To threaten me? To cast another dark-fae spell and banish me to oblivion?

I'll never know, because at that exact moment, another voice shatters the intimacy of our little father-daughter brunch, shrill and stomach-churning and attached to the *last* person I need to deal with today.

Fucking Eloise.

CHAPTER TWO

WESTLYN

"Westlyn Patricia Avery!" Eloise shrieks as she barrels through the narthex doors and into the nave. "Thank the *darkness* you've finally decided to grace us with your presence."

In that moment, I'm glad I didn't touch the food. I would've gagged on it at the very sight of her.

She saunters down the aisle toward Verrick and me, head held high, hips swishing. Despite the show of confidence, she looks a lot worse than the last time I saw her. Her skin is pale, her hair unkempt. Dark circles line her eyes, and her clothing—a dark gray pantsuit with a cream-colored silk blouse—looks as though she slept in it.

"Your highness," she coos as she approaches the altar. "You're looking well."

Great. So they know each other. That... can't be good.

Verrick's fingers tighten around his fork, but he says nothing.

She bows her head slightly, her eyes remaining fixed on Verrick. Rather, on the golden crown atop his head.

Of *course* that's what she's after. For a social-climbing harpy, it doesn't get much better than dark-fae royalty. It wouldn't surprise me in the slightest if she was after the title of Wintermoon queen.

"I came as soon as I received your message," she continues. "I was so relieved to hear that Westlyn finally heeded my warnings and—"

"*Finally*, yes," he says smoothly. He sets down his fork and sips his wine, his gaze locked on mine even though he's speaking to her. "You assured me, shadow witch, that the binding ceremony would be completed weeks ago."

"Yes, well..." Eloise clears her throat and stands up straighter. "The girl was... less cooperative than we'd hoped. And her father—"

Verrick sets down the goblet hard, wine sloshing over the rim.

"I... beg your pardon," she says softly. "I was merely speaking of... of the man who raised her. He was supposed to—"

"Your excuses are tiresome, witch." Verrick extends a hand, and another chair appears at our table. "Sit."

"I..." Eloise hesitates. "Thank you, but I've only just eaten lunch. How about I wait for—"

"It was *not* an invitation."

Swallowing hard, she finally nods and totters up to the top of the altar, her breath quickening as she lowers herself into the offered seat.

She's doing her best to maintain her composure, but I know her well enough to see the cracks beneath the facade.

That bitch is terrified.

Verrick returns to his meal, taking several excruciatingly long bites of roasted quail and herbed parsnips before finally addressing her again. "Many years ago, I was assured by the Archmage himself, along with various other high-ranking members of his organization, that you could handle the task."

Eloise smooths her hands over her thighs. "I didn't anticipate the complications with—"

He holds up a hand, silencing her, then continues. "Instead of ushering my daughter into her great destiny, you took it upon yourself to finance her torture at the hands of childhood bullies. Through them, you abused and belittled her, wrung her out until she was little more than a shell of a girl with no access to her magic, fearful of her own shadow. You never even told her about the alliance, about the importance of her role in our—"

"I beg your pardon, highness," she says, a note of irritation creeping into her contrite tone, "but that's an unfair categorization. I was merely following your orders in preparing her for the ultimate sacrifice, just as the Forsythes prepared—"

I didn't even see him move, but suddenly Verrick is towering over her, sword drawn, blade held to her throat.

"On the ground," he commands.

"I... I'm s-sorry," she stammers, holding up her hands in surrender. "I meant no disrespect. I was—"

"*Now!*"

With a pathetic yelp, Eloise slides out of her chair and prostrates herself at his feet, a sniveling shell of the tyrant I once knew.

Despite my own dire circumstances, it's hard to keep the smug satisfaction from twisting my lips.

Oh, how the mighty have fallen...

He takes another step toward her and slides the tip of his sword beneath her chin, forcing her to look up at his imposing form.

"P-please," she whispers. "I was wrong to speak out of turn. Forgive me, highness."

Still chained to my chair, I have little choice but to watch this dark drama play out. Truthfully, though, I'm not sure I could look away even if I *did* have a choice.

Ever since my wedding night, I've fantasized about killing her.

Ever since she tried to kidnap me the night of the car crash, I've fantasized about making it *hurt*.

I wanted her to suffer. To die slowly at *my* command, either from my magic or the deep slice of one of Jude's blades, or even by my own hands wrapped snugly around her neck as Jude cheered me on from the sidelines, eager to carve up her bones.

Just like we killed the mages she paid to torture me.

But looking at her now, Verrick's blade gleaming in the afternoon light, all I can think is...

Do it. Just put that sword right through her fucking throat and end it...

I can almost hear her gurgled screams, almost smell the coppery tang of her blood pooling on the altar. I grab a fork from the table, my hand tightening around it as if I were holding the sword and sinking it into her flesh...

It's only when I hear Verrick's dark chuckle that I finally snap out of my fantasies and tear my gaze away from my stepmother's terrified eyes.

I have no idea how long I've been staring at her, but when I finally glance up at the fae king, I find him watching me intently, his lips tilting ever-so-slightly upward at the corners, eyes shimmering with a mixture of curiosity and pride.

"Perhaps I should let you do the honors, my moon," he says.

I tighten my grip on the fork, but remain silent.

Abandoning Eloise on the floor, Verrick crosses the altar to stand before me, his sword dangerously close. In a soft, almost soothing voice, he says, "The thought of executing her stirs something inside you. Something primal and dark and utterly, unshakably right."

I don't deny it. I *can't* deny it, because he's not wrong.

Far from it.

Again, the imagined scent of her blood wafts toward me, filling me with a sick pleasure I'm terrified to name.

Verrick fingers a lock of my hair, making me shiver. "Westlyn of Wintermoon. Was there ever any doubt that you were my child?"

Westlyn... of Wintermoon?

At this, I finally regain my senses. Jerking free of his grasp, I glower at him and say, "I don't doubt that I'm your biological offspring, Verrick. I just despise it."

The proud gleam in his eyes dulls a fraction, and he sighs. "Ah, well. I suppose that's to be expected. All children go through a rebellious phase, do they not?"

"This is no childish rebellion," I assure him. "You *disgust* me. The only reason you're even here is that you tricked me into hocus-pocusing you into existence."

Another dark chuckle. Another sigh. "You are as willful and fiery as your mother, and yet—"

"Do *not* speak about my—"

His sword is at my throat, freezing me in place. "Tell me, daughter. Does the idea of spilling the shadow witch's blood tempt you? Fill you with a sense of power that makes your nerves sing, your heartbeat quicken, your very life force hum with pleasure and possibility?"

I'm not sure if he actually expects an answer, but with his sword at my jugular, I don't dare move, not even to nod or draw a breath to speak.

"The sheer power of holding another being's fate in your

hands," he continues, "the simple brutality of a sword pressed to a helpless throat, the inexplicable joy of watching the light dim from the eyes of the unworthy... These images *intoxicate* you as surely as they intoxicate me..." His words fade into a seductive whisper, his sword biting into my skin.

A shuddering hiss escapes my lips, and I close my eyes, unable to hold his penetrating stare.

Unwilling to admit just how close to the bone those words actually cut.

A tear slips down my cheek as Verrick continues to peel back my layers and flay open the darkest parts of my heart, one unnerving declaration at a time.

Auggie believes I'm a good person, and he's partly right —I *have* been good. So far. But all it takes is one decision, one small action to put yourself on the other side of a line you *swore* you'd never cross, and then what? You draw a new line, a little farther out. Then you cross that one, too. Another line, another step, and... *Goddess.* I've already crossed all those lines. I freaking *obliterated* them the night I carved up those mages... and I enjoyed every second of it.

What if I *am* like my dark-fae father? Draegan told me the Wintermoon fae are the worst of the worst. And Wintermoon isn't just some trendy fashion choice like vintage punk or boho chic—something you can try on and discard at will.

It's a bloodline.

And maybe that bloodline is more a part of me than I want to admit.

"Dusk approaches, sire," a deep voice murmurs from somewhere behind Verrick, scattering my thoughts. "We need to make the preparations."

Verrick holds my gaze another beat, his cruel smile lingering, then finally slides the sword back into the scabbard at his hip. Turning toward the man behind him—one of the shadow mages, I now see—he says, "Help the woman to her feet and clean up the altar."

He does as the fae king asks, helping an unsteady Eloise to stand. She brushes the dirt from her suit, refusing to meet my eyes.

"And the girl?" the mage asks, nodding toward me with a look that says I'm last week's trash and he doesn't want to touch me.

"Put her in the sacristy," Verrick replies, and with a snap of his fingers, my chains vanish.

I try to bolt to my feet, but my legs collapse beneath me, and I fall right back into the chair.

Damn it.

"Give her another shot," Verrick says. "Only a half dose this time—just enough to calm her nerves and keep her still."

"No!" I shout. "No shots. I'm fine. I won't run. I'll—" Before I realize what's happening, the mage is jamming a needle into my neck. A sharp sting, then warmth floods my veins, and everything inside me turns as heavy as lead.

"What of the other prisoner?" the mage asks. "Should we relocate him?"

Prisoner? There's another prisoner?

I try to speak, but my lips are swollen, my throat tight, everything inside me shutting down.

"Yes!" Eloise practically shouts. Then, at Verrick's sharp glare, she lowers her head and says, "I mean, I think it's best to keep the prisoners separated, but—"

"But *what?*" Verrick asks, his voice as smooth as silk.

"But I... I defer to his highness in this and all matters, of course."

"Good choice. Now, luckily for my daughter, I'm not as merciless as you, *witch.*" Verrick's eyes glitter with anything *but* mercy as he turns to look at me once more. Then, through a grin as sharp and cold as his voice, "I think it's only fair we give them an opportunity to say goodbye."

Say goodbye?

Fear squeezes the last of the breath from my lungs. *Oh, goddess. No...*

It's not dark yet—the guys are still in their stone forms. There's no way Verrick would waste precious time and energy dragging them all the way here from upstate. Besides, he can't get to them—not physically. He can't cross Rook's protective wards. He indicated as much when he was taunting me earlier.

You walked out into the darkness beyond the wards, straight into my waiting arms...

It's a small comfort, but I can't imagine who else they could've captured.

"Who... who is the... other?" I finally manage, fighting

against the pull of oblivion as Verrick's drug works its way through my system. I can't pass out now. Not when I have no idea if I'll even be allowed to wake up again.

I focus on Verrick's cold, calculating gaze. On the mage's grip around my arm as he jerks me up out of the chair. At the faint smell of candle wax from the chandeliers overhead. But all of it is blurring together, my thoughts slowing, my tongue fat and useless in my mouth.

"I will see you in a few hours, my moon." Verrick touches my cheek, his tone suddenly kind. "Worry not. After tonight, everything will be different. You'll see." He leans in to kiss my cheek with ice-cold lips, and then he's gone, heading out through a plain wooden door behind the altar, waving for Eloise to follow.

She rushes to obey.

The mage drags me across the altar and into the sacristy, where he dumps me on my ass in front of the vestment cabinet and heads out without a second glance, locking the door behind him. I'm slumped against the hard wood of the cabinet, my legs stretched out before me, but I can't move them. Can't feel my arms. Can't even scream.

My head pounds against my skull, and all I want to do is fall into a dreamless sleep. But just before my eyelids flutter closed and the darkness sweeps me under, I catch sight of the man watching me from across the room, blood staining his shirt, tears staining his face.

"I'm... sorry," he chokes out. "I'm so, so sorry."

My mind has slowed to a crawl, my vision dark and

blurry, and I'm not even sure my heart is still beating. But through the fog, one thing is painfully clear.

The other prisoner isn't a gargoyle. Not even a glamoured one.

He's...

"Dad?" I whisper, because it's the only name I've ever called him.

And then the world goes black.

CHAPTER THREE

DRAEGAN

The gargoyles and I feel it before we see it—the kind of deep, dark dread that pools hot in the gut, nameless, yet nevertheless horrifying.

Still, when the sun finally sets over the grounds of Blackmoor and releases us from our stone prisons for the night, none of us is prepared for the brutal confirmation that we were not, in fact, trapped in a nightmare.

This terror is absolutely real.

Our senses awaken to a sky choked with thick, roiling smoke, ash floating in the air like the gentlest snow, Lucinda and Huxley circling us with frantic caws. The scent of burning wood is overpowering, and before my men and I so much as glance at one another, we leap from the manor rooftop and soar toward the glow of the strange fire.

Flames stretch into the sky, hungry and devastating. We land on the ground in front of the inferno, unbearable heat radiating from the strange fire—a fire that rages high, but hasn't moved beyond the structure it consumed.

It's so unexpected, so disconcerting, it takes me a full minute to realize what I'm actually looking at.

A pile of flaming ash where just last night the library stood in stately, quiet pride.

It's... gone. Just gone. All of it. The barn. The books. Rook's computer equipment and the loft and the damn Cerridwen Codex and—

"Westlyn," I say suddenly, my heart slamming against my ribcage. "Where is *Westlyn!*" It's not so much a question of her whereabouts as a command to find her, and in a single breath I'm charging back across the lawn to the manor, the others scattering behind me to scour the property.

The ravens are going mad with worry.

She wasn't in the library, I tell myself. *She had no reason to be out there. The sun has only just set. She's asleep in her bed, right where I left her after visiting her room last night.*

Right where I left her... Right where I left her...

I repeat the mantra in my mind a dozen times as I tear through the manor and up the stairs. I repeat it as I call out to her, again and again, with no response. I'm *still* repeating it when I open the door and step into her room and find it utterly empty, her scent everywhere, the shape of her impressed upon the mattress as if she's only just risen from sleep.

I can't seem to make myself breathe. To force my heart to beat. But then, after an impossibly long moment, it starts up again. And in the echo of it, amidst the eerie cacophony of squawking birds and the shouts of the other gargoyles searching the premises, an inexplicable void opens inside me.

Westlyn.

She's gone. Not in the bath, not tucked away in one of the other bedrooms. Just... gone. I know it as sure as I know the scent of her skin.

But... *no*. That's impossible. I was only just here with her... I came in to apologize after our argument last night, but found her asleep. I knelt beside her and ran my hand over her hair and she stirred, reaching for me, whispering my name as she tried to draw me close...

Sleep, little mortal, I told her. *Just sleep...*

I can almost see her here now, almost feel the warmth of her breath against my lips, but the bedding is ice cold beneath my touch. Beside the pillow, her fae amulet lies inert. I pluck it from the bed. It's as cold as the sheets.

Lucinda skims the air over my shoulder and lands on the headboard, pacing. Silent now as her black eyes lock on mine. She seems to be waiting for something from me—an answer to this terrible riddle. A promise that I know what to do. That I *will* find a way to fix this.

Whatever *this* is.

She caws at me, piercing and accusatory, and something inside me fractures. A tremor begins in my heart and radiates out through my limbs, my wings shuddering as pure darkness threatens to pull me under.

The last thing I said to Westlyn—the last thing she'll remember, anyway—was... nothing. After our dalliance in my bathroom, her cheeks still dark with desire, she'd looked into my eyes and asked me if I was ready to be fully honest with her. *Use your words,* she'd said. And I stared back into those endless turquoise depths and said... absolutely *nothing.* Not a single fucking word, and now she's gone and the fire rages outside and I—

The floorboards groan behind me, and I whirl around and grab the closest gargoyle by the throat.

Fucking. Jude.

"Where. The fuck. *Is she?*" I can barely speak through the blinding fury, the terror, the gnawing black pit in my chest, but I choke those words out and glare at him and wait and wait and fucking wait for an *eon,* and still, he has the gall to remain silent.

Not so much as a breath, not so much as a shove against my chest and a demand to release him.

Jude Hendrix. The gargoyle who never backs down from a fight. Who never lets a moment of silence pass without filling it with a threat or an inappropriate joke or some inane babble about blood and bones and violence.

"Jude, I..." I blink rapidly, trying to focus. Trying not to lose the last of my control.

I don't even know what I mean to say to him, only that I can't bear seeing him like this.

I release my grip on his throat and clamp a hand over his shoulder.

"I... can't," he finally whispers. His eyes are rimmed in red, muscles rigid and trembling beneath his gray skin. "She's not in the workshop or the kitchen or the study. She's just... I can't lose her, Draegan. I just fucking... can't."

The fear in his voice is fathomless and bleak and so unlike him it cuts me right to the fucking core.

This is really happening.

This is really *fucking* happening.

"No sign of her in the orchard or the darkroom," Augustine says, barreling up the stairs in a breathless rush. Rook trails behind him, laptop open and balanced on his hand as he frantically taps its keys.

"Tell me you've got something," I say to Rook, grateful that his mind has the ability to lock away fear and grief and the horror of his lost library so he can focus on this singular, all-important mission. "And tell me it's not evidence of our witch being anywhere *near* that fire."

"I'm pulling up the security footage now. Give me a minute—this thing is slower than the tablets, which are flaming goo at this point. I don't understand how it could've happened. Come on, come on... There it is. Hang on." He hits a few more buttons, the screen a blurry reflection in his glasses.

"Well?" I demand.

"Wait. That's..." His words trail into a shocked whisper. "Oh, fuck. No... How the fuck... no. No!"

"Who's responsible for this?"

No response but the paling of his skin, his head shaking in disbelief.

"Damn it, Rook. I need to know who did this. They took Westlyn. They bloody *took* her. They've probably got her stashed away somewhere right now, very possibly hurt, and we're standing around with our dicks in our hands trying to... *Fuck!*" I'm out of my mind with it, barely holding on as the walls seem to close in around us. I snatch the laptop from his hands, but in my haste I accidentally turn off the video. "Which of our enemies *dared* to steal her from her bed while she slept? Tell me, so I can—"

"Draegan," he finally says, his eyes flicking up to meet mine. The horror there is just... it's as indescribable as Jude's silent fear. "They didn't take her from her bed. She... she was there. She walked out of the house and straight into the library this morning."

My world shrinks. Darkens. Dies.

The library. The pile of smoldering ash and flame. It... cannot be.

I fall to my knees, nearly dropping the laptop. Rook saves it at the last second.

"Wait," he says. "There's more. We need to see the rest. We need to see what happened."

CHAPTER FOUR
WESTLYN

I don't know how long I'm unconscious this time, but when I finally wake up, I'm still in the sacristy. I'm lying on my side, my entire body aches, and my head feels like it's full of angry hornets... but I suppose that's better than being completely numb and conked out, vulnerable to who knows what.

Goddess. Why am I even here? What the hell does Verrick want with me?

With great effort and a lot of huffing and puffing, I drag myself into a sitting position. It takes nearly all my energy, and my legs are still numb. Glancing around, I try to get my bearings.

That's when I feel his gaze on me, the sound of his wheezing breath cutting through the fog in my mind.

I look up to find my father—Brian—watching me. He's bound to one of the bishop's chairs, roped and chained like I was. Unlike me, however, he took a serious beating. Black blood has dried on his swollen face. His shirt is stained and torn, knuckles split like he put up a fight.

"Westlyn?" he asks, his voice cracking under the strain—or maybe the guilt.

A storm of conflicting emotions erupts inside me—relief that he's alive. Gratitude for the small comfort of a familiar face.

But mostly? Anger.

He tried to sell me off to a demon prince. No matter that Eloise is clearly his enemy now, I can't let myself forget how this all started.

Ever.

"Why are you *here*?" I grind out, grateful I can actually speak.

He flinches at my words, at the obvious hatred in my voice, and closes his eyes, hanging his head in shame or avoidance. Maybe both.

He's silent for such a long time, I doubt he's going to speak to me again at all. But then, finally, he says, "I'm here —we're *both* here—because I failed."

I nearly laugh at the feigned regret in his voice.

Am I supposed to feel sorry for him?

"Oh, you failed!" I scoff. "Right. Failed to deliver me into the hands of your demon-worshipping mage cult so they could bind my life to a prince of hell and usher in the end of the world. No wonder they've got you chained up.

They must be so disappointed in you, *Dad*. Well, we've got that in common at least."

Tears blur and burn, but even if I could lift my arms, I wouldn't bother dashing them away. I welcome them. They remind me *exactly* who this man is. Exactly what he did to me.

"You were supposed to protect me." I don't even mean to say the words out loud, but there they are. The ugliest part of this truth between us.

Genetics aside, Brian Avery was my father. He was supposed to look out for me. To do everything in his power to keep me safe, not trade me away to the monsters the moment that power ran dry.

When he finally deigns to meet my gaze, tears streak his face, too.

If that man has ever cried in front of me before, I can't remember it now, and the sight of it lances my heart.

Despite my best efforts to hate him, some part of me actually feels sorry for him.

Something went off the rails in his life—a great many somethings. Happy, content people don't just wake up one day, join an evil cult, and make plans to sell their kid off to a demon prince.

Even if I wasn't really his kid to begin with.

"You don't understand," he says. Soft. Broken. "It wasn't the mages I failed. It... it was your mother. It was you, sweet girl. I failed you. And that has already become my biggest regret."

The admission is the closest thing I've ever gotten to any acknowledgment that his parenting was less than stellar, and part of me wants to forgive him, instantly and completely.

But that's just the ridiculously immature response of a love-starved child still longing for the approval of a father who could never be bothered.

"It's a little late for self-reflection now, Dad," I say. "I mean, Brian. *Goddess*, I don't even know what to call you anymore."

"You found the letters, then."

"And the amulet, for all the good it did."

"That amulet likely protected you from the worst of Verrick's influence and allowed you to tap into your fae magic without having it take over your mind. It was crafted by a fae witch from the Summerdale Court—and at a great, great cost. It's very likely the reason you're still alive even after summoning the fae king."

"No. My gar—" I cut myself off, not wanting to explain the gargoyles' otherworldly presence in my life. I don't owe him that. I don't owe him *anything*. So instead, I say, "My friends are the reason I'm alive. Because unlike you, they actually care about me."

I hate the resentment in my voice. It reminds me of Eloise, and I know it's hurting him. But I can't waver. The best defense is a good offense, and if I let my guard down even for a moment, Brian will find the words to make this all right.

And I can't let that happen. This can never be all right. What he did to me... It's unforgivable.

"My mother would be ashamed of you," I bite out, ignoring the twinge in my heart when I hear him suck in a pained breath. "But I get it now—why you kept me at arm's length all those years. Why it was so easy for you to hand me over to the Forsythes. You couldn't punish her for the affair because she died, so you took it all out on me instead. And why not? I was born inept, and another man fathered me. You had no reason to protect me. No reason to—"

"That's *enough*," he snaps, some new fire igniting inside him. "A great many terrible things have happened to you, and yes, I'm absolutely to blame for most of them. But you are wrong about your mother and wrong about my feelings for you. When it comes to protecting you, I had the *only* reason that matters—love. I loved your mother, and I loved you."

"But how? She cheated on you! I'm not even yours! I'm..." I close my eyes and lower my head, the rune on the back of my neck burning as if it can sense my resentment. "I'm *his*. A child of Wintermoon. As dark and vile as Zorakkov himself."

The anger fizzles out of Brian as quickly as it reared its fiery head, and when I glance up at him again, his eyes hold only longing and regret. "You're nothing like the demon, Westlyn. And no, your mother never cheated on me. Goddess, what happened between us... It was so much more complicated and beautiful than that."

"Explain."

"Madison and I were best friends in high school," he says, "but the truth is, I was always in love with her. She knew it, too—neither of us had ever bothered to pretend otherwise. But she didn't feel that way about me, and she was absolutely clear on that. I accepted it. It didn't change how I felt about her, but I accepted it. Knowing where she stood on the matter, I never pushed her for more. Never tried to change her mind or win her over like some reward for a good effort. I think that's why we were able to remain friends."

"But... she married you. She left me in your care. I know she eventually fell in love with Verrick, but... surely she *felt* something for you. Otherwise why did she marry you in the first place? Why did you marry *her*?"

"The answer to both of those questions is the same." He catches my gaze again, and a sad smile touches his lips. "For you, Westlyn."

"I... don't understand. I wasn't even..." *Yours*, I almost say again. But he doesn't need the reminder.

Brian nods. "That never mattered to me. I don't expect you to believe me or to even understand, but I truly loved your mother. All of her. You were just another part of her. A part she loved with her entire being from the moment she realized you existed. How could I not love you too?"

Tears glaze his eyes, and that sets me off all over again.

Love? How dare he throw around that word. Does he have any idea what it even means?

"Apparently, you loved the gaming tables a little more," I snap. "So let's say we skip the father-daughter trip down memory lane and—"

"It was a ruse, West. Every casino or racetrack I ever set foot in, every bet I ever placed, every card I turned over was all part of the plan your mother and I set in motion the moment she returned from Faerie and realized she was pregnant."

My head is still throbbing from the fae drugs they stuck me with, my limbs useless, and Brian's confusing words are making everything worse. I don't even know how to respond to him anymore—what questions to ask, what to deny, what to demand.

Whether I should even care.

So instead, I close my mouth. Lean back against the cabinet. And wait for him to shine a light on the dark secrets that have haunted my existence since the moment Verrick and my mother danced at a royal ball and rolled around in a moonlit Faerie field.

CHAPTER FIVE

WESTLYN

"She was missing for months," Brian says. "I was a wreck, but deep down, I knew what'd happened. Your mother was a powerful witch, but she never quite fit in among the magical circles around us. She'd been dabbling in fae magic for a long time, experimenting with new spells, dangerous rituals. She was utterly obsessed with connecting with the fair folk—no one could talk her out of it. She'd been venturing out alone more often, staying out until all hours, heading off on retreats upstate to find the most isolated spots in the woods for her casting. But she always checked in with me within a day or two, never more than that." He exhales, his head shaking. "Four nights passed. Then five, and I knew it'd finally happened. She'd gone to Faerie, like she always wanted, and I had little choice but to just... wait. To hope she'd actually come back home."

My mother had said as much in her diaries, but hearing

it now, from the perspective of someone who cared about her... Goddess. I can't even imagine what that must've been like. The worry. The fear.

It's probably a lot like what the guys are feeling right now.

I take a deep breath, trying to keep my own worries at bay.

They have each other, I remind myself. *Whatever happens, they're not alone in this.*

"Three and a half months after I'd last seen her," Brian continues, "Madison waltzed into my apartment for dinner one night, acting as if she'd only been gone a few days. She truly believed it, West. She had no concept of the days she'd lost. When I told her how much time had passed, she was absolutely beside herself. She knew she'd been tricked—in more ways than one."

"What do you mean?"

"It wasn't long after that when she realized she was pregnant."

He tells me the story as my mother relayed it to him, rehashing a lot of what I'd already read in the diaries, smoothing out some of the rough edges.

It can't be easy for him, reliving all of this. But to his credit, he doesn't hold back.

"You were conceived from your mother's endless love," Brian says, "but you were also conceived from your father's endless deceit. From the moment she returned to me and awoke from her Faerie-induced stupor, your mother understood what kind of fae Verrick was, even if she still had a hard time resisting his charms. She didn't know exactly how Verrick's threats against you would manifest—only that they would. She was utterly terrified. All she wanted to do was keep you safe."

"So she asked you for help," I surmise.

"She didn't have to ask, West. Maddie was my world. I loved her. A deep, profound love that went beyond all else. There was and continues to be nothing I wouldn't do for her, *or* for her child."

Ignoring the surge of affection shining in his eyes, I say, "So you married her and agreed to pretend to be her baby daddy?"

"That was just part of it, but yes. It wouldn't fool Verrick, of course, but we thought it might buy us a bit of time in the human realm. We had no idea whether he'd gotten to anyone else in our world, no idea who might be working for him. We needed time to figure things out. To devise a plan that would keep you safe from him."

"I see. So you agreed to marry a woman who didn't love you back and raise her daughter as your own all to protect her from a fae king, only to turn around and pawn her off to a demon prince instead?"

The anger is back, churning up all that bitterness again.

Damn it. I need to move. To work off some of this excess rage before I start dreaming of clawing my own eyes out. Or his.

"Westlyn, no. No, it wasn't—"

I shake my head, cutting him off. Right now, it's taking all of my concentration just to try to feel something in my arms and legs. For a brief instant, there's a slight tingling in my foot, a twitch, but... that's all I've got. I can't even curl my fingers into my palms.

I lean back against the vestment cabinet, biting back a string of curses. Whatever they dosed me with is no fucking joke.

When I get my strength back, I'm going to murder every last one of you assholes with my bare hands...

"Are you all right?" my father asks.

"Peachy."

"West, you look a little unsteady. Maybe you should—"

"Maybe you should just continue your story, before I start making plans to jab something sharp and pointy into your eyeball."

Channeling Jude? Yeah. Apparently that's my new stress response.

If only I could channel him for real. Call him up with a bit of spellwork, bring him right here with the other guys. Blow this cathedral wide open, along with everyone in it.

Clearing his throat, Brian finally continues the tale. "Not far into her pregnancy, your mom began to suspect you were far more than just a fae-witch baby. She dreamed of you wearing a crown in a kingdom of ice, and always Verrick was there, taunting her, threatening. Whispers of a prophecy were growing louder among the covens—it was said that a fae king made a bargain with a high-ranking demon centuries earlier, and the demon was finally looking to collect the promised prize—a child born of both light and darkness. But more than that, she just... she just *knew* Westlyn. Deep inside, she knew how special you were."

"Special. Right." I close my eyes as the words from the prophecy scroll through my mind, straight out of the Codex.

> *A child conceived 'neath moon so bright*
> *Born of the union of darkness and light*
> *Blessed is the babe who inherits the crown*
> *Blessed is the blood that brings the world down*

If I had even a *slim* chance of denying the prophecy was about me, Brian just obliterated it. I was conceived beneath a full Faerie moon, a union of my light-witch mother and dark-fae father. Verrick already told me I'm to inherit his crown—my so-called "legacy."

The only thing that hasn't yet come to fruition is the part about bringing the world down, but something tells me the king is already cooking up a plan for that.

"What sort of bargain?" I ask, hoping to find some clue that will allow me to unravel the whole damn thing. "What *exactly* did the fae king get in exchange for handing off his oh-so-special unborn daughter centuries after the fact?"

"No one ever knew the specifics, but most believe the demon granted the fae king use of hell's magic for some sort of dark curse against the enemies who'd taken up arms against his kingdom. In exchange, the fae king agreed to one day, when the timing felt auspicious, conceive a child with a powerful light witch. A child that would later be bound to hell, intended to reunite the demons and dark fae bloodlines of old and lead—"

"Lead the newly joined forces to everlasting glory on the human realm," I recite, recalling what Rook shared about Tatiana's research. "Yeah, I've seen this show before."

And I *know* the so-called "enemies who'd taken up arms." Know them *intimately*.

After all our research, our work on the Codex, our speculation, all the pieces are finally sliding into place. Sharp and broken, each one cutting deeper than the last.

No wonder the gargoyles and I always felt such a strong connection. The threads of our fates were woven together the moment Verrick and my mother locked eyes across that ballroom. My conception—my very life—was the promised payment for the demonic magic Verrick used to bind the gargoyles' brutal curse.

My life in exchange for their endless torment.

My life in exchange for their very souls.

The room spins, and I have to close my eyes and suck in deep gulps of air to keep from passing out again. Maybe it's the sudden rush of blood to my veins, or a flood of adrenaline, but somehow—with a will I didn't know I possessed —I finally manage to draw my knees up to my chest, and I rest my forehead against them, trying to convince my heart not to pound right out of my chest.

Just when I think this story can't get any worse, that no more enemies can rise up from the darkness to torment us, the hits just keep on coming.

"Your mom and I spent the long months of her pregnancy searching for everything we could find about the prophecy," Brian continues. "We'd hoped to find a loophole, something that would allow us to sever your connection to Wintermoon or to craft a spell of protection that would keep you out of his clutches. But there was very little written information available, and we couldn't cast too wide a net among occult scholars for fear that anyone with knowledge of the prophecy could already be in the king's service."

"Eloise," I say, lifting my heavy head. My arms are tingling, the feeling slowly returning to them. "She's connected to the Archmage and to Zorakkov, obviously. But you... you married that evil shrew. How did that even happen?"

"Eloise... She had her claws in our family since Verrick's people lured your mother to Faerie." Brian shakes his head, as if he's still admonishing himself for that particular life choice. With a heavy sigh, he says, "She's half demon, West. From a lesser demon family eager to win favor with the royals. And somehow, she decided the best way to impress *them* was to destroy *us*."

"Wait. Eloise is half demon? Are you *kidding* me?" I nearly laugh. Because of *course* the evil stepmother from hell would *literally* be from hell.

"She doesn't have much power," Brian continues. "The lesser demons rarely do, and her human witch lineage is fairly watered down as well. Her entire life has been an endless quest for magic and status, for some sort of acknowledgment that the whole of her parts is better than her individually weak bloodlines."

"How did you know she was involved with Zorakkov and the Forsythes?"

"The moment I saw her in the delivery room with your mom, I knew what she was—a shadow magic society witch with demonic blood. I'd never seen her before, but I could sense something dark and cruel through her painted smile. Maddie was still having contractions when her doctor was called away for an emergency consult, and Eloise came to sit with us. Said she was passing by and sensed we could use some company, but everything about her felt wrong. There was a whisper in the back of my mind—*she's here to hurt the baby.*

"I vowed to stay close, but then your mother went into labor and the doctor was nowhere to be found. Two other nurses rushed in with a doctor I'd never seen before, and they dragged me out—called security to keep me away. It all happened so fast... By the time I fought my way back through security and barged into the room, Eloise was holding a screaming baby, and Maddie... she... she was silent, and I... It never occurred to me that they'd hurt your mother. I was so focused on you—on your mother's visions about the danger you were in. I was sure they'd try to steal you, to claim you were stillborn and take you right out of that room. And maybe they would have if I hadn't arrived at that precise moment, but I did. And your mother... She never even got to see you, or..." He closes his eyes, emotion choking off his words.

I feel it too. The loss of the mother who loved and wanted me but never got to hold me. The loss of that first hug, that warmth, that tiny grip around a finger, that tender brush of lips on a downy-soft head. The loss of love and guidance over the years, and all the things we could have made together as a family—magic and laughter. A life. Happiness.

No, maybe it wouldn't have turned out exactly like that. I'm sure there would've been arguments and disasters along the way. But we never even got a *chance*.

And Brian lost his best friend. A woman he loved—that, I believe. I can hear it in his every word about her, see it in his eyes. His entire life was rerouted because of the vow he made to her.

Eloise robbed us both.

"She... she murdered Mom?" I whisper.

Back when Rook and Auggie were looking through the old hospital records and helping me put the pieces together about Hunter's medical treatments, I'd wondered if and how Eloise could have been involved in my mom's death.

But this? *Goddess.*

"I don't know, Westlyn. I don't know if it was Eloise herself, or one of the others with her, or some dark-fae trick of Verrick's, cursing her to death at the moment of your birth. There was no proof of anything, of course. Her doctor eventually returned and the cause of death was determined to be complications from childbirth, but there were no inquiries beyond that. I wanted to fight it, to demand they open an investigation, but how could I? I had no choice but to let it all go, because I made a promise to Maddie, and suddenly I had this tiny, precious newborn to... to protect."

My heart cracks in half. All of this—it's too much to bear. Yet I *need* to know. I need to know every detail. I need to feel the echo of her actions right down to my core, let it all stoke this fire inside.

Because when I kill Eloise—and I *will* kill her, make no mistake about that—she's going to know that it's no longer about what she did to me.

She's going to feel every ounce of this rage. This loss. This heartache.

She's going to *suffer*. Suffer in ways I never even allowed myself to fantasize about before—not even earlier when Verrick threatened her. Before, I didn't want to admit I had that kind of darkness and depravity festering in my heart.

Now?

I *welcome* it.

CHAPTER SIX

WESTLYN

When Brian finally looks up at me again, his eyes are clear. Determined.

"I continued to search for a way to break your bond to Wintermoon and protect you from all of this," he says, "but... Goddess, it was all so complicated. So many dark entities involved. Ancient curses. Demonic bargains we could only guess at. I thought Eloise, at least, was out of the picture. But a few years after you were born, she began showing up in my circles—a ritual feast here, a coven meeting there. She always made a point to seek me out, her flirtations obvious from the start. Of course her interest in me was feigned, but her interest in *you* was genuine—she'd ask about you as though you were family, always wanting to know how you were getting on without your mother, how your magic was progressing. It was all I could do not to slit her throat, but that would've made things even more dangerous for you."

"But I *had* no magic," I say. "She had to know that."

"Well, yes and no. Your magic was there, it just hadn't visibly manifested yet because of your bond to Verrick—the dark fae part of your bloodline was dominant, overpowering the witch side, and fae magic doesn't come in fully until adulthood. Verrick would've known this when he conceived you—would've known he could keep his claim on you secret until the time was right."

The fae rune burns again on my neck like a warning, and I've got just enough strength in my arms to wrap my hand around it. The skin feels hot against my fingertips, but I still can't access my magic.

You will, girl. Just need to wait it out...

"Eloise likely knew all of this," Brian says, "but she didn't know that *I* knew, so I had to play the part of a confused and overwhelmed mage father concerned about his witch daughter's lack of magic. I began speculating to fellow coven members that you'd been cursed by a dark witch or a demon. I needed those rumors to spread, needed anyone who was in on Verrick's plans to believe that your mother never told me about their dalliances. So, like any good mage father who believed his daughter was magicless, I had to take you to healers. Had to act baffled and frustrated by your so-called lack of progress."

He tells me the rest of the story—how Eloise ensured their paths crossed more and more often. How she began whispering to him about the shadow magic society, what a fine addition he'd make. How he could no longer ignore her blatant attempts at flirtation and finally began dating her, despite how deeply he resented her.

"It was exactly what she wanted," he says, "and though it made my skin crawl and my stomach turn, I reasoned that if I could get close to her, gain her trust, I could gain some insight about the Archmage's bigger plans, which was what I'd wanted all along. I kept her away from you as long as I could."

A chill creeps down my spine, making me shiver. I can't even imagine having to pretend like that, to feign affection for a demonic witch who very likely killed the woman he truly loved and wanted nothing more than to steal away their daughter.

Eloise must've reveled in it all.

Despite my anger at Brian, I can't help but hate her for what she did to him. Can't help but use it to add a bit more fuel to that fire smoldering inside me, waiting to be unleashed.

"Of course, she never really trusted me," he says. "The more time we spent together, the more obvious it became that she didn't think very highly of me. She pretended to be interested in my magic, in my reputation among the city's light mages, but she was laser-focused on you. So, I had to change tacks. Instead of trying to win her trust and approval with my magic and reputation, I decided to amplify her perceptions of me as weak and ineffective. I stopped attending meetings and practicing my magic, and started visiting the casinos instead, draining money from my accounts to make it look like I was going bankrupt. Didn't take much on my part to convince her I was obsessed and useless. She started underestimating me, stopped paying attention to my day-to-day activities. Her dismissal gave me time away from her, time I could use to keep searching for ways to break your bond to the fae."

"I don't understand that part." I shake my head, the logical part of my brain still grasping for some other explanation. "Your so-called gambling debt is what allowed you to make the alliance with the Archmage and sell me off into a demonic marriage in the first place. If not for that debt, none of this would've even happened. Now you're saying the debt didn't even exist?"

"Some of that money went into my research expenses. But the rest..." A faint smile touches his lips. "It's all in a series of offshore accounts. Set up to transfer to you upon my death. You'll be financially secure for many, many years."

My eyes widen. "You think that's what's important to me? Goddess, Dad. I would've traded away all that for a chance at a normal life with you, even if our family wasn't exactly ideal. Instead, your so-called debt is what gave the Archmage the perfect opportunity to propose the demon marriage, and—"

"No, Westlyn. The alleged debt just lent credibility to my so-called feebleness and put me into the society's debt —a position I hoped would grant me better access to their plans. They were going to bind you to Zorakkov either way. You were promised to him by the dark-fae king—he created you solely to fulfill his end of the bargain and bring the prophecy to fruition. I thought if I could get in close with the society, perhaps I could stop Zorakkov from manifesting in Hunter Forsythe, but even that would've been a temporary Band-Aid to a problem that required major surgery. I thought I'd have more time, but in the end..."

I finish the sentence he clearly can *not*. "In the end, you put your best friend's daughter on the altar with a prince of hell."

He nods, smart enough not to deny it.

Then, with another smile—this one bringing a sheen of pride to his eyes, "But no one suspected you'd stab him and flee."

"No one suspected me of doing *anything*," I snap. "That was the point. I was docile and powerless. Everyone let me believe it. And in the end—"

"We all underestimated you. Something tells me we're *still* underestimating you." He's still smiling, still looking at me as if he really is a proud father. "No one was more surprised *or* thrilled at how that night played out than I was. But I couldn't let on. I had no choice but to go into hiding with Eloise, pretending to fear the Archmage's retribution. Somehow she made arrangements with the Forsythes to capture you and return you to them, but by then my nerves were fraying. I couldn't... I couldn't keep pretending. I couldn't be part of it. I left her, but eventually, the shadow mages caught up with me, too."

"And here we are," I say with a deep sigh.

At this, the sadness and regret return to his eyes. "And here we are."

I lower my head to my knees again, unable to hold his gaze as every one of my memories rearranges itself to align with this new knowledge.

Goddess, there are so many moving parts to this story. To my history. My future, if I've even got a chance at one.

Verrick. Eloise. The botched wedding and binding ceremony. The Archmage and his shadow magic society. The bullies who tormented me throughout childhood at Eloise's behest.

I close my eyes and bite back a sob. I wish Rook was here. He'd help me map out all the different plot lines, weave them all together into a tale that made sense. A tale with an ending I could actually alter before it destroys us all.

But he's not here.

None of my guys are here. They're upstate, and I'm trapped in this cathedral, locked away from them because of the monsters who've been pulling the strings on my fate since long before I was born.

I don't even know who started it. Verrick? The demons? Whoever authored the prophecy? The common ancestor demons and dark fae supposedly shared?

At this point, I guess it doesn't even matter who started the game.

All that matters is I'm fucking *done* being everyone's pawn.

"You should've told me, Dad," I say, my voice cracking on the D-word, but I push on. I push on because he's absolutely right—he *did* fail me. No, not because he couldn't stop the Archmage's plans, not because he couldn't unravel a dark prophecy that was millennia in the making. He failed me because he lied. Because he didn't trust me enough to let me in. Because he let me grow up thinking I was power-less, a burden, a girl who killed her mother just by being born. He let those bullies torment me, let me move from school to school, never dealing with the issue. He let me walk down that aisle into the arms of a demon prince.

And in the end, he still couldn't find a way to save me, because here we fucking are.

I tell him all of this, shouting at him until my voice is raw, my throat burning with twenty-two years of pent-up rage and tears. With grief. With confusion. With loneliness for a family that never could have been.

With fear of what's to come.

But before he can respond, her cruel, terrible voice shatters the air once more.

"Aww, what a precious family reunion!" Eloise glares at us from the doorway, her eyes sharp and cunning, her smile twisted.

I have no idea how long she's been standing there eaves-dropping, but I can't really bring myself to care.

The immensity of everything Brian confessed feels heavier than Eloise's petty vendetta against me, her stupid demon deals with the Archmage, her whole ridiculous, backstabbing life.

But I can't dismiss her outright. I'm still a prisoner here, and she's still pulling the puppet strings.

She's wearing a dress now, black and elegant, her hair swept up, makeup flawless. Two mages stand behind her, both in ceremonial black cloaks. One of them stalks over to me and jabs me in the neck with another needle before hauling me to my feet.

The feeling rushes back to my body in a wave of heat that leaves me dizzy. The moment I feel my strength return, I try to run straight for my evil stepmother, hoping I can at least get in a left-hook before they catch me.

But they're expecting it. The mage grabs me before I take a single step, locking me in a vise grip.

"Fuck you, asshole," I hiss, but he only tightens his hold.

Eloise clucks her tongue at me. "Still, with the language? Honestly, Westlyn. It's unbecoming."

Frustration burns inside me. All I want is to curl up by the fireplace with my gargoyles and tell them everything. I want Rook to talk through all the angles with me, to offer his theories about the prophecy. I want Jude to describe in gory detail all the pieces of art he's going to carve for me out of Verrick's bones. I want Auggie to make me a latte and apple scones and kiss me until I forget about all the bad things in this world.

And Draegan... I want him to fold me up in his wings and whisper in my ear, *Everything will be okay, little mortal. I've got you...*

But I'm here, as far away from them as I've ever been.

But I can't give in. Not like this. Not while there's still a chance.

My father's words come back to me.

Something tells me we're still *underestimating you...*

He's right. They *are* still underestimating me. They've only ever seen me as powerless. Rebellious at times, perhaps. But never strong. Never truly powerful.

And that will be their greatest mistake.

I'll make damn sure of that.

"Can you behave yourself?" Eloise asks.

"Y-yes," I stammer, forcing exhaustion and defeat into my voice. "I'm... too tired to fight."

I repress a grin as Eloise eyes me up and down, nodding once at the mage to release me.

This time, I don't make a move. I let her think she's cowed me again.

"Good. Now get dressed, Westlyn. It's time." She tosses a swath of fabric at me—a simple sleeveless dress in dark violet. "Don't turn your nose down, child. It's the best we could do on such short notice, and considering how you *ruined* the last dress I had made for you—at great cost to myself, I might add—you should be grateful I'm not putting you in rags tonight. Honestly, I will never understand how..."

Her rant blurs into an indiscernible din as my attention snags on her first words, throbbing like a pulse through my mind.

Get dressed. It's time. It's time. It's...

"Time for what?" I blurt out.

Her terrible smile is all the answer I need, but she drives in the knife anyway, unable to hide the glee in her voice. "Your *wedding*, dear stepdaughter. And this time, it will go off without a hitch. Guaranteed."

CHAPTER SEVEN

ROOK

Books.

For fifteen hundred years, I've relied on them for knowledge. For history. For companionship when I'd lost almost everyone else who'd ever mattered to me in this world.

Mostly, I relied on them for answers.

But for the first time in my long immortal life, I'm faced with something so deeply unsettling, so far outside the realm of possibility, so ridiculously nonsensical... there are no possible answers to be found in books.

Even if my library *hadn't* burned to the ground.

Westlyn, my wild girl, my witch, the woman I've fallen hopelessly in love with... She's gone, taken by some dark magic we've yet to discern. And there's no comfort I can seek—not even in the most logical, most reasonable parts of my mind.

There, I find only chaos.

The fact that I'm still standing is a fucking marvel, and I'm pretty sure it's only instinct keeping me going at this point. Instinct to keep pushing, to turn over every stone and shine a light upon every shadow until we figure this out and bring our witch back home.

So, with a steadying breath and a great shoring up of my heart, I hit the key to bring up the security video again.

Drae's still on his knees, so the rest of us crouch down beside him, huddling close around the screen, and I recognize the dubious look in their eyes; they want to believe this isn't real. That I misinterpreted the images, that there's dirt on the lens, that something glitched with the cameras or the transmission to make it look like West was in that barn when the fire started.

I want to believe it isn't real, either. That it's *anything*—any impossible, ridiculous thing other than the brutal truth.

But the cold feeling in my gut tells me that what I saw so far can only mean one thing.

It was all real. She was there.

With a shaking finger, I hit the button to restart the video.

Through the eyes of the exterior barn camera, the four of us watch our witch pad across the lawn just after sunrise, not long after the four of us retired on the roof. Her movements are quick but graceful, bare feet leaving soft footprints in the still-dewy grass. She's wearing nothing but an oversized T-shirt and a thin pair of yoga pants—no hoodie, no shoes—but if she's cold, she doesn't show it. She makes her way to the library as if she's in a trance.

Sensing the motion at the threshold, the cameras switch, giving us a view of the barn's interior. The library is deathly quiet inside, dark in the murkiness of an early fall morning. The only light comes from the Cerridwen Codex on the table. It pulses with indigo-violet magic, brightening at her approach.

"What is she *doing*?" Draegan asks. He can barely hold his head up.

I reach over and squeeze the top of his wing, gesturing at the screen for them to keep watching. This is as far as I got before. The rest is as new and terrifying to me as it will be to them.

We all hold our breaths as West places her hands on either side of the book. The words on the page glow furiously, reflected in her glazed eyes. Her expression is blank, devoid of life and laughter and any spark that even *remotely* resembles the woman we love.

Jude reaches out and touches her face with a claw as if that alone can put the light back in her eyes.

It doesn't, of course.

It's fucking heartbreaking. All of it. Watching her under the influence of this dark magic, feeling the fear and rage radiating off my brothers, seeing that dead glaze in her eyes, and worst of all—wondering if we'll be forced to watch through the goddamned security cameras as the love of our immortal life is utterly incinerated.

But I keep watching. We all do. Because whatever it is, we need to know how this ends.

West glances up from the book, the rune on her neck blazing to life and igniting her magic, dark indigo light surging from her palms, flickering in the eye of the cameras.

Yet through it all, her face remains blank.

And then, with nothing more than a deep breath, she begins to chant. Soft at first, the words gathering power and volume with each repetition.

Blood of my blood, my magic, my fire
I call unto you, my king and my sire
Return to this realm to claim what is ours
By flame and by force, so shall we devour

She recites the words three times—something from the Codex? Something she made up? Some dark enchantment forced upon her by the mages? The fae?

"What the bleeding hell is that?" Jude asks, and we watch, awestricken as indigo flames gather in her palms and stretch up both arms and across her chest.

"What must I do?" she whispers.

"Who the fuck is she talking to?" Auggie asks. "There's no one there."

She seems to be waiting for an answer, but if she gets one, it's not something any of us can hear. There's a quick shake of her head, and she hesitates, as if she's debating whatever she's about to do.

But it's only a few seconds before she's dismissing whatever doubts stayed her hand.

Her face finally changes, a spark of life where before there was only emptiness. But the vicious smile stretching across her mouth doesn't belong to her. It's dark and cruel and terrible.

Ugly.

And then, like something out of my worst nightmares, she heads for one of the shelves and holds her flaming hands to the books.

They ignite in a whoosh of blue flame, the strange fire devouring everything it touches in a matter of seconds. Shelf by shelf she moves through the ground floor of the library, setting it all ablaze.

The cameras start to flicker, the screens cracking, circuitry melting.

In the very last seconds of footage, we watch in shocked horror as Westlyn falls to her knees and laughs, palms outstretched as if she's waiting for a blessing. She laughs and laughs and *laughs* until the sick sound of it is lodged so deeply in my memory, I'm sure it will haunt me for the rest of my life.

But she doesn't burn. She doesn't fucking burn.

And as the video finally fizzles out and turns black, as Draegan launches to his feet and smashes his fist through the wall, as Jude lets out a howl that pierces my eardrums and Auggie just shakes his head over and over again, tears staining his cheeks, I hold on to that final image.

Westlyn, her skin silver-blue in the light of her magic fire, that eerie laugh reminding me that she might have actually survived this.

It's a hope as thin as gossamer, but it's the only one we've got, and I'm not about to let it go.

I get to my feet, taking the laptop with me.

"Stop it," I command. "All of you. Pull it together, for fuck's sake."

Auggie and Jude look up at me with wide, shocked eyes. I can't recall a time when I ever raised my voice at them. Not like this.

Draegan whirls on me though, new fire blazing in his eyes. "Don't you *dare*—"

"We don't know the outcome here," I say. "Yet you've already written her off as—"

"The fucking barn is a pile of dust!" he shouts. "We watched her ignite that blaze and fall to her knees in the center of it. There's no way she..." He shoves a shaking hand through his hair.

"We didn't actually see her burn, Draegan."

"Because the fucking cameras melted!" He shoves me in the chest, making me stumble backward.

"I don't care about the fucking cameras!" I shout, refusing to back down. "We didn't actually see her die, which means there's still a chance. There's a fucking *chance*. If the situations were reversed, you know damn well she wouldn't give up on us. Hell, even if she'd seen a full-color HD video of our deaths, she still wouldn't believe it until she felt our cold, dead corpses for herself. She'd fight for us until the bitter end, and that's exactly what I'm going to do for her. So if you want to stand here smashing your fists through the walls and tearing apart the whole damn house, be my fucking guest. But me? I'm going to do everything in my power to prove our girl isn't a pile of ash. And then I'm going to find her and bring her back home. And you know what? I'd *really* appreciate some backup on this, but if all of you can't figure out how the fuck to pull your horned heads out of your asses, fine. I'm on this mission either way. Excuse me."

I shoulder my way past the gargoyles and head down to the study, dropping onto the sofa with my laptop. Grabbing my phone, I pull up the tracking app and sync it up with my computer, fingers flying over the keys, everything inside me still clinging desperately to that gossamer thread.

This has to work. This fucking has *to work...*

"Rook, wait." Draegan sighs as he enters the room a moment later, the others right behind him. He's clutching West's amulet in a tight fist, its luminous violet-and-amber magic absent. "I didn't mean... That is to say, I was only... You're right. Tearing apart the house isn't going to..." Clearly flustered, he blows out another big sigh and says, "What are you doing, exactly?"

"Trying to track her. If I can confirm she left the property, I may be able to find out where."

"What? How?" He crosses the distance to stand behind the sofa, peering down at the screen over my shoulder. Jude and Auggie follow, the gargoyles once again crowding around the laptop—the only apparent lifeline to our witch.

"I gave her a smartwatch and synced it with my phone," I say. "It was designed for... other purposes. But now it might just lead us straight to her."

"A smartwatch?" Jude smacks the back of my head. "You could've led with that, mate. *Fuck*."

"Forgive me, oh wise one," I retort. "My thoughts aren't exactly focused at the moment."

"Guys." Auggie glares at them. "Shut the fuck up and let the man work his tech-magic mojo. *Please*."

Silence descends, the only sounds the clicking of the keys and a series of beeps as I pull up a map of the entire region and try to home in on a signal.

Nothing.

"*Damn it*," I growl.

"What is it?" Drae asks.

"Signal's dead now, but that could mean anything. Dead battery, most likely. Or the watch was damaged, or she's in a place where she's not getting service, but... Hang on."

A few more clicks, a few more hacked relay towers, and... *boom*.

"Yes. Yes!" I'm damn near out of my skin with relief as the green dots illuminate a clear path on the map. "This is a map of her location—at least, the watch's location—starting last night and ending a few hours ago, presumably when the battery or device itself died."

"How are you getting all this?" Drae asks.

"It's the tracking signal. When it's working, the device pings the towers at regular intervals. See, this is Blackmoor Manor last night." I zoom in and check the time stamps. "She was in her room, probably sleeping at this time. Then you can see the slight movement here—now she's in the library."

We watch as the light shifts on the screen.

"And then?" Auggie asks, his breath warm on my cheek as he leans in closer, all of them awaiting confirmation that the signal didn't die in that library.

That somehow, she got away.

"There. There!" Draegan jabs his finger as a new series of dots lights up along the road leading off the property. "That means she left Blackmoor, right?"

I blink back tears of joy. "Yes. That's exactly what it means."

The collective sigh is audible, a weight evaporating from all our shoulders.

But now we've got a new problem, because it still means she's gone, and we have no idea what the circumstances were that led her off the property.

"So she just... wandered off?" Jude asks.

I check all the timestamps. "No, the signal is moving too quickly for that. She must've gotten into a car."

"Or she was *put* into a car," Auggie says.

"Where?" Draegan asks. "Where the hell could she have gone? And with whom? None of our vehicles are missing."

We watch as the lights blaze a trail straight into downtown Manhattan.

"That's it." I point to the final dot on the screen. "The towers received a signal from this same location for about ten minutes before the transmissions stopped for good."

"You got an address?" Jude asks.

I plug in the GPS coordinates to get the exact location.

"Fuck," I breathe. "That's Thornwood. Which means... The fucking shadow mages. It has to be them."

Draegan curses. "Tell me the cathedral security cameras are still operational."

"Should be. I never turned them off." A few more clicks of the keys, and I've got the feeds from Thornwood pulled up.

The candlelit chandeliers flicker over a scene that chills me to the core.

"Is that live?" Auggie asks.

Taking in the sight of all those black-hooded mages gathered in the nave, I swallow hard. "Yes."

Because past the mages, trembling on the altar in a thin dress, her hair a mess, her eyes wide with a mix of fear and determination, is Westlyn.

"She's alive," I whisper. "She's fucking alive."

"But what the bloody *hell* are they doing to her?" Jude barks out.

A hot, sick feeling tears through my gut, chasing away the chill. There's only one explanation for all of this—the kidnapping. The mages. The cathedral. Westlyn in a dress on the very altar where she once stabbed her betrothed.

"They're binding her to Zorakkov," I say. "And... oh, fuck. That's... Fuck *me*. How is this even possible?"

It's not just the mages, which are bad enough. A new player has just entered the game.

There's no mistaking that golden crown. Those cold, cruel eyes. The satisfied smile.

"Fucking *Verrick*?" Draegan seethes behind me, rage rolling off him in hot waves. "How the *fuck* is he even here?"

"A better question," I grit out, my teeth clenched so hard my jaw aches, "is how the fuck can we send him back to Wintermoon, and how can we make it hurt bad enough that he never comes back?"

"I've got plenty of ideas on that front," Jude says. "Bloody ones."

Auggie looks ready to spit fire. "Dark fae, dark mages, demons, fucking Verrick... This is all so fucking—"

"We need to go. Now." I slam the laptop shut and rocket to my feet, punching the contacts button on my phone. To Jude, I say, "Find the ravens, lock them in the manor. I don't want them following us to the cathedral and getting hurt. That's the last thing West needs right now."

"Who are you calling?" Auggie asks, right on my heels.

"More backup."

The ancient vampire-witch answers on the second ring, and her words from the other night echo through my mind.

Whatever lies ahead for you and your rune bearer, something tells me you're going to need allies in this. I just want you to remember you can always count me among them...

I hope like hell she meant it.

"Tatiana?" I say by way of a greeting as the four of us charge outside, ready to hit the skies. "We've got a situation."

"Rook Van Doren," she says with her usual drawl. "Is this your way of asking for my help?"

"Pretty sure we don't stand a chance without it."

"Tell me what I can do," she says, the teasing gone from her voice.

"How many witches in your immediate circle do you trust with your life and all your secrets, because I'm going to need to trust them with mine."

"Two," she says. "Fleur and Laney Archer. They're sisters, humans, and the *only* witches I trust without reservation."

"How soon can you meet us in lower Manhattan?"

"Text me the address and whatever else I need to know." I hear the rustling of clothes being thrown on, a door creaking open. "I'm already on my way."

CHAPTER EIGHT

WESTLYN

There's no bouquet of poisonous flowers tonight. No elaborate music or choreographed marches down the aisle, no delicate clinking of champagne toasts among the guests before the main event.

Standing at the head of the cathedral, bound by royal dark-fae magic stronger than any chains or magical drugs to remain on this altar until my task is complete, I glance out across the sea of hooded shadow mages gathered in the nave and I realize with shocking clarity...

This is very likely the night I die.

Either that or I'll become the worst kind of prisoner, magically trapped in my own mind while the mages, demons, and dark fae use me to carry out their wicked plans—a fate even worse than death.

On the altar table behind me, an indigo light pulses from an open book, the edges crackling with magic.

The Cerridwen Codex.

It didn't burn in the library as I'd feared. Apparently, I saved it. I brought it to Verrick after using it to summon him last night, just as he intended.

I feel its power calling to me now, touching the edges of something inside me. Searching for a magic it once knew, but can no longer find.

I'm trembling in the cheap, skimpy dress Eloise provided, but it's not fear or cold that's got me shaking like the autumn leaves in the orchard now.

It's *fury*.

Fury at Verrick for thinking he has any sort of claim on me. On the magic inside me he's locked up with some terrible spell.

Fury at Eloise for her role in my mother's murder, for using Brian, for orchestrating the plot to turn me into a demon prince's slave.

Fury at Brian for not trusting me enough to let me in on all the secrets. For not allowing us to build a real relationship before it was too late.

Fury at my mother for dying, as ridiculous as that is.

But mostly, I'm furious with myself.

I promised my gargoyles I'd find a way to break their curse. But if I can't figure out an escape plan in the next few minutes, the only thing I'm going to break is their hearts.

The sun set a couple of hours ago. They're certainly awake by now, and yet the fact that they're not here yet tells me they don't know where I am.

They probably think I'm dead. And if not, they'll be out of their minds with worry. Even if they somehow figure out who took me and where I am, there's no way they'll be able to stop this ceremony before the dark deed is done.

It's too late for that.

Once again, I find myself standing at the altar and wishing for a rescue.

But fuck that.

This time? There are no gargoyles hiding in the bell tower, waiting to answer my pleas.

This time, I'm truly on my own.

But this time, I'm no longer that same scared, powerless witch who cowered at the feet of evil all those weeks ago.

Ignoring the greedy, sharp-eyed mages staring up at me from the pews, I close my eyes and try again to reach for my magic.

Come on. You're there. I know you're in there. Answer me. Come to me...

No luck. Not so much as a flicker.

Verrick made sure of that.

I close my eyes and take a deep, calming breath. I have to trust myself. I have to trust this magic inside me, because wherever it came from—witches, dark fae, destiny, some otherworldly force I can't even begin to contemplate—it's mine. It's real.

And I've been waiting my whole life to unleash it.

Heartbeat steady once more, I open my eyes to find Eloise emerging from the sacristy, Brian lumbering behind her, chained and obviously drugged. His movements are even more sluggish now, his head lolling on his neck as if he can barely hold it up. Blood leaks from a fresh gash down the side of his face, dripping onto his already ruined shirt. His doting *wife* guides him to the front pew and he takes a seat at her command, just like he did the night of my first sham wedding.

We lock eyes for the briefest instant. This time, he doesn't look away in shame.

It feels like a goodbye. Like he's going to die tonight, too.

"If you're waiting for your birds to swoop in and save you, you can forget it." Eloise waltzes up to the altar, fluffing her hair as she does so, her smugness so huge it may as well have its own dress. "Not even your monsters can help you tonight, Westlyn."

"The only monsters here are you and your secret society of wannabe minions," I reply. Then, leaning as close as I dare and forcing a smug smile of my own, "And you have no idea who you're trifling with tonight, *demoness.*"

She blanches. It's only for a second, but I see it. Hesitation in her eyes. The tiniest flicker of fear.

A murmur ripples through the crowd of mages, and I look over their dark heads to see a pair of well-dressed guests slowly sauntering down the aisle. The woman is dressed in a blood red gown overlaid at the bodice with sheer black lace, the elegant satin skirt hugging her figure and spilling into a long train behind her. Her escort is dapper in a cream-colored ceremonial robe, the edges trimmed in gold.

My heart lurches. I would recognize those mages anywhere.

The Archmage Lennon Forsythe, and his wife Celine.

They barely spare me a glance as they ascend the altar, all their attention focused on the Codex splayed open behind me.

"It's... breathtaking," Lennon whispers, his eyes glazed in holy revelry as he reaches out to touch the edge.

A bright purple spark sizzles across the pages, and he yelps, yanking his hand back.

"Ouch," I mock, unable to help myself. "That looks like it hurt." I reach over and trace a fingertip down the center of the book, stirring the magic back to life. It swirls and dances for me, a pleasant tickle across my skin, fading only when I draw back. "I don't think it likes you."

He finally makes eye contact, his gaze dark with malice. "You will burn tonight, witch. And your sacrifice will be all the sweeter when the Codex and all its power are transferred to me."

"To *us*." Celine grips his elbow, her smile tight. Then, attempting the same we're-all-family-here tone she used on me the night she tried to kidnap me from the restaurant, she says, "Westlyn, dear. I'm so glad you've finally realized the error of your ways."

"Hmm." I smile right back at her. "Have I?"

"You're here, aren't you?"

A frisson of magic skitters down my spine—the first I've been able to feel it since Verrick took me. Hope stokes the embers inside me to a slow, flickering life.

"As are you," I say, still smiling. Then, lowering my voice to a whisper, "But I wouldn't count on that for too much longer."

"I beg your pardon? I'm—"

"*Ignore* her, Celine." Eloise rolls her eyes. "If my useless husband had spent more time raising her properly and less time trying to find a way to derail a destiny that was written in the stars long before she was even conceived, perhaps we wouldn't be subjected to—"

"*Enough.*" Verrick's voice booms across the altar as he steps through the wooden door behind it, his presence more fierce and powerful than I've ever seen him.

He's dressed in dark pants and a silver tunic embroidered with black and violet snakes that slither and move over the fabric, their eyes glittering with tiny inlaid rubies the same color as the jewels in his crown. Shadows gather around him like smoke, eating up all the light as he comes to stand at the altar table.

He places his hands on the table on either side of the Codex, close but not touching it. After a single nod of acknowledgment at the Forsythes, he turns his attention to me, his eyes sparkling with something terrifying and possessive.

That same magic slides down my spine again, warm and

tingling, stronger than before. As if in response, the book glows.

"Be seated," Verrick says to the Forsythes and Eloise, and at once they obey, shuffling off to arrange themselves in the front pew with Brian.

Best seats in the house.

Verrick winks at me, and I try not to shiver.

Then, two black-robed men enter from that same wooden door.

A high priest I've never seen before, with thick, angry brows and a pockmarked face, his shoulder-length hair a yellowing shade of white.

And a hunched, mangled figure that's nearly unrecognizable by sight, limping slightly behind the priest, his eyes black as pitch, sections of skin melting from his face like candle wax, his hands gnarled as old tree roots.

My heart turns to ice as he comes to stand next to me.

Zorakkov.

His body—*Hunter's* body—is failing, just like Jude and Auggie suspected after they tortured the intel out of the doctor who'd been treating him.

"No tricks tonight, witch," he hisses, his speech slurred, the scent of his breath like rotting garbage on a stifling summer day.

A scream lodges itself in my throat, but I clamp my mouth shut before it can escape, determined not to show fear.

Not to give anyone here an *ounce* of satisfaction.

"Shall we begin?" the high priest asks as he joins Verrick behind the table.

"Get it done," Zorakkov says.

Ignoring the stench of my groom, ignoring the way my skin crawls at the raspy sound of his voice, I hold my chin high and say with as much force as I can muster, "The sooner we begin, the sooner we will *end.*"

The Codex glitters with indigo sparks. My skin heats, nerves prickling. I sense a ripple in the magical barrier that's got me locked on this altar.

My magic is waking up again.

The priest gestures for Zorakkov and me to face each other, and I wait for him to bring out the ritual grimoire and recite the old marriage rituals, just like the other priest did last time. But this one merely nods at Zorakkov, and the demon prince retrieves the athame from his robes.

The same athame I stabbed him with.

My fingers itch to wrap around that jeweled handle. To shove the blade in deep. To feel his blood coating my skin...

"Dismiss those vile thoughts from your vile mind," Zorakkov hisses. "This will be over soon enough."

With that, he grabs my hand and slices a deep gash, then makes a similar cut on his own, mashing our palms together. Our blood mingles, and just like before, the pain is an unbearable torment. His vile demon blood burns a path up my arm and across my chest, exploding through my heart like shrapnel.

The priest doesn't ask me to speak the vows this time,

to offer myself in servitude to this ghastly creature as if I ever had a choice.

Those words were already spoken.

All that's left now is the final proclamation—the part left incomplete last time when I stabbed my groom and fled.

I try to wrench out of his hold now, but his grip is unrelenting, his voice in my head a dark warning.

You are mine, witch. You belong to me, magic and soul and blood. Together, we shall usher in a terror greater than any mankind has ever witnessed...

"By the bonds of blood and magic," the priest says over the sound of my panicked breaths, my blood boiling hotter with every word, "with the blessing of the old gods and the new, so shall this oath be sealed. Zorakkov, demon lord of the underworld, and Westlyn Avery, witch and fae of Wintermoon, you are hereby forever bound."

"Forever bound," the mages in the pews call back, rising to their feet as hundreds of black candles flicker to life in their hands, their faces twisting with eerie shadows beneath their hoods.

With a final explosion of blinding agony in my chest, the intensity of that demonic fire inside me finally relents. It no longer burns, but I can still feel it—pure evil running through my veins, my own magic melding with it, forming some new, unholy alliance.

The ceremony is complete.

Zorakkov and I are forever bound.

But apparently he's not done with me yet.

"Hold still, witch," he growls, grabbing my other hand and jerking my arm close. The athame glints in the candlelight, and with a quickness I don't see coming, he drags it down my arm. A gash opens up from elbow to wrist, blood spilling over my skin.

The high priest rushes forward with a small metal bowl, shoving it under my arm to collect every drop. I'm lightheaded and dizzy, barely able to stay upright as he hands the bowl to Zorakkov.

The demon kneels on the altar, dipping two fingers into the bowl. Then, using my blood as paint and the altar as his canvas, he draws a summoning symbol.

It glows red when it's complete, and the demon prince tosses aside the bowl and presses his wounded palm to the symbol.

The mages' candles snuff out at once, filling the cathedral with smoke as some horrifying new agony rips me apart inside, dropping me to my knees.

I thought the pain of the binding ceremony was unbearable, but this? Goddess, I'm not going to survive.

I lean forward, dry-heaving, the room spinning before my eyes.

"Just breathe, little moon. It will pass." Verrick is suddenly crouched at my side, stroking my hair and back as a real father might. "You can feel it, can't you? The power. The great rising. Soon, this will all be ours..." His comforting tone shifts into something greedy and hungry, his words trailing off as I try to find the source of this devastating pain inside me.

This power.

Verrick's right—I *can* feel it. And when I finally lift my eyes and look out across the nave, I see it, too.

What I thought was the result of hundreds of candles being extinguished wasn't actually smoke at all, but the demonic souls of hell.

Made of darkness and shadow, they rise from the ground in droves, seeking a connection to this realm. Seeking human vessels among the dark mages—mages who are all too willing to sacrifice themselves for the cause.

I watch in stunned, sickened horror as the demons claim their new hosts. Hoods fall back, revealing black eyes glittering in pale faces, mouths stitched shut.

Only the front pew remains unpossessed. Eloise. Brian. And the Forsythes, whose soulless eyes are as hungry and desirous as Verrick's.

Zorakkov gets to his feet and lifts his hands skyward, like some kind of God on the mountain.

"Bow to your master," he booms, his voice dark and powerful, making the still-burning candles in the chandeliers flicker. "*Bow!*"

But the newly risen demons do *not* bow to the prince of hell.

They do not bow to the Archmage who sacrificed his adopted son to be Zorakkov's vessel.

They do not bow to the Archmage's wife, or to my stepmother, or even to Verrick of Wintermoon, arguably the most powerful being in this entire cathedral.

The newly risen demons turn toward the lone witch the world continues to underestimate.

And they bow to *me*.

CHAPTER NINE

AUGUSTINE

After Rook coordinated with Tatiana for the meet-up and Jude finally lured a frazzled Lucinda and Huxley into Drae's bedroom with a mountain of crackers, three different kinds of imported cheeses, and enough dark chocolate to thoroughly ruin Draegan's expensive sheets for good, the four of us left the manor in a flurry of wings and rage, no time to strategize beyond the basics.

Get West. Torch our enemies. Bounce.

With a little luck, we'd be home in time for an epic night breakfast and a round of *very* stiff drinks.

Done, done, and *done*.

But now that we're here... Fuck. It's painfully obvious that our simple plan needs a little more, well, planning.

First clue this wasn't going to be a quick rescue-and-destroy operation? The fucking mages put up some kind of magical barrier, preventing us from getting within twenty feet of the cathedral. We tried. It was like hitting a damn invisible wall. An electrified one that damn near fried my dick off.

Whatever mojo they've got working in there gummed up the cameras, too. Rook keeps checking the feeds on his phone, but all we're getting is static.

So for now, the gargoyles and I are gathered on the rooftop of a shuttered Greek restaurant directly across from the cathedral with Tatiana and her two companions. With shrewd, wise gazes and confident command of their magic, Fleur and Laney Archer seem like they've been around the block a few times and know how to handle themselves in a bad situation.

I truly hope they can be trusted, but it's too late for regrets. They know we're gargoyles—we're in our true forms. Rook had to tell them about West's connection to Wintermoon, too. About our suspicion that she is, in fact, the child spoken of in the so-called Moon Blessed prophecy.

A prophecy that may very well be coming to fruition tonight.

For now, the witches seem genuinely determined to help us, which is a relief. Judging from the waves of dark energy rolling out of that fucking impenetrable cathedral, we're gonna need all the help we can get with this shadow-mage shitshow.

"They've already completed the binding," Tatiana says

now, shaking her head. "I can feel it—a dark power gathering between the realms. We can deal with breaking it later, but for now, you all need to prepare yourselves. The Westlyn you know... She's very likely going to be different."

"Different how?" Draegan asks. He hasn't stopped pacing since we landed, his body crackling with energy just waiting to be unleashed.

"Depending on how she reacts to the demonic connection," Tatiana says, "she could be severely weakened. Or, depending on which bloodline ends up being more dominant, the demon's blood could end up fueling Westlyn's inherent magic instead, amplifying the darker aspects of her fae nature."

"Darker aspects?" I ask. "What does that mean?"

"She may experience intense feelings of bloodlust," Tatiana explains. "A need for utter destruction. An all-consuming rage that can only be quenched with extreme acts of violence."

Jude lights one of his witchweed cigarettes and inhales a deep drag. Then, with a slow exhale through that psychotic grin, "You say all that like it's a bad thing, Tats."

"Fucking *Jude*." I roll my eyes.

"What? I'm just saying—"

"Well, say less. We need an actual plan here, and you're not helping."

He lifts his hands in surrender, and Tatiana continues.

"Regardless of the bond, Westlyn should still recognize

and trust you. However, she may be reluctant to leave her demon mate behind."

"That *monster* is not her mate," Rook seethes, his ire rivaling Draegan's.

Tatiana places a hand on his arm. "I mean it in purely magical terms. The forced bond between them will, by its very nature, draw them close together. She'll feel compelled to obey him. Your task will be to convince her she needs to leave the area with you and return home, leaving the demon behind."

"We won't be able to break the bond if Zorakkov remains close," Fleur says. "He'll do everything in his power to prevent that from happening."

Laney nods. "If she won't come willingly, you'll have to force her in any way that you can. No matter how angry it makes her, no matter how hard she fights you. It's her only chance."

"We won't let it come to that," Rook says confidently. Then, removing his glasses and polishing them with a cloth, "Right now, we've got two big advantages. One, they don't know we're here. And two, they don't know we've got three powerful witches on our side. The witches will break the barrier, giving us a short window to get in and grab West. That's our primary objective right now. Like Tatiana said, we can deal with breaking the bond later."

I nod, squeezing the back of Rook's neck to let him know I'm with him on this. It's rare to see him step up when Drae's usually the one calling the shots, but this isn't some hit job on a crooked city councilman. This is Westlyn we're talking about here. We need finesse. We need logic. We need the kind of calm, rational approach that only Rook can provide.

"As soon as the sisters and I break the mages' protection spell," Tatiana says, "you'll feel the barrier drop, like a shockwave rippling through the air. We'll hold it down for as long as we can, but the moment you feel that ripple, you need to *move*. Get in, take down as many of the mages as you need to, but above all else, get your witch."

"And get the hell out of there," Rook adds.

Jude's nostrils flare, witchweed smoke billowing out of them. In a deadly voice, he says, "I'm not leaving until we've choked the bloody life out of *all* those shadow magic bastards. And I'm taking Forsythe's fucking femurs, and I'm gonna use them to crack open Eloise's skull like a rotten egg, and I'm gonna gather up all the pieces and make a lovely tile mosaic for our kitchen."

"Let's just make sure West is safe," Rook says. "You can indulge in your creativity later. Deal?"

Our resident psycho grins again, but his eyes are deadly serious. "You've got yourself a deal, genius."

We review the basics one more time. Then, the witches join hands and close their eyes, magic crackling between them as they begin their spell, and the rest of us quickly move into position.

High atop Thornwood Cathedral, the stained glass

windows glow ominously, and a cold dread settles into my gut.

Hang on, witchling. We're coming.

From their timeless perch around the bell tower, the stone gargoyles of Thornwood watch me and Rook fly circles overhead, their eyes impassive as ever.

The last time we saw them was the night of the first wedding. Draegan had taken some notes about their deteriorating condition, hoping we might find ways to patch them up. Protect them from the elements.

Sadly, we never got the chance. Everything happened so quickly that night with West, and it feels like we haven't been able to take a breath since.

I look them over now, though, as we circle above the invisible barrier and await the witches' signal. Jude and Drae are on the ground, preparing to charge through the doors on the main level—Jude in front, Drae in back. Rook and I will come down the bell tower stairs. Between the four of us, we should be able to spot Westlyn and get to her fast.

To save her from whatever darkness fate—and her cruel, fucked-up family members—have planned for her.

Nervous energy has me hot and twitchy, and I stretch my wings and sweep around the tower again, trying to calm myself in the stately presence of the old gargoyles. I've photographed them so many times and from so many different angles that I know every shape and shadow by heart. Every chip. Every fissure.

I knew them as men, and while their human faces have long since faded from my memory, their strength and courage has not.

I borrow it now, reciting their human names in my mind. Remembering them.

Tonight, I will honor them in the best way I know how —by keeping the ones I love safe.

A hacking cough breaks into my thoughts, scattering them. I fly around to Rook, who's got a fist pressed to his chest, his eyes squeezed shut in obvious pain.

"Rook?" I ask. "You okay?"

Head still bowed, he sucks in a deep breath, almost like he can't get enough air. But after a beat, it passes, and he stretches out his wings and meets my gaze once more, sharp-eyed and alert behind the glasses.

"Still feeling that library smoke in your lungs?" I ask. Every time I take a deep breath, I can taste it. The char. The ash.

But Rook shakes his head. "Nah, I'm good. Just anxious to get our witch."

"Any minute now," I say. "As soon as we feel that ripple, we're—"

"*You have no claim on me, monster!*" Westlyn cries out from somewhere inside the cathedral, her voice dark and powerful, and a burst of cold, otherworldly magic tears through the night, a great shattering of stained glass and metal and wood that rumbles up from the foundations and radiates into the air above, nearly knocking us both out of the sky.

When we stop spiraling and get our bearings again, the air is charged with electricity, my head ringing from the blast, and two things become abundantly clear.

The magical barrier has been obliterated.

And so has half the fucking cathedral.

Dark power surges inside, eradicating the lingering effects of the mage drugs and whatever spells Verrick cast on my body. The magic imprisoning me inside the altar space falls away, and I get to my feet.

The demon legions watch closely, silent and obedient. Awaiting orders.

"Rise," I command, the voice not truly mine. The *thought* not even mine. It's as though I've been possessed too, right along with the mages.

But one look at Verrick, at his proud smile, at his silver eyes, and I know without a doubt that it *is* mine. All of it.

My voice, my thoughts, my demons.

My power.

My legacy.

Finally free, I step down from the altar, and the hooded masses rise at my approach, heads bowed low, the hems of their black robes whispering against the floor. They don't speak through those horrifying stitched mouths, but I hear their collective voice in my head, scraping inside the walls of my skull like a thousand dull knives.

We are yours, Moon Blessed. Witch-queen of the forgotten realms. Yours to control. Yours to command.

Desire flickers inside me like a black flame, and dozens of runes appear on my arms, glowing as bright as the moon.

Mine to control. Mine to command...

As humans, the shadow mages were fiendish and vile. But as vessels for demons? They're straight out of the land of nightmares.

I can feel their evil, their darkest instincts brought to life by *my* blood.

Not Zorakkov's. Not Eloise's. Not the great Archmage of Manhattan's.

But mine.

Mine to control. Mine to command...

Desire licks a hot path up my spine. Alarm bells ring in my head, but I tune them all out.

What do you demand of us, Moon Blessed? The scrape of that multi-layered voice fills my mind once more, calling my magic to life. It crackles in my palms, hot and eager.

Still spread open on the altar table, the ancient Cerridwen Codex pulses in time with my heartbeat.

Take what's yours, daughter, it seems to say. *Take all of it.*
All of it.
All of it.

I spread my arms before the demons, smiling at them like a benevolent goddess...

Mine to control. Mine to—

"What is the meaning of this treachery?" The Archmage shouts, his voice cutting through the haze of my strange thoughts. As his shocked and horrified face comes into clear view, I know at once this wasn't part of the deal. Not the deal the shadow mages agreed to, anyway.

But Verrick?

This little show is playing out *exactly* as he intended.

My lips twist into a smirk. Like my thoughts, it doesn't feel wholly mine, but I claim it anyway.

That silver-eyed, dark-fae motherfucker—my father— just double-crossed the Prince of Hell.

He bound me to Zorakkov. Allowed him to use my blood to summon hell's legions into the bodies of the awaiting shadow mages.

The last line of the prophecy comes back to me once more—*Blessed is the blood that brings the world down*—and as I look back at the demons silently awaiting my command, I realize that this is it.

This is how it starts.

"Stop!" Zorakkov shouts, hobbling toward me on shaky legs, his body still a hot mess even after the binding. "I command you to obey me!"

I don't know whether he's speaking to me or the demons, but it doesn't matter.

The demon legions aren't going to answer to him.

They're going to answer to the witch whose so-called "blessed blood" called them forth from the abyss.

Verrick knew this would happen, and now that it has, he wants to use *me* to achieve his ends.

I can hear it in his hungry voice, feel it in the greedy whispers of fae magic still prickling across my skin.

He thinks he can coerce me.

He thinks I have no real power.

Ignoring Zorakkov and the Archmage's furious protests, he comes to stand at my side now, his voice cool against my neck as he murmurs his twisted, dark-fae spells. His magic is a coarse, ancient language I don't understand, but every word unlocks another image in my mind—the same visions that have haunted my nightmares. The same visions I saw when I got a glimpse into Eloise's twisted thoughts.

But in Verrick's vision of the future, Eloise and the shadow magic society suffer the same fate as the humans he intends to enslave, torture, and execute, paving the way for the dark fae to reclaim the earthly realm as their own.

The demon army—*my* demon army—will carry out his will, obliterating all of humanity.

Another whisper of magic, his fingers cool on the back of my neck, and suddenly I can hear their screams. Smell the blood running red in the streets.

I whirl around to face him. He smiles at me like a proud father, and power blazes in the air between us. The red jewels on his crown sparkle in the candlelight, and my runes respond in kind, blazing on my skin.

His runes.

His fucking claim.

"Taste it, my moon," he whispers, his magic a sweet seduction as it winds around my heart. "The power. The darkness. All of it will soon be ours."

I smile at him in earnest. In the inky black of his pupils, I see my reflection, my own eyes glowing bright. Sparks of violet magic arc across my chest, the demon legions feeding me their power. Their hatred. Their malice.

"No, Father," I whisper, my lips brushing Verrick's ear. "All of it will be *mine*."

The pride in his eyes falls away, replaced in a heartbeat with pure, uncut rage.

"Do *not* presume to claim the power that my blood has bestowed upon you. I am your—"

"*You have no claim on me, monster*!" I roar, slamming my palms into his chest. A burst of wild, indigo magic explodes from my very soul, the force of it sending him flying into the nearest pew. The wood splinters beneath him, and the floor cracks, a deep rumble shaking the cathedral.

Indigo and silver light bursts out of the cracks in the floor, blinding me, a shocking pain splitting my skull.

The cathedral groans, timber beams cracking. A chandelier crashes to the ground, then another. Windows shatter overhead, and the side wall crumbles. I have just enough awareness to drop and roll under a pew before a thousand stained-glass shards fall to the floor in a deadly rain, slicing through the demon army.

Chaos erupts as the legions scatter, slipping on blood and gore, choked by the dust of the falling walls. Zorakkov and the Forsythes run into the fray in a vain attempt to corral the demons, but the Archmage and his family have no power over my dark army.

I glance over at the broken pew where Verrick landed, but he's gone. I can't find Eloise or Brian, either, but that doesn't matter now.

Out. I need to get the fuck out.

But glass continues to rain down, the remaining chandeliers swinging precariously overhead. Candles fall, flames igniting wooden beams. Black robes catch and burn.

I'm about to make a run for it, take my chances in the chaos, when I spot a familiar shadow sweeping over me.

Wings.

Seconds later, strong arms haul me out from under the pew and pull me against a muscled chest, those beautiful, impenetrable wings arcing over us, shielding us from the falling debris.

"Hang on, witchling," a deep voice growls in my ear. "You fucking hang on."

Augustine.

The feel of him, the warmth, the solid arms around me... All of it brings me back to myself. Back to him.

The runes on my skin fade, but the magic inside me crackles as hot as the burning cathedral.

I catch sight of the other gargoyles in my periphery— Rook heading for the Archmage, Draegan going after

Celine. Magic and violence clash, blood spilling, wood cracking all around us.

I find Jude just in time to see him tear out the heart of one of the robed demon-mages.

And there, right behind him, the awkward gait of the black-eyed demon prince.

"Put me down," I demand.

"No can do," Augustine says. "We're leaving. Now."

"No! I'm not leaving here like this. Not while Verrick and Zorakkov still breathe."

Auggie sighs, almost as if he's... disappointed?

That makes no sense.

"Auggie, what are you doing? Put me down! I'm serious!" I struggle against his hold, but he doesn't budge.

"Witchling, you can hate me for this all you want, but I can't let you do this. You're not yourself right now. It's the demon bond. It's forcing you to obey him, and—"

"*Obey* him?" I laugh. "Augs. Look at me."

He meets my gaze, scrutinizing me.

"I'm ready to fucking *destroy* him," I grit out, magic pulsing in my hands. "Verrick too, along with all these demons and anyone else in on this sick, fucked up game. So either put me down and help me, or I'll put *you* down with a spell that'll knock you so hard on your ass, you'll turn back into a human."

For a second, Auggie doesn't speak. Doesn't even breathe.

But then... a slow grin, that dimple finally making an

appearance. A sparkle in his hazel eyes. And finally, a deep rumble of laughter vibrating through his chest, making his whole body shake.

"It's really you," he says.

"It's really me."

He sets me on my feet, takes one more look at what's left of the ceiling to make sure nothing else is about to fall on our heads, then grabs my face and plants a searing-hot, all-too-brief kiss on my mouth.

"I got your back, witchling," he says, finally releasing me. "Let's take these motherfuckers *down*."

CHAPTER ELEVEN

JUDE

Ahhh, the delicious scents of fear and freshly spilled blood. The soothing sounds of splintering wood and breaking glass. The unholy screams of the innocent.

Oh, *fine*. Eloise and the Forsythes are not exactly *innocent*. And they're not so much "screams" as "tormented wails of the eternally damned," but I digress.

Serenity—that's what I'm talking about. That's what this night has become.

Because after I spent the first part of the night crawling out of my skin thinking I'd never see my girl again, there she is, safe in Augustine's arms on the other side of the cathedral.

The demon-mages are running around like headless chickens—all the more fun because some of them *are* headless, thanks to me and Drae. And even Rook's witches have joined in on the fun, lighting up the whole place with a show of magic and lights that even Disney World couldn't compete with.

"Jude! Watch your back!" Rook shouts, and I spin around just in time to catch another demon-mage by the throat. Motherfucker was about to set my arse on fire with his spooky little candle and a little hocus-pocus hell magic.

I lift him off his feet, grinning at him through my fangs.

"Black robes? Really?" I punch my other fist through his chest and rip out his heart, tossing it to the floor like rotten meat. "You'd think the most powerful mage society in all of Manhattan wouldn't have to resort to the post-Halloween bargain bins for their formalwear. Then again, I suppose it hides the blood pretty well, doesn't it?"

He doesn't answer. Poor blokes can't talk, what with their mouths sewn shut and all.

I drop his arse on the floor and take down three of his mates, their blood coating my skin. Rook's right by my side now, smashing skulls, tearing out vital organs.

But for every demon we take down, another seems to spring up in its place, like we're standing at the very gateway to hell.

Fucking demons. Fucking shadow mages. Fucking hell magic bullshit.

So much for serenity.

"We need to get the fuck out of here," I say to Rook, his hands buried in another demon chest. "Where's Drae?"

"Jude!" Westlyn shouts, her voice clear and commanding, cutting through the din. "Move!"

I grab Rook and the two of us leap out of the way just as our girl throws out a blast of purple lightning—wild and angry, as beautiful and terrifying as she is. It hits home, scorching three bastards in one perfect shot, melting the flesh from their skulls.

The scent of fried demon makes me all kinds of warm and tingly, and the sight of Westlyn after fearing the worst all night makes me feel all kinds of something else, and that's it. I need to touch her. To hold her.

Right fucking now.

Path clear for the moment, I run to her, scooping her up in my arms and giving her a big kiss. With extra tongue, just how she likes it, the dirty girl.

Laughing and breathless, she wriggles out of my hold and says, "Did you see that last move? With the zap, and the whole lightning thing?"

"I saw everything, scarecrow. And I couldn't be more proud of you. Not to mention grateful you're alive. Fucking hell, woman. I thought you were..." I shake my head. Can't even bring myself to say it.

"Honestly? I thought so too." West laughs, nervous and relieved both, brushing her wrist across her forehead. A trail of blood streaks her skin.

Fuck, that's sexy.

Fuck, I should not be thinking about how sexy she is right now.

But fuck, I can't help it.

I steal another kiss, sweeping my tongue into her mouth, damn near eating her up right there.

But all too soon, the demons are rising again, and Draegan's shouting something behind us about the Codex, and Westlyn's face falls, and then she's bolting away from me, headed straight for the altar.

I spin around and see Verrick and the Archmage both diving for the Codex, magic pulsing from its pages like the very lightning West used to attack the demons, dark and violent and deadly.

"Burn in *hell*!" she shouts at them, snatching the book away just as her enemies crash into the table. She clutches the Codex to her chest, tendrils of silver and indigo magic snaking out from inside it, winding around her arms like serpents.

"Where the fuck is Auggie?" Rook shouts, joining me again. "We need to get West and—fuck. Incoming!"

I tear my gaze away from West and catch a half dozen demons charging toward us. Tatiana's right behind them, her eyes widening with some horrifying realization I can't even guess at. Her lips move rapidly, and I feel the warmth of her magic washing over me just as the tendrils wrapped around West explode in a flash of blinding silver magic that knocks us all to the ground.

There's nothing but that light. That eerie magical light, and a pain like nothing I've ever felt before, like my entire body is being turned inside out and scrubbed with a wire brush, which is way less fun that it sounds.

I'm spinning. I'm floating. I'm sinking. I'm drowning. Every last one of my cells is being rearranged, reformed, and I can't fucking see...

Westlyn. Where are you? Where the fuck are you...

A burst of cold air floods my lungs, shocking my body back to consciousness. When I finally open my eyes again, I'm ninety-nine fucking percent sure we're dead.

And a *hundred* fucking percent sure we're in hell.

"Is everyone all right?" Tatiana says, helping Fleur and Laney out of a snowdrift.

I do a quick scan—all gargoyles are bloodied but present and accounted for, but... fuck. Westlyn.

Right there. Standing in the middle of the group, still clutching that Codex, shivering her tight little arse off, but alive.

And really fucking angry about it, too, judging from the fire in her eyes.

"Why is it snowing in the cathedral?" she shouts up at the sky, fat snowflakes landing on her cheeks and melting against her skin. "And why do I feel like someone tried to turn me into a smoothie? Somebody better explain this before I absolutely lose my shit!"

She's dangerously close to losing said shit, not that I blame her. None of this makes a damn bit of sense.

I trudge through the snow and put a wing around her,

blocking out the cold as best I can as I scan the area, trying to get my bearings.

We seem to be in some sort of town square straight out of the middle ages, complete with its own gallows and pillories. A guillotine too. A few dozen dilapidated buildings and homes line the street, and on the edges of this pathetic little town, a dark, lifeless forest encroaches, bare black trees reaching up through the snow like corpses rising from the grave.

A gust of wind buffets us, bringing with it a silence so dark and complete, I want to weep.

"Jude," West whispers, teeth chattering. "Is this... Are we in hell?"

"No, darling," I say softly, the realization finally hitting me. "Worse. We're in the Court of Wintermoon."

She shivers beneath my wing, and when I look into her face, tiny threads of that same dark magic skitter across her skin. Still held in her protective embrace, the Codex gives off a faint glow.

"This doesn't look like the Wintermoon I remember," Auggie says, spinning in slow circles as he takes it all in. There's not a soul in sight. No *life* in sight—fae, animals, birds, evergreens. Even the snow itself feels like death. "How did we even get here?"

"There's a fae portal above Thornwood," Drae says. "I assumed it was no longer operational, but Verrick must've triggered it."

"Why the fuck would he bring us here?" Auggie asks. "The place is a damn ghost town."

"I'm wondering the same thing, mate." I draw my little scarecrow a bit closer, more for myself than for her, if I'm being honest. This whole fucking place is giving *me* a case of Auggie's infamous heebie-jeebies. "If only the coward had the balls to show his face, we could ask him."

"Verrick didn't bring us here." Tatiana glares at West.

My hackles raise, but it's not accusation in the old witch's eyes.

It's wonder.

"She's... she's right." West blows out a breath, fogging the air before us. "I'm pretty sure it was me. Rather, the Wintermoon magic in my blood. I can't explain it. I grabbed the Codex and felt this surge of magic—the same kind of magic I felt last night when I supposedly brought Verrick to our realm and—"

"Wait." I cup her face, gazing into her eyes, bright blue-green against the endless sea of white that surrounds us. "You brought him to our realm? Why?"

"There was a spell for it in the book. He tricked me." She gives us the highlights-version of her dream. The cauldron and the fire. Waking up in the cathedral to come face-to-face with the monster that fathered her.

And later, face-to-face with the one who raised her.

My blood boils all over again, hungry to sink my fangs into Verrick's throat. Brian's too, for being such a damned coward.

But neither bastard is anywhere in sight.

"When I saw Verrick and Forsythe going after the Codex, I just knew I couldn't let them get their hands on it. But the moment I picked it up, I felt that overwhelming surge. It was like my magic was being pulled in two directions. Part of it felt like it was trying to protect me. The other part felt like it was trying to..." She closes her eyes, a shiver rattling her from head to toe.

"Trying to what, darling?" I say softly.

When she looks up at me again, that same magic whispers across her skin. "To bring me home."

"Wintermoon *isn't* your home," Draegan says, as if by his firm command he can make it so. But even he knows the truth.

Westlyn is the Wintermoon princess. She may not choose to live here, but this court is her ancestral homeland.

"How do I get us back?" she asks the witches, her words no more than a whisper of white in the air. "Do any of you know how to cast a portal spell? As in, on purpose?"

The witches look at her with serious gazes, which is all the answer we need.

"That's what I was afraid of," West says. "Damn it."

"It's all right," I tell her, though I'm pretty sure it's not. "We'll figure it all out. Maybe there's something else in that book of yours. But right now, we just need to get in out of this cold. Maybe find something to eat. Yeah?"

At the suggestion of food, she brightens a bit, and we all

head out in search of a place to take shelter, preferably one that's not one stiff breeze away from toppling into dust.

Preferably one that's not fucking haunted, either, but by the looks of this town, that might be a bit too much to hope for.

CHAPTER TWELVE

JUDE

Drae takes point with Auggie. I stick close to West. Rook brings up the rear with the witches, his sharp eyes taking in every detail.

"When the magical bomb went off, for lack of a better descriptor," our resident genius says, "it felt to me as if the entire cathedral got sucked up into the vortex."

"It very likely did," Laney replies. "If Westlyn cast a portal spell, consciously or unconsciously, it would've impacted every living being it touched."

"I don't see any signs of the others, though," Rook says. "Verrick, the Forsythes, Eloise. Not to mention all those mages. Demons. Whatever the hell they were. Did they end up in a different realm?"

"No," Tatiana says. "They're all here in Wintermoon with us—for whatever reason, I'm getting a strong sense of their presence. The portal spell wasn't specific—everyone who crossed over was essentially scattered to the winds, so to speak."

"Then how did we all remain together?" Rook asks.

"That was my doing." Tatiana sighs. "The moment Westlyn picked up the Codex, I felt a portal opening. I had no idea where we were going, only that we *were* going. There was just enough time for me to cast a temporary spell of connection on our group to ensure we wouldn't be separated on the journey."

"Smart thinking," he says, the admiration in his tone clear.

"This is not my first encounter with portal magic," she says. "Though I can't say it's my preferred mode of travel. Goddess above, I'd rather be stuck in bumper-to-bumper traffic on a packed bus in the Holland Tunnel than go through that again."

"That makes two of us, Tats." I pull out my witchweed, grateful it made the journey with us, and turn to offer her one. "Ciggie?"

"You know, I don't mind if I do."

I light one up for her, then offer the pack to the rest of our rag-tag crew, but they all decline.

Guess it's just me and Tats with the oral fixation, which is fine by me. I've got no idea how long we'll be stuck here, and I'm not keen on running out of these babies.

We finally come upon an old tavern and inn that looks to be in pretty good shape, aside from a thick layer of dust coating every surface inside. Not sure what the upstairs holds, but on the main level there's a decent sized kitchen, two bathing chambers, and a bar and dining area that opens into a big common room with a couch and overstuffed chairs and a gloriously massive hearth.

An untouched stack of wood leans against the stones, and I get to work building a fire to chase away the chill, if such a thing is even possible here.

"Where are the demons, then?" West asks the witches, joining me at the hearth. "There were so many... It's weird that we aren't seeing any evidence of them."

"The demons likely haven't materialized," Fleur says. "They're here, but not in physical form. They were only just summoned from hell, bound to the mages whose bodies they inhabited. But the mages themselves died the moment they were possessed, which means *those* bodies are still in the cathedral. The demonic entities... They have nothing to tether them to this realm yet. So they merely... exist."

"And what of the diabolical residents of Wintermoon," Draegan muses, more to himself than to anyone else as he paces the perimeter of the rooms, inspecting the shelves and cupboards. Tension radiates from his every muscle, his eyes alert for danger.

"I don't think there's anyone left," Tatiana says. "I can sense energies, and this place is... It's dead. But there's an undercurrent of anger here, too. Resentment. Same sort of echo you might find after a person has been murdered. Whatever happened here, it affected scores of people. It was sudden and unexpected, and it didn't happen all that long ago. A few weeks, perhaps."

"What makes you say that?" Rook asks.

"It's the intensity of the energy. The sharpness of it. I can almost taste their fear, their anger." She glances around the space. "The fact that the inn seems to be in relatively decent condition speaks to that as well. It doesn't have the same feeling of utter neglect that places get after they've long been abandoned."

"I'm feeling it too," Auggie says, his face pale. "A lot of darkness. Rage. Strong, strong vibes."

"The question is," Rook says, "if all these fae were murdered, where the hell are the bodies?"

Tatiana shakes her head and closes her eyes, holding out her hands as if she's trying to literally feel for an answer. "Whatever event took them, it was magical in nature, and it was evil. Pure evil. That much, I can say with certainty."

A collective shiver ripples through us all.

"Augs. You good?" Sensing his discomfort more than anyone else's, I nod for him to join me and West by the fire, which is just starting to crackle to life. "You don't look so good, mate."

"I'll... I'll be okay. Just need to shake off this bad mojo. I'm gonna go clean up, then check out the food stores in the kitchen. See if there's anything salvageable."

While the rest of us wash off the blood and gore from the attack and the humans find some warmer clothing to change into, Augs manages to cook up a stew of potatoes and herbs and carrots and some sort of dried beef I don't bother asking him to name, because it's hot and hearty and that's what matters most right now. Westlyn, of course, gets the veggie version. We even found some wine and ale in the cellar, and between that and my fire fit for a king, the mood is considerably lighter.

As we all go in on seconds on Auggie's stew, a thing that pleases him immensely, Westlyn fills us in on the rest of the details about what happened in the library last night: her strange nightmares, the woman from the Judgment card in the Tarot, all the things Verrick told her when she came to consciousness in the cathedral.

She tells us about Brian and his alleged attempts to protect her from this fate, about her apparent command over the demons, and her suspicions that Verrick double-crossed Zorakkov and the Forsythes, intending to steal the demonic army for his own dark deeds.

"But now that we're here," West says with a sigh, "I really don't get it. He said he wanted me to rule in his stead in Wintermoon once he reclaimed the earthly realm for the dark fae. But... *what* dark fae? And who, exactly, did he want me to rule over? This whole realm feels like a ghost town. Does he have all his minions stashed away somewhere, awaiting his triumphant rise to power in our realm?"

"All questions that need pondering," Tatiana says, "and answering."

I pass her another witchweed cig, sensing she's about to get philosophical, and light one up for myself.

The witches are just starting to get into the nitty-gritty on all that Moon Blessed prophecy lore and West's connection to the Codex when I decide that in addition to the weed, the conversation also needs more wine.

I'm about to head down to the cellar to find a few more bottles when Westlyn suddenly bolts up from the table, a look of sheer panic in her eyes.

"He's here," she breathes, and her skin comes alive with glowing fae runes.

It's all the warning we get before Verrick crashes through the front door on a frigid wind.

"Give me my daughter and the Codex, or all of you will *burn*." The fire surges brightly at his ominous threat, flames licking the top of the hearth, smoke swirling into the common room, choking out the breathable air.

Chaos erupts as the gargoyles and I charge at him, the witches calling up more spells, the fire roaring like a living beast as we grapple with the dark fae king and magic sizzles in the air and dishes clatter to the ground and then, all at once, the bastard is just... gone.

He's gone.

The fire is back in its place. The smoke has cleared.

Drae, Augs, and I look around at each other and the space between us like we just hallucinated the whole damn thing.

"Where the fuck *is* he?" Draegan demands. "He was right bloody here in my grasp, and then he just—"

"No... Oh, goddess, no. *No!*" Westlyn's cries slice

through the confusion, and we turn to find her on her knees in front of the fire, tears glittering on her cheeks, her hair wild.

In her hands, she holds a pair of broken glasses like it's the most precious thing she's ever touched.

My fucking heart drops.

Because right beside her, towering over her like a silent, protective sentry, is a horned, winged statue of solid stone.

A *gargoyle* of solid stone.

Rook.

CHAPTER THIRTEEN

DRAEGAN

There's no safety to be found here. No security.

Rook's transformation is just one more reminder of the ticking clock hanging over us all, as sharp and deadly as the guillotine outside.

From a bedroom on the second floor an hour after the attack, I gaze out the window, trying to see beyond the dark, snow-covered street. Trying to gauge how far this town is from Verrick's castle, assuming that's where he might've gone. Trying to pick out the best route.

Trying to do something other than stand by while my men to turn to stone and the woman I love falls into the clutches of her evil father, cursed to roam this desolate land as the souls of her gargoyles will be cursed to wander the halls of hell.

I've just decided that no one route is better than the

other—that I must simply choose a direction and fly until I find him—when I feel her approaching the doorway.

It's her presence I sense first, the warmth on the air, the way my heart beats faster when she's near. Her scent comes to me next, apples and sweetness, newly tinged with a magic all her own.

When I finally hear the creek of her soft footsteps on the wooden floors, I turn from the window and look her over.

Before dinner, she traded in her thin dress for some warmer clothing she must've found in one of the rooms—a soft tunic and trousers, wool socks that are a bit too large, slouching on her feet—and despite her show of power at the cathedral, she looks young and soft and far too vulnerable.

"You're planning to go after him," she says quietly. They're the first words she's directly spoken to me since our argument in my bathroom—feels like a lifetime ago now.

But those words are not a question, so I don't answer them as such.

"This is yours," I say instead, handing over the amulet I found in her bedroom at Blackmoor. "You... left it behind."

It glows bright at her touch, violet and amber light reflecting in the depths of her eyes.

"It feels stronger here," she says, tucking it into a pocket in her trousers. "Everything does—the amulet, my magic. My..." She swallows hard. "My connection to Verrick. Even when he's not with me, I feel him trying to get inside my mind. Trying to manipulate me again."

My blood simmers, my jaw clenching tight.

"All the more reason for me to—" *End him*, I want to say, but don't. That would require admitting that yes, I *am* planning to go after him—an admission that would only lead to a prolonged argument in which she tries to talk me out of it and I try to justify it and then, once again, we part in bitter silence.

"What happens when the sun rises and your stuck outside somewhere?"

"It isn't our sun. It won't affect us the way it does back home."

Westlyn folds her arms across her chest and leans against the doorframe, scrutinizing me. "You have a plan, then?"

Damn it.

I did *not* want to get into this with her tonight, but... "Yes."

"Care to enlighten me? Preferably with something other than a grunt and a one-word answer?"

Biting back a sarcastic retort, I say firmly, "You and the others will hunker down here. Eat some more food, drink some more ale. Warm yourselves by the fire and get some rest. Tomorrow, you'll—"

"And where will *you* be while we're all having this Christmas-card-worthy gathering?"

"I'll be... taking care of Verrick."

"Oh!" Westlyn laughs. "In that case, please. Continue. You were saying?"

I glare at her.

"*Tomorrow*," I repeat, "you'll put your heads together and figure out how to open another portal, and by the time I return, we can—"

"Put our heads together. Right." She lets out a laugh like the bitterest wind, but the tears glazing her eyes are borne of nothing but grief. "You know *damn* well which one of us would've figured it out. Rook. Rook Van Doren. But he can't. Why? Because he's locked in stone. A thing that could happen to any one of the rest of you, at any moment, without warning."

"Which is why I need to go, Westlyn. Can't you see that?"

"Go where? We're in the middle of nowhere, dead of winter. Dead of everything."

"I need to find Verrick's castle, where he's very likely hiding, licking his wounds. The sooner I take him out, the sooner we—"

"Take him *out*? Draegan. The king of Wintermoon isn't some petty criminal you can intimidate with a wave of your gun and a few salacious photos. You're talking about the monster who tricked me into burning down Rook's library and bringing him to the earthly realm. The monster who doubled-crossed a prince of hell. The monster who cursed you. Who slaughtered your family and probably spent the last fifteen centuries dreaming up ways to torture you and—"

"I know *damn* well who I'm talking about, far better than you, so unless you've got something constructive to add to this conversation, you're wasting my time."

Anger chases the grief from her eyes, but she doesn't rise to my cruel bait. Not tonight.

Guilt, my old friend, gnaws at my insides, and for a long time, we just glare at each other in the moonlight.

I would give anything to know what she's thinking, but I can't bring myself to ask.

I haven't earned the right.

"Celine Forsythe is dead," I finally say, my voice soft in the dim space.

Westlyn gasps, a look of true surprise in her gaze. "I saw you go after her, but then I lost track."

"She managed to escape me in the chaos, but I grabbed her again just before the portal spell surged. Her magic was tapped out, and she opened her mouth to... I don't know. Beg for her life? Offer some dark bargain? I didn't give her the chance. I ripped open her throat, then bashed her fucking head against the wall. It was gruesome and terrible and I didn't feel an ounce of remorse."

I step away from the window, crossing the room until I'm standing so close to her she has to tip her head back to meet my eyes, and that face—that lovely, heartbreaking face that's etched so deeply into my memory—suddenly unleashes a rage inside me so complete, I see only blood and fire.

"I didn't fucking *hesitate* to destroy her, Westlyn, because on your first night at Blackmoor I made a vow that I would take down *all* of your enemies. That counts doubly now for the dark-fae king who's already made demands for your surrender tonight. So no, I will *not* remain here and warm idle hands by the fire while he plots his next attack and you are still a target and this nightmare *fucking* realm is—"

"You don't think we all feel that way?" she snaps, jabbing a finger into my chest. "No one wants to sit around with our thumbs up our asses, Drae. We want to fight. And we *will* fight, but we need to do it together. None of us is strong enough to take him down alone. Not even you. I don't care what you—"

"I'm sorry, but there's nothing you can say to talk me out of this. I'm leaving."

She huffs out a breath and takes a few steps back, the cold rushing in to fill the space. "So that's how it is, then?"

"That's how it is."

A tiny shake of her head, and she lowers her gaze to the floor, staring at a dark spot in the wood for so long I wonder if it might ignite.

After what feels like an age, she finally meets my gaze again.

In a small, hoarse voice, she says, "How many times have you saved me?"

I fold my arms over my chest and sigh.

"How many?" she presses. "Ballpark."

When I can't produce a number for her, she says, "Yeah, I lost count too. Lost count of how many times you saved my *life*, Draegan. My life! So if you think I want you to risk yours on some suicide mission against your oldest foe, you can go fuck yourself right into the nearest snowbank, because I—"

"Westlyn, you don't understand! Never mind my past with him. The fact is, Verrick will never stop being a threat to you. Hunting you. That is *all* the reason I need to tear out his fucking heart."

She closes the distance between us again and I brace myself for another jab to the chest, another barrage of angry words.

But her face falls, a sad but gentle smile touching her lips, and she places her palm on my cheek, surprising me with the warmth of her touch.

"I love you," she whispers, and the raw simplicity of the declaration nearly bowls me over. "And that's all the reason *I* need to ask you, one last time, not to walk out those doors. Stay with me, Draegan Caldwell. Please stay."

She brushes her thumb across my lips, then turns and walks out of the room with my whole heart in her hands, her retreating form little more than a blur through the shock of tears in my eyes.

CHAPTER FOURTEEN

DRAEGAN

I don't know how long I stare out the window, frozen with guilt and indecision and an aching heart, when I feel another presence behind me.

"What is it, Jude?" I ask softly, not turning from the window.

After the conversation I had with Westlyn, I've got no fight in me for another sparring match, especially not with the gargoyle who best knows how to get under my skin.

The ropes beneath the bedding creak as he takes a seat. There's a rustling, then the flick of a lighter, the crackle of a cigarette flaring to life.

"I know what you're thinking about," he finally says, smoke lacing the air. "What you're feeling."

"Oh, really?" I laugh. "Care to enlighten me, then? I seem to be having a bit of trouble sorting it all out for myself."

Another crackle. A deep exhale.

"What happened with Verrick," Jude says softly, "the bloody wars, the bloodier aftermath, this fucking curse... For fuck's sake, Draegan. None of it was your fault."

Outside, dark clouds slide across the moon, blanketing the snowy lands in darkness.

"I led you into a losing war and gave you a death sentence," I say simply, because that's the honest truth. "All of you. I'm *still* giving you—"

"You gave us *hope*. And while you can certainly be a right pain in the arse on the best of days, you're also my fucking brother, and I've let you carry this burden for far too long. It was never yours to bear, but you did it anyway, and we let you. We fucking let you, Drae, and *that* is my one true regret in life. Not that I fought by your side. Not that I sacrificed everything for a losing war. Not that I'm cursed. But that when the dust finally settled and we realized everything we'd ever known and loved was gone, *you* picked up that shame, and I stood by and let you carry it off. You're *still* carrying it, and I'm trying to tell you... Fucking hell, Draegan. Let it go."

His words cut me right to the core, hollowing me out inside, but he's not done yet.

"I'm not just talking about the war and the curse, either," he continues. "I'm talking about *all* of it. Westlyn. Rook. Fucking *Verrick*. The way everything went tits up before our eyes tonight and all we could do was just stand there with our dicks in our hands... It's a bloody damn mess, yeah. But our girl's right. You can't fight him alone. We're all stronger—and smarter—when we stick together. Going off half-cocked is the surest way to end up ashes in a box, and after what happened to Rook, I'm *damn* well not gonna stand by and watch you sign your *own* death warrant just because you're convinced you've signed ours." He pats the bedding beside him. "So come over here and take a load off, or I'll be forced to take it off for you, and I'd really rather not. I've only just gotten the last of the mage blood out from under my claws."

I manage a weak laugh at that. Then, with a heavy sigh, I finally turn away from the window and join him on the bed, stealing his pack of witchweed smokes.

I pluck the cigarette from between his lips and use it to light my own, then hand it back, taking a deep drag. I haven't smoked in years, and the effects are immediate, my head already swimming with a pleasant, mellow buzz.

"Was a time when you would've relished the idea of me going off on a suicide mission," I say, exhaling a plume of smoke.

Jude looks at me as if I've just hit him, and it takes me a hazy beat to realize he's actually affronted.

"Is that what you think?" He shakes his head, eyes glazing. "For all our long years, the four of us have walked side by side with death. We've spilled rivers of blood, broken enough bones to build a full-sized replica of the city, and fought each *other* enough it's a wonder we never destroyed the manor. But if I'd ever lost any of you—truly lost you—

fucking hell, Draegan. It would've gutted me. Do you understand? Westlyn... she's not the only one who... who loves..." He trails off and turns away, sucking in another drag. "Think whatever you want. But *no*, you won't be sauntering about Wintermoon tonight like some lone wolf with a score to settle. Westlyn might not be able to stop you on her own, but there are two gargoyles in this tavern who can still draw blood, not to mention a bevy of witches who I'm sure would be more than happy to practice some of those sparkly attack spells on your cocky arse."

"Oh, all right. For fuck's sake." I laugh again, though whether it's from the witchweed or something else, I can't discern. "What's your plan then? Frankly, I'm all out of ideas."

"Tonight? We drink the rest of that wine. We sleep. We take turns keeping watch over each other and that Codex. We take care of Rook in whatever way we can. And most of all, we protect our girl, because *she's* the only reason we've got a fighting chance in this life at all. Agreed?"

She's the only reason we've got a fighting chance in this life...

I know Jude's not talking about her magic, her unwavering determination to break our curse.

He's talking about what she's brought back to us—the humanity we lost. The bonds of family we'd taken for granted with each other for so long before her arrival.

Love, in all its forms.

I shake my head, still shocked by the miracle of it. Just when we were ready to finally succumb to the darkness, in walked Westlyn Avery, shining a light so bright we couldn't help but follow it.

Jude's right. Westlyn's right. We all need a breather tonight. A chance to shore up our defenses and come up with a plan better than 'fly out the window and hope for the best.'

And most importantly, we need to stick together.

"Agreed," I finally respond. "But one night, Jude. Just one night. We rest and regroup. And tomorrow, we—"

"*Tomorrow*, brother..." Jude sucks down the last of his cigarette, then grins, sharp fangs glinting through the smoky haze. "Tomorrow, we're out for fucking *blood*."

CHAPTER FIFTEEN

ROOK

We've lived with the threat of a dark-fae curse hanging over our heads for fifteen centuries. Plenty of time to brood about it, to plumb every dark part of our worst nightmares for ideas on how it would eventually claim us.

I thought I'd covered all the bases. An endlessly wandering soul, never to find peace. The fear of eternal damnation. The particular torture of being trapped in stone for eons upon eons, conscious but unable to move. The incredible sense of loss for a life lived on someone else's terms.

Verrick's terms.

But even with all my dark imaginings, *nothing* could've prepared me for how it feels to be locked in a stone prison when the woman I love is out there worried sick over it. Her every tear is a knife through my heart, and her determination to find a way to set me free only makes me ache for her all the more.

This is not how she should be spending the prime of her life. Fending off dark curses, chasing a monstrous father through a deadly realm. Fighting battles that never should've been hers to begin with.

This is worse than a death sentence.

My witch is sitting with the other witches on the floor before the fire, right at my feet, yet I can't reach out and touch her.

I can't hold her and stroke her hair and promise her we'll find the answers.

I can't pore over book after book by her side, answering her questions, watching her eyes light up with new discoveries.

I can't kiss away her pain or make her laugh or flirt with her until she's begging for a kiss that could set us both ablaze.

And worst of all, I can't fucking protect her. Not from the agony of losing her gargoyles. Not from more of Verrick's twisted magical attacks. Not from whatever new threats lurk just beyond the tavern doors.

And it's driving me absolutely mad.

Right now, the only thing keeping me even marginally sane is the fact that the others are still able to take care of her, and we're no longer alone in this fight. Tatiana and the witches are with us, doing everything they can to find a way to defeat Verrick and the demons and get us all back home.

As for Westlyn... My wild witch may be down, but she's certainly not out.

Even after facing down Verrick twice tonight, she's still ready to fight. I could no more convince her to stop searching for a key to unlock my stone prison than she could convince me to stop loving her.

Now, while the guys clear away the dinner mess and do an inventory of the food, weapons, and supplies at the inn, West and the witches are hard at work too, poring over the Codex for clues about the Spell of Unmaking, the elder witches helping West learn to channel and control her magic.

With the way she handled herself in the cathedral, it's easy to forget this is all brand-new to her, but it is.

And my favorite student is more eager than ever to learn.

I just wish I could be part of this. Teaching her, guiding her. Filling up a whole new library with all the new discoveries she's going to make about herself.

"Thank you for helping me with all of this," she says now, as Laney returns from the bar with a fresh round of tea for the witches. "The Codex is still such a mystery. To be honest, I'm still trying to process the fact that I've got any magic at all, let alone that I'm a dark-fae princess with the power to read this ancient book."

"You aren't *just* a dark-fae princess, Westlyn," Tatiana says, glancing down at the Codex spread open before them.

"Or just a witch, for that matter. The fact that you *can* read this text can only mean one thing."

"That I'm cursed, too?" West forces out a laugh, but it quickly fades into her teacup.

Tatiana's face turns serious. "That you're a Daughter of Cerridwen. Descendant of the ancient witches who transcribed the original fae carvings of the text."

West looks up from her tea, her eyes wide. "But... how can you be so sure?"

"The book would not have chosen to reveal its secrets to you otherwise."

Holy shit.

No wonder none of us could ever read it. We couldn't even get near the thing. Only West. In all my research on the Cerridwen witches after we stole the Codex from Forsythe, I never came across anything about this.

"But it didn't," West says. "Not at first. It fought me tooth and nail just to open its pages."

"That was very likely Cerridwen's magic interacting with the dark-fae magic in your blood," Fleur explains. "Almost as if it sensed a threat. Not from you specifically, but from the Wintermoon fae. The dark-fae magic within you does *not* want its secrets revealed, yet the Cerridwen witches did reveal it. Spell by spell in this Codex. Now, those secrets are yours, handed down through your line."

"What changed?" West asks. "As far as I know, I've still got the Wintermoon blood running in my veins. If anything, it's even stronger now that I'm here. So why am I finding it easier to read the spells now?"

"Think of it like a new relationship," Tatiana says, and I'm hanging on every word, my fingers itching for my tablet or a pen to write all this down. "You need time to get to know each other. To build trust. Yes, you've got Winter-moon blood, and there's a lot of dark power inside you. But that doesn't make you evil or undeserving. The blood of Cerridwen's witches is equally powerful, equally accessible to you. You can achieve great works with both magics, or you can commit great atrocities. It's all in what you decide to do with the power granted to you."

Laney reaches across their circle and touches West's knee. "Your task, Westlyn, is to decide what kind of witch *you* want to be. Not the witch the Archmage and his ilk wanted you to be. Not the one Verrick is attempting to control and manipulate. Not the witch some ancient prophecy has dictated for you, generations before you were even born. Not even the witch you believe your gargoyles want. But the truly powerful, divine witch of your heart and soul."

"Goddess, this is all so..." West blows out a breath, her eyes shining with the same wonder I feel inside. "I spent my whole life believing I was useless. That I had no magic at all, no gifts, nothing to offer anyone but the burden of my exis-tence. Now, I find out nothing could be farther from the truth. I'm a dark-fae witch born of two powerful bloodlines

—a witch at the center of an ancient prophecy fated to bring together demons and dark fae in a new world order that's sure to destroy humankind. I have all this magic inside me—light *and* dark. And I'm getting stronger with every passing hour. And yet..." She lowers her gaze, a tear slipping free.

"What is it, child?" Tatiana says softly.

At this, West turns her face up toward mine, her eyes so haunted it breaks my heart. "I feel like I can't do a damn thing to save the men I love."

Tatiana places a hand over West's, smiling at her with the same gentle affection and patience that earned my trust all those years ago. "It's not that you *can't*, Westlyn. It's that you just haven't figured out how."

"Rook is still trapped either way. The guys are still bound by this curse. We're all stuck in Wintermoon, and... I don't know. Why do I have all this magic if I can't do anything useful with it? It's not much different from when I couldn't do any witchcraft at all. It's almost worse, actually, because this?" She runs a fingertip down the center of the book, the pages alighting with indigo sparks. "It just feels like a tease."

"Witchcraft is more than magic," Laney says. "It's a craft —just as the name suggests. And craft takes time to hone."

"But you have to believe you deserve it," Fleur says. "That you deserve the magic of your birthright. The more you question it, the more you resist it... You're blocking yourself from receiving its many blessings."

"How do I open up to it?" she asks, some of her

haunting sadness fading in the wake of a new curiosity. The desire, as ever, to learn and grow and become. I've seen that look in her eyes in the library so many times during our sessions together, and seeing it return to her now is just...

Hope. That's what it is. Pure hope.

"Become its vessel," Tatiana says. "Know that the ultimate source of the magic in your blood comes from life itself—from creation, from destruction, from the air you breathe and the ground you walk upon. It comes from the trees and the sky, from the rivers, from fire. From love. Allow all of that to come to you, to flow through you, and eventually you'll learn to channel it back out through your intentions."

"Intentions like bringing Rook back? Breaking their curse?"

Tatiana nods.

"I dreamed it would happen," she whispers. "Rook, turning to stone. But it didn't play out the same way. In my nightmares, we were on top of the Blackmoor Capital building in the city. Manhattan was burning. Rook wanted me to go through the portal there, but Verrick showed up. Then he sort of became Zorakkov... It was all kind of jumbled up. I stepped on Rook's glasses in the dream, too. So when that happened tonight, I just... Goddess, I just knew what was coming next. I feel... I feel like it's all my fault. Like I should've seen this coming and done something to stop it."

Oh, my sweet, wild witch. No...

How I wish I could take that blame from her shoulders. Hell, I've been fearing this fate for a long time now. The signs were there—the stiff wings, the aching back, the tight lungs.

Every night, it was taking me longer and longer to awaken from my stone slumber—longer than the others. Those aren't normal symptoms for immortal beings. I was very likely already turning, cell by cell.

Whether it was an attack from Verrick or merely crossing through the portal into Wintermoon, the process just accelerated.

Short of obliterating the curse, she couldn't have done anything to stop it.

But even if I could speak, she wouldn't trust those words. She's carrying the weight of our curse almost as much as Draegan is.

I worry it's going to destroy them both.

Tatiana rises to her feet, then comes to stand at my side, brushing her fingertips over my arm. Her touch is as grounding and comforting as ever.

"The gargoyles are under a powerful curse," she says. "Dark and terrible, crafted with fae and demon magic both. This tragedy was bound to happen one way or the other. The visions in your dreams may have given you glimpses, just as any divination method might—Tarot, pathworking, even reading the tea leaves. But destiny is never fixed. We always have choices."

"I guess that's good." West sighs, gazing into her teacup. "Because in my dreams? Verrick destroys us all."

The flames in the fireplace hiss and pop, and the witches fall silent, finishing their tea and gazing into their mugs. Searching for clues about their destinies, perhaps.

But I don't need to read the tea leaves to know *my* destiny.

The wild, Cerridwen witch and dark-fae princess of Wintermoon seated beside me? She sealed my fate the moment she walked into my library with her ravens, smiled at all my books, and stole my heart.

CHAPTER SIXTEEN
AUGUSTINE

Silence blankets the inn, a quiet restlessness settling into the cracks and crevices as we try to get used to our new accommodations and cobble together a few half-baked plans.

One to find Verrick and put a sword through his heart.

One to hunt down the Archmage and Eloise, and eliminate them from the chessboard too.

One to find Zorakkov and the demonic legions, and send those dickheads straight back to hell.

And finally, one to get our asses back home to the human realm.

Oh, and did I mention we need to stay alive for all this? That's kind of important, too.

Yeah. Talk about a stacked deck.

But of all the new worries dropped onto our proverbial

doorstep since last night, the one that's got me the most twisted up inside is Westlyn.

After her fireside meeting with the witches tonight, she's barely spoken. When Fleur and Laney volunteered to put fresh linens on the beds upstairs and set up rooms so everyone could get some sleep, West declined, preferring to remain on the sofa where she could keep an eye on Rook.

Hours have passed, and the elder witches have long since retired. But my witchling remains, steadfast in her loyalty, fighting sleep with strong tea and even stronger herbs she found in the kitchens.

Jude, Draegan, and I have been trading off shifts keeping watch outside, doing regular flyovers to scan for threats. The two of them are out there now, circling, but I wanted to come check on our girl.

Some part of me was hoping she'd decided to go upstairs and get some rest after all, but...

No such luck.

I get the sense she's not in the mood for conversation, so I grab a piece of charcoal and some old parchment I found behind the bar, and take a seat in one of the worn chairs in front of her.

"Do you mind if I sit by the fire with you?" I ask softly.

West shakes her head and smiles, but doesn't say anything else.

Not wanting to push her, I remain in my chair, stealing alternating glances at her and Rook, my hand moving across the parchment almost as if it's got a mind of its own.

I'm not sure how much time passes, but the fire has burned to embers when West finally speaks again, and somehow, I've managed to sketch a complete portrait of her and our stately stone gargoyle.

"Getting back in touch with your roots?" she asks, her voice low in the quiet darkness. "You've been in another world for an hour at least."

I'm so relieved to see a faint smile touching her lips, I can't help but grin right back at her.

"Before the invention of cameras," I say, "this was how I spent most of my free time—scrounging around looking for something to draw with. Charcoal, pigments I mashed together out of plants. I could almost aways find something —even if it was just a charred piece of wood and a curl of tree bark to sketch upon."

Westlyn draws her knees up and wraps her arms around them, her eyes softened by the amber glow of the smoldering fire. "You've always been an artist, huh? Since the very beginning."

I nod. "It's funny, though. I never considered myself an artist—that word always felt too formal to me. Something that required an apprenticeship with a master. For me, it always seemed like I was more of a... a messenger, if that makes sense? Like, the portrait or scene already exists somewhere, even if we can't yet perceive it with our limited senses. So it's my job to remove everything else in the way of that perception—to bring it to life for others to enjoy." I glance down at the parchment in my lap. "When I sketch like this, I'm removing some of the empty space by adding in the shadows, and in that way, it just... *becomes*." I shake my head, an uncharacteristic warmth blooming in my cheeks. It's so rare that I ever talk about this stuff anymore —I forgot what it feels like to be shy. "I don't know. It makes sense in my head."

"No, I get it. I love that interpretation." She glances around the cozy space, then up at Rook, his protective form looming over her. "Beauty is everywhere, always. Sometimes it's hard to remember it's there when all that other stuff is getting in the way. I think we could all use the reminder. Art is the very best messenger for that."

My throat tightens at her words, and we slip into a comfortable silence again, a lone flame licking one of the logs in the fireplace before us, refusing to give up. In its flickering light, I see the shapes of us all—gargoyle wings and tails, West's long dark hair, the apple trees in our orchard, the feathers of her ravens, the bones lining the shelves of Jude's workshops, the sharp angles of Draegan's face... All the light and shadow of our word.

The knot returns to my throat, and a wave of longing washes right through me.

For the first time since I became a gargoyle, I miss our life at Blackmoor.

Because for the first time since I became a gargoyle, I realize I had a life worth missing. Not a perfect life, but a real one. Three fiercely loyal brothers. Our home. Our apple trees.

And when Westlyn came to us, it felt like the only missing piece had just clicked into place. Like we'd all been saved.

And now we're here, fighting for that life all over again. Fighting for the mere privilege to build and cherish something that should be ours by rights.

Rage brings a glaze of raw emotion to my eyes, blurring that lone flame before me. But before I can sink too far into my anger and despair, Westlyn's pulling me right back to the surface.

Like she always does.

"Will you show it to me?" she whispers, and I turn to meet her gaze, her eyes brighter than they've been all night. "The sketch, I mean. Unless it's private."

Thrilled to be asked, I join her on the sofa, showing her the parchment.

She scans the portrait, a hand pressed to her chest. "Auggie, that's... Wow. The details are so... And Rook... This is just... It's beautiful. I mean, look at this!"

But I don't look at it. I look at her. Only at her.

"*You're* beautiful," I whisper, setting the parchment on a side table and tucking a lock of hair behind her ear. She's still got her knees drawn up, and now I pull her in close, wrapping a protective wing around her, holding her tight. She melts into my embrace and lets out a long, shuddering sigh.

And then she falls apart in my arms.

"I'm sorry. Goddess, what a mess." Westlyn finally sits up again, her eyes puffy from crying. "I shouldn't have done that. I need to focus on solutions, not lose my shit at the first sign of—"

"Hey. None of that, now." I tuck a finger under her chin, turning her gaze toward mine. "You can cry or scream or freak out all you want. Whatever you need to do, because witchling, this whole thing fucking *sucks*. Rook is... I'm sure he's hurting in there, and I can't... I *won't* lie to you about that. We're *all* fucking hurting."

She nods, snuggling in close again. "I just feel so helpless. I hate that feeling."

"I know. I do, too."

Devils balls, do I ever. And Verrick? Nothing gets his dick harder than making everyone else around him feel completely fucking helpless. He did it when he murdered our families and robbed us of our homeland. He did it when he cursed all the soldiers who fought by our sides to become gargoyles, and cursed the four of us to remain living as we watched all those friends and allies turn to stone and crumble.

Those brutalities... They were the hardest things I've ever had to witness.

But never before did I have to watch one of my brothers suffer that same fate.

Seeing Rook now... Fuck.

No. I can't even allow myself to *think* we won't find a way to fix this. To get Rook back. I know we may not have much time left before the curse ends us all, but even if it's just a few months or days... I don't want Rook's final moments to be locked in stone.

"Thing is, witchling," I say, "we're *not* helpless. We can't be—I refuse to accept it. You and I, Drae and Jude, the witches... All of us are still here, still drawing breath against all the odds. Even Rook is still here. Trapped, but alive. So yeah. We'll find those solutions you mentioned. I know we will."

She nods, drifting into that space of quiet contemplation once more, and I rest my cheek on top of her head and close my eyes, anchoring myself by the familiar scent of her hair.

Home.

A little while later, voices outside the door tell me that Jude and Drae are back from watch, and I need to head out —I promised Drae I'd help him search the nearby dwellings, see if we might turn up some more food and weapons, maybe some maps.

"Try to get some rest," I say, gently extracting myself and helping her stretch out on the couch.

When I turn to add a fresh log to the fire, she says, "I'm afraid to sleep, Auggie."

And my heart breaks all over again, because I know it's not just fears of an attack keeping her up.

It's Rook.

"Right now," she continues, "as long as I can see him, I can still *feel* him. I'm still connected to him. But I'm terrified if I close my eyes, that thread will snap and he'll just—"

"He won't." I turn back to her, running a hand over her head. "But I get it. You don't have to go upstairs. Stay here. Stay with him for as long as you need to. He knows you're here, West. He can feel you, too. I'm sure of it."

A tiny smile. A glimmer of hope. A balm on my fucking soul if ever there was one.

West takes my hands in hers, trailing light fingertips over my charcoal-smudged skin. "Thank you for drawing me," she says softly. "It's an honor. I mean it."

"I always want to draw you."

Another smile. "You do?"

I nod. "The first time I saw you in that cathedral, walking down the aisle in your black dress, I swear my heart stopped. And every night I've spent with you since, my fingers itch to reveal you on the page. But I could never do it justice, witchling."

"Personally, I think you did a pretty damn fine job tonight. But once we get back home, we'll have lots of time to practice."

Her newfound hope is downright infectious, and I can't help my answering smile. "Yeah?"

"I can feel it."

"Good. Then it must be true." I lean down and kiss her forehead. "I need to head out with Drae for a bit, but I'll be back to check on you in a few hours."

"Where are you going?"

"Not far." I tell her about the scouting mission.

She tries to protest, but I press a kiss to her mouth, silencing her. When I finally force myself to break away, she smiles up at me again, hopeful and bright, and whispers, "Just... just promise you'll both come back to me. Okay?"

I lean down and steal one more kiss for the road. "I promise, my witchling. We will *always* come back to you." Then, brushing my fingertips over Rook's wing as I head out, "*All* of us."

CHAPTER SEVENTEEN

JUDE

After conferring with Augs and Drae and sending them off on their little scavenger hunt, I head back into the common room to check on my girl, unsurprised to find her on the couch next to Rook's towering form, a tattered blanket pulled tight around her shoulders.

She's doing her best to stay awake, but her lids are heavy, dark circles forming beneath her eyes, her gaze lost in the flames of the fire.

Not waiting for an engraved invitation, I sit down next to her and wrap a hand around her neck, soft and warm underneath all that dark, gorgeous hair. "Can't sleep, darling?"

She shakes her head, but her comfortable stare remains fixed on the fireplace. "You?"

"I haven't even tried. Besides, I'd much rather spend the night sitting here with you, if you don't mind."

"I'd love the company."

"Good to know, because the company loves you." I run my thumb up and down the side of her neck. "You know, I was thinking—"

"Jude Hendrix, *thinking*?" She finally tears her gaze away from the flames and looks at me, brow crinkling as she presses a hand to my forehead like she's checking for fever. "Do you need medical attention? Should I see if we can scrounge up a fae healer?"

"You are *so* damn cute when you're trying to be funny. You know that, right?" I flick the tip of her nose and laugh, but it's not long before the weight of everything chases off the levity.

Here in the looming shadow of our stone brother, it's hard to hold on to laughter.

"The last thing I want is to sleep," she says. "Rook... He needs me. Don't ask me to explain it."

"No need. I get it. And you're right—he does need you." I shift to the end of the couch, then pull her feet into my lap. "How about I just help you relax, then? No sleeping required."

"You? Help me 'relax?'" She makes air quotes around the word, the tiniest smile twitching at the corners of her mouth. "Is this a trap? It feels like a trap."

"When have I ever laid a trap for you that you haven't happily waltzed right into?"

"Fair point."

"But no, this is not a trap. I'll have you know I'm *very*

good at relaxation techniques. Certain ones, anyways. You don't know what you're missing, scarecrow."

"Oh, I'll bet." She nudges my thigh with her foot. "Does that line actually work?"

"Hmm." I remove her baggy wool socks, then press my thumbs into her bare arches, massaging them with deep, slow circles. "You tell me."

"Oh, damn. That feels..." A blissful sigh escapes her lips. "Okay, fine. I'll admit it. Maybe you *do* have some secret relaxation skills that even a cranky, overtired, dark-fae witch freakshow can't resist."

"No, you can't, my little freakshow. So you might as well lie back, close your eyes, and let your man Jude take care of you." I press a thumb into her foot again, squeezing her heel with my other hand.

She moans in pleasure, but she's not lying back like I told her to. Not closing her eyes. Not relaxing in the slightest.

Propped up on her elbows, she's glaring at me like she's about to unleash some new brand of hell.

"What is it, darling? You can't possibly tell me this doesn't feel good."

"It feels amazing."

"Then what's the problem?"

"The problem is..." She rolls her eyes. "Do I really need to spell it out?"

"Apparently. I'd blame the witchweed, scarecrow, but

your very presence muddies my mind on the best of days, so—"

"Ugh. Fine. I don't really want you to rub my feet, Jude. Is that clear enough?"

"Oh. Well, how about a shoulder massage, then?"

She bites her lip in sheer frustration—fucking adorable—and shakes her head.

"Neck? Scalp? I don't know... Elbows?" I laugh. "Throw me a bone here, darling. If I start naming other body parts, I'll have no choice but to remove your clothing, and then we're—"

"Yes," she says firmly, sitting up so her knees are brushing my thighs, her lips close enough to kiss.

"Yes, what?" I whisper, threading a hand into her hair and dropping my gaze to that soft, lush mouth.

"Yes, I want you to name other body parts." Her breath mists across my lips. "I want you to *touch* other body parts. I want you to peel me out of these hideous clothes and put your mouth on my skin until I forget all the awful things that've happened tonight, and I want you to make me so fucking hot and wet for you that I forget all the awful things that are going to happen tomorrow, too. So, Mr. Relaxation Techniques, if you're not in the mood to get naked with me and—"

"Hey! Don't put those blasphemous words in *my* mouth, scarecrow. When it comes to being naked with you, I'm *always* in the mood. Hell, I could literally be on fire and I'd still be begging for a chance to make you writhe beneath me."

She slides a hand up my thigh, soft fingers brushing against my cock, already hard. "Then what's the holdup?"

Fucking hell.

Twenty-four hours ago, I would've had her pinned down by now, my tongue between her thighs, my name echoing up to the rooftop like a wicked curse from her lips.

Now, I glance up at Rook, wondering what the cheeky bastard would say about all this. Wondering if this is even remotely okay.

Then I damn near laugh, because I know exactly what he'd say.

Carry on, then. I'll just be over here getting an eyeful while I jerk off to the sound of her moans...

"Are you sure this is what you want?" I ask, returning my full attention to Westlyn. To her silky, seductive touch that's sending shivers straight down to my balls.

She closes her eyes and nods. "I need to feel alive. And nothing makes me feel more alive—more connected—than when you're inside me."

Fuck *me*. This whole situation is beyond fucked, but I can't *stand* to see her in pain. There's nothing I won't do to erase the ache in her heart, even if it's just for an hour.

And Rook?

Hell, I know he'd feel the same way.

"Please, Jude," she whispers. "Touch me."

Every last protest I can think of dies right there.

I grab her wrist and bring it up to my mouth, drawing a delicate circle with my tongue that leaves her trembling.

"You want me to fuck you in front of the fire, little scarecrow?" I whisper. "While our naughty professor watches?"

Another smile peeks out from the darkness, and she nods. "I think he'd approve."

"So we're doing this for Rook, then," I tease.

"Oh, absolutely. One hundred percent."

I glance up at Rook and wink. "Taking one for the team here, resident genius. You're *definitely* gonna owe me when you get back."

I swear he winks at me in return, and even I'm laughing a bit now.

But we all know the real deal here. Death is a constant companion. And nothing keeps it at bay quite like raw, unfiltered passion.

I peel her right the fuck out of those clothes, then push her down on the couch and stretch out behind her, bringing her back to my chest.

She lets out a soft sigh and rests her head on my arm, the fire crackling, the rest of the main floor dark and quiet.

Fucking heaven.

I skim my palm down her ribs and slide it across her belly, slowly circling lower and lower. Goosebumps pebble on her soft skin.

"Are you cold, darling?" I whisper, kissing her bare shoulder.

"No. I'm perfect."

"Then arch your back for me and spread your thighs."

She does as I ask, and I pull her closer, sliding one of my legs between hers. Her naked flesh is warm and wet on my upper thigh, my cock stone-hard as it presses against her backside.

All I want is to fucking *spear* her, to claim her body in all the filthy ways I love to do.

But tonight isn't about what I want. It's about taking her away from this epic shitshow and giving her even a few precious moments of sheer bliss.

"Thank you, Jude," she whispers.

"Shh. Close your eyes and take a deep breath, and let me take care of the rest."

She does as I ask, and I feel her relax against me, melting like the sweetest chocolate on a summer's day. With slow, deliberate kisses, I bring my mouth from her shoulder to her neck, then up to her earlobe, nibbling the soft skin as I tease one of her nipples with the gentle scrape of a claw.

"Can you... talk to me?" she whispers, her hips already rocking as she seeks the friction of my thigh.

"Hmm," I murmur. "Any particular topic?"

"No, I mean... I like it when you... *talk* to me. During... you know."

I let out a soft laugh. "Has my little scarecrow gone shy all of a sudden?"

"Considering we're lying here naked with an inn full of people, I don't think shy is the right word."

"Then use your *other* words, darling. Tell me exactly what you like, and I promise to deliver."

"I like... I like when you tell me about all the things you want to do to me in bed."

"Oh, now that's a tall order, scarecrow. There are hardly enough words in English *or* fae for all the things I want to do to you in bed. But for you? I'm willing to try."

I pinch her nipple, tugging it into a tight peak, making her moan for me.

"First, I want to taste your skin. Like this." I press my lips to the back of her neck, teasing her with hot, delicate kisses. "You taste like apples and sunshine, darling. Like all the best things. The very first time I kissed you, I was already addicted. Do you remember?"

"The night you finally admitted to stalking me?"

"And *you* finally admitted to liking it."

"I still can't believe I let you into my bed that night." A quiet laugh. "You were beyond creepy."

"Creepy? Please. You were a goner the moment you saw the size of my—"

"Wingspan?"

"*Tongue.*" I unfurl it all the way now, licking a path straight down her spine, swirling it around her tight little arsehole as I bring my tail around the front to graze her clit.

"Jude," she whispers against my arm, her hips rocking harder, seeking my cock.

"Is this what you want?" I whisper, arching my hips so the tip of my cock teases her from behind. "My cock sliding into your greedy little cunt? Because that's what *I* want. I want to fuck this tight, wet hole until we're both coming so hard we make a mess of this couch."

"Please," she whispers, fingernails digging into my arm. "Say more."

I bite her shoulder, then drag my mouth back to her ear, my breath hot and heavy on her skin as I bury my face in her hair, increase the pressure of my tail on her clit, and slowly—ever so slowly—push the tip of my cock into her wet heat.

In and out. Circling. Stretching. In and out once more, but never more than the tip, teasing her until she's writhing and whimpering in my arms.

"You're so hot and wet for me, darling. So fucking... so fucking *good*." I close my eyes and try to force myself to keep up this long, delicious tease, but everything inside me is so ready to fucking *claim* her, my balls heavy with need, my cock aching to sink deep, all the way in, and I—

"*Fuck*," I grit out, grabbing her hip and burying myself to the hilt, unable to hold back for another moment.

She rocks back to meet my thrust, and together we find a perfect rhythm, fucking slow and deep on that couch, chasing away the ghosts, the pain, the fear of what's to come.

I replace my tail with my fingers, desperate and needy to touch her, my skin gliding over her clit as I continue to fuck her from behind.

"I can't stop touching you," I whisper, leaving another

trail of kisses down her neck. "Kissing you. Being inside you and fucking you so perfectly and just... oh, fuck. That's... Westlyn, I'm..."

All my words are tangling up, spiraling out into the ether as I lose myself in the feel of her wrapped so perfectly around my cock, her body rocking softly against mine, the fire crackling, my fingers circling her clit harder and faster as she pulses around me, so close, so fucking close to that white-hot end...

"Jude," she whispers, a prayer rather than a curse, her hand wrapped tight around my arm, squeezing me as hot tears fall on my skin. A sob wracks her body, but she's still arching back against me, still chasing bliss. "You feel so good. You feel... I want... I just want to scream."

"It's okay, darling." I press a powder-soft kiss to the shell of her ear and cover her mouth with my hand. "No one will hear you. So for tonight, right now, just let it all out. Your fears, your nightmares, all the things still tying you up in knots. For Rook, darling. Let it all out."

Here beneath the shadow of our stone gargoyle, I feel her draw in a shaky breath and hold it, tears still hot and wet on my arm.

But then, all at once, a sob finally bursts free from her chest, her cries muffled against my palm, and her body tightens around me, trembling and hot as she rocks her hips and I fuck her harder and faster and bury my face in her hair and whisper her name over and over as I come inside her, hot and hard and devastating, claiming her with everything I've got, the very last, very best thing in this whole bloody realm.

In my whole bloody existence.

She's shivering now, the last of our momentary bliss fading away like the stars in the sky. I'm still inside her, but I'm not ready to leave yet. I reach behind me for her blanket, drawing it across her naked form and arching a wing over her.

But then I feel it.

A sudden chill in marrow of my bones. A prickling in my nerves.

My wings, sensitive to even the slightest breeze, are suddenly numb. And so is my arm. My chest is tight, lungs burning as I try to suck in a breath.

"Jude? What's—"

"Move. Now!" I shove her off the couch and leap to my feet, the movement sending a bolt of pain up my spine, straight into the base of my skull. I grab my head to keep it from fucking exploding.

It's the last fucking thing I feel.

A dark, devastating horror sweeps across Westlyn's face, and I know.

I'm stone.

"Jude!" she cries. "No. No, no, no. Come back, Jude.

Please come back. Come back to me. Come back. Come back! Tatiana, help!"

She snatches up her clothes and hastily dresses, calling up to the other witches, her eyes frantic.

But before anyone else can respond, there's a flicker of movement at the bar, and then...

He's here. An apparition come to life, sauntering toward us with malice in those terrible silver eyes.

Verrick.

I'm trembling with fury... At least, I *should* be trembling. It *feels* like I'm trembling. But it's not possible. Nothing inside me will fucking move.

"This is but a taste of what awaits you unless you surrender yourself and the Codex to me now," he says.

Westlyn's gaze darts to the Codex, sitting on a shelf behind us. When she looks at Verrick again, the horror and fear are gone from her eyes.

Now, there is only rage.

"I'm not yours to claim, *Verrick*," she hisses, calling a ball of glittering magic into her hands. "And neither is the Codex. So release whatever spell you've cast on the gargoyles, or you'll get a taste of what awaits *you*."

Verrick's power seems to flicker in response, black veins darkening beneath his eyes, like he's crying tears of ink.

Like he's trying desperately to hold on to it, but doesn't have the strength.

"Westlyn! Move!" Drae's voice cuts through the darkness as he and Augs crash through the front door and take in the scene, then charge straight for the fae king.

Verrick curses, and West hurls the sphere of lightning at him, but he dodges the attack, then lunges for her just as a bright silver light opens up behind them, like a tear in the very fabric of the universe.

Another portal. *Fuck.*

The witches descend the stairs just in time to see him vanish, taking our girl with him.

Draegan roars like a wild animal and barrels through it after her, and then that silver light—that cruel fucking silver light—closes around them both, plunging the rest of us into darkness.

CHAPTER EIGHTEEN

DRAEGAN

Pain lances through my chest as the portal spits Westlyn and me out into a blinding white blizzard. I barely manage to grab her and roll us out of the way before a massive snowdrift plummets from a rocky cliff above, burying the spot where we'd only just landed.

She's shivering in her borrowed clothes, no coat or boots, and I have no idea how far we've traveled from the inn. The only thing I know is we're somewhere in the mountains of Wintermoon, and if I don't find shelter soon, she'll freeze to death.

Verrick, of course, is nowhere in sight.

Tomorrow, we're out for fucking blood...

Jude's earlier words are a cruel echo.

I spot an opening in the rock face a few dozen yards ahead, and hope like hell it's big enough to fit inside.

"It was all a trap," Westlyn says to me now, her teeth

161

chattering. "If he wanted to turn you *all* to stone back at the inn, he could have. He wanted to separate us—make us easier to pick off one by one, because that's the kind of game he wants to play."

"I don't think that's it, love." I scoop her into my arms and trudge through the snow toward that dark crevice. "He may have wanted *you* to chase him, but I don't think he intended for me to follow. He's not looking to pick us off—I don't think he even has the power for it."

"What do you mean?"

We reach the opening in the rock face, which is—mercifully—an entryway to a large cavern, uninhabited like the rest of the realm, and dry.

"Something isn't right about all this," I say once we're out of the wind, gathering some dried brush from around the entrance and following her deeper into the cavern. "His magic seems to be fading. He's taunting us, yes, but I'm not sure he has the power to mount a full attack. He certainly doesn't have any armies. Not even a small guard."

"He wants the Codex."

"And you. Do you think you can light this for me?" I ask, setting the brush into a small dip in the rocky ground. "Anything will help—even a spark."

She closes her eyes and holds out her hands, magic sparking to life at once. The kindling catches easily. It won't last long, but for now, it's something.

Westlyn sighs and slumps to her knees, staring into the small fire. "Draegan, Jude is..."

"I know, love. I know." I sit down beside her, wrapping a wing around her shoulders.

"I'm glad you decided to stay with us, though. Thank you."

I nod. It's all I can manage. The thought that I even *considered* leaving them before makes my gut burn with shame.

"Are *you* okay?" she asks.

"I'll be better once we eliminate the threat and return home."

"I mean... physically. You don't have any pain or stiffness or..." She shrugs, unable to finish the sentence.

I can't finish it, either, only this time, it's not because I'm trying to deflect her or start another argument.

It's because I truly don't know how it feels to be turned to stone against my will without the ability to change back.

Of all the ones who've turned before Rook and Jude...

None of them ever came back to us.

But that's not what she needs to hear right now, so I force a tight smile and say, "I'm fine, little mortal. No symptoms. I promise."

It's not a lie—physically speaking, I'm one hundred percent. But I don't tell her my suspicions—that the only reason I'm in such an unaffected state is that Verrick is low on power and saving me for last. One more cruel trick to ensure the most egregious suffering goes to the man he believes is responsible for the fae wars against his people.

People who no longer even exist.

None of it makes sense, yet here we are.

"And you?" I ask. "Are you... still cold?" *Damn it.* It's the first thought that comes to mind—an obvious and relatively minor discomfort, something I could actually do something about. Because I can't bring myself to ask about the true source of her pain—her worry over Rook and Jude. Her fears about the curse. All the unknowns about Verrick and his true motives for wanting her and the Codex.

"He's with me," she whispers, pressing a hand to her heart. "He's always with me now."

"What do you mean?"

"When I first woke up in the cathedral, Verrick told me I was the one who brought him to our realm. We're linked somehow. I can feel him trying to draw on my power—it's like an incessant tugging. And whenever he's close, it's like... like ants crawling all over my skin." She shivers and rubs her arms, but before I can draw her closer, she's shooting to her feet, alarm blanching her face.

"He's here, Draegan. He's—"

"Be reasonable, my moon." Verrick strolls out from an adjacent passageway, silver eyes flashing. His crown is missing, dark hair hanging lank over a pale face, those strange inky marks still visible on his skin.

But he's *here*. Solid and real and very, very determined to take what he believes is his.

I'm on my feet in an instant, but with the careless flick of a wrist, Verrick's magic slams me back against the cave wall. I struggle against the force of it, but it's useless. I'm completely pinned, my wings crushed behind me.

"Please!" Westlyn cries out. "Let him go!"

Verrick takes his time sauntering over to her. At first, I think he's doing it to taunt her further, but there's a slight wobble to his gait, an unsteadiness as each foot lands. Westlyn notices it too, her eyes tracking his movements.

Tracking the sword shining from a scabbard at his hip.

Don't do it, little mortal. Whatever you're thinking, don't take that chance...

She raises her hands, a hint of indigo light gathering between them.

"I wouldn't," Verrick says calmly, and with another flick of his wrist, I'm gasping for air, my lungs nearly crushed.

She drops her hands at once. "Please, Verrick. It's me you want. Let him go."

"Now, what good would that do?" He's right in front of her now, reaching out to finger a lock of her hair.

Westlyn stiffens at his touch, but he doesn't release her.

"Unhand... her," I grit out, but my words are barely audible, and he doesn't even acknowledge me.

"Draegan and his soldiers are not long for this world," he continues, his tone bored. "Or your world, for that matter."

"So undo the curse!" she shouts. "You said it yourself—you want the human realm, and you want me to rule here. You don't even need the gargoyles anymore. Set them free. Please!"

"Ah, yes. The dreaded curse. Is that what your little crusade against me is all about?"

"It's not a crusade, Verrick. I'm asking you to let them go. Break the curse and give them the choice of remaining immortal or... or moving on."

Verrick laughs, the sound of it like knives on a blackboard. "Why do you even care, my moon? Soon you'll have more riches than you could even want—riches that can buy you all manner of... Oh. But wait. I see." He drops her hair and looks her over, a sneer curling his lip, mockery filling those silver eyes. "You're in love with them."

Westlyn says nothing.

Again, I fight against the binding magic, desperate to get to her. To end him. But the hold is too fucking strong. Too painful.

"You know," he says, tapping his lips as if he's actually thinking about helping her, "the curse *does* have one loophole."

"Tell me," she breathes, and Verrick's smile stretches wide.

Too wide, and I know whatever he says next will be nothing but a trick, even if there's some truth to his words.

A silver lining with a rotten, bloody core.

"Westlyn," I say with a gasp. "Don't... don't listen to him."

But it's too late.

She's spent too many long, sleepless nights searching for

a loophole, and now she thinks he's going to hand it over, just like that.

I can't blame her for it. Haven't I been searching for it too? For fifteen hundred bloody years, against all the odds, all the shadows in my heart that only sought to remind me again and again that Verrick would *never* grant our freedom through something so simple as a loophole?

"If the curse should be broken by one whose love is true," he says, "the gargoyles *will* be granted that choice."

Bloody hell, it's the kind of drivel straight out of a fucking fairytale, yet even *I* can't help but wonder. Hope.

But all too quickly, Verrick's smile twists again. "Obviously, you love them. It's a pity you can't be the one to break it, little moon."

"Why not?" she asks. "You said it yourself—I love them. So tell me how to break it. Tell me, and I'll give you the Codex. I'll wear the crown. Whatever you ask of me, just tell me!"

His eyes glitter, but it's not because of her offer—as much as he wants all those things.

It's because he's about to twist the knife in a little deeper, just like he always does.

"Oh, I *would*, daughter," he says. "Absolutely. But I'm afraid it's just not possible. The curse is demon- and fae-made both, tethered to an immortal bloodline that ensures its eternal source of power."

"What does that even *mean*?" she demands, the tremor in her voice echoing off the cave walls.

"A curse of such immense power is much more than a simple spell," he says. "It must be tethered, for lack of a better word, to an external source of magic to ensure that its potency never fades."

"I still don't understand," she says.

Verrick sighs. "For all your spells and witchery, for all your fruitless searching for the Spell of Unmaking, the only way to actually break such a powerful curse is to break the tether, and the only way to break the tether is to break the bloodline it's tied to—the bloodline whose magic ensures the curse is truly eternal. Quite ingenious, really. All the best curses are, of course."

"Whose bloodline?" she asks, but she already knows the answer.

We both do.

Verrick answers anyway.

"*Mine*," he practically hisses. Then, with one last cruel, ice-cold smile, he delivers the final blow. "And if I shall meet an untimely demise, the tether passes to my heir. Yes, child, you *are* fully immortal—make no mistake about that. So you see, my moon, the power to end the curse of the gargoyles may *technically* be within your grasp, but breaking the tether requires my death as well as your own, and surely that would defeat the whole purpose of setting the men you claim to love free. Quite a sticky dilemma, is it not? Anyway, now that we've settled the matter of the curse, it's time to—"

"You're lying!" she screams, but deep down, I know he

isn't. The twisted, sharp-edged riddles of curses and tethers are just the sort of trickery the dark fae thrive on.

"I'm not," he says with a simple shrug. "You know, Westlyn, most people would consider it an honor to be entrusted with such a valuable tether. Alas, there's no need to prostrate yourself. Consider it a father's gift to his doting child."

"Yeah?" Westlyn laughs, cold and empty. "Then consider this your doting child's thank-you note, *asshole*."

For the briefest instant, I swear her eyes shine silver like her father's, and I know—I know with a sickening, terrifying realization what she's about to do.

"*Westlyn*," I warn, nothing but a quiet rush of air, but it's too late. She's already lunging for that sword.

Verrick is so shocked by the move, it takes him a beat too long to realize she's stolen his weapon. Without hesitation, she stabs at his chest, but she's untrained and he easily dodges the attack, grabbing her wrist and using her momentum to throw her to the ground.

His boot is on her chest in a flash, the blade retaken, and before I even realize what's happening, he shoves that blade right through her.

"No!" I roar, the force around me snapping like a rubberband, launching me toward them.

But Verrick vanishes in another flash of silver magic, and I fall to my knees at Westlyn's side, the light fading from her eyes, her blood a ruby-red stain on the black rock beneath us.

CHAPTER NINETEEN

DRAEGAN

The fire rages. The storm rages. My fucking *soul* rages, but all I can do is pace a groove into the old wooden floors of an abandoned cabin and wait.

And wait.

And fucking *wait* for her to wake up, my heart about to beat out of my chest.

After Verrick's attack, a brief pause in the storm gave me just the opportunity I needed to find warmer shelter—an abandoned, one-room hunting cabin nestled among a copse of dead trees not too far from the cave. As gently as I could manage, I carried her out of that dreadful darkness, bleeding and unconscious, never before so grateful for a wooden shack in the middle of nowhere.

I lit a fire in the hearth, heated water to bathe her in the small chamber off the main room. I cleaned and inspected the wound—a long, gaping gash between her arm and shoulder that had already begun to heal.

A miracle for which, ironically, we've got her Wintermoon fae blood to thank.

Then I wrapped her in a soft robe I found and tucked her into the small bed, dragging the whole thing close to the fire just as the storm kicked up again in earnest.

She's been unconscious the entire time, and I've been pacing.

Fuck. From the moment we chased Verrick through the portal at the inn tonight, all my thoughts have been on Westlyn—on keeping her warm, on protecting her, on figuring out how to get her back to the inn. But now, in the deadly silence of this infernal waiting, my thoughts turn to him.

Verrick was supposed to be dead by now. By *my* hands. Instead, he lives to see another day. To hatch another plan against us. To continue to fucking *exist*, while the woman I love remains wounded and unconscious, and all I can do is fucking crawl up the damn *walls* of this place until—

"Draegan?"

The voice. The sound of my name. The warmth in it...

I rush to her and kneel at the bedside, clasping her small hands. When she finally blinks her eyes open and meets my gaze, it takes everything in me not to fall to the floor and weep.

Bloody hell, little mortal. You're truly going to be the death of me.

Gingerly, she sits up and glances around the tiny cabin, taking in the scene—a single main room with a modest cooking area along one wall, some sort of animal-skinned rug tossed on a wood-planked floor before a small hearth, the bathing chamber off the back.

"I see we've upgraded our accommodations," she says, her voice still weak, but her eyes bright. "What the hell happened?"

Outside, the storm continues to lash the walls and windows, snow slipping in through the chimney and making the fire hiss, but the cabin holds together.

Somehow, I manage to do the same.

"What do you remember, love?" I ask, tucking a lock of damp hair behind her ear.

"Verrick showed up, talking all that bullshit about the curse. I tried to get his sword, but..." She rubs her shoulder, shaking her head at the lack of pain. "I could've sworn he stabbed me. Like, *really* bad."

"He did."

"Then why am I not dead?" She meets my gaze again, then shakes her head, a soft laugh escaping. "Oh, no. *Please* tell me you didn't save me again. I'm seriously going to have to start marking it off on the calendar."

I grin at her, if only to hide the sheer immensity of my relief that she's not only alive, but still has her sense of humor. "I've got a reputation to uphold, Miss Avery. Thankfully, you've grown quite skilled at giving me ample opportunities to meet my quotas, so—"

"*Groan*. Goddess, Drae. You are literally the *worst* hero ever. You're not supposed to brag about it!"

"Clearly, I need more training. Not that I'm suggesting you throw yourself into danger again anytime soon, mind you." My smile fades, my thoughts drifting back to the cave. To her blood. So much blood... "Anyway, I brought you here and cleaned you up, but you mostly healed yourself. I've just been keeping watch."

And damn near losing my mind at the thought of you not waking up again...

"I... healed myself? That's a thing now?"

"Dark-fae magic. Comes with the territory. Being in your ancestral homeland is clearly amplifying your innate fae powers."

She glances down at her hands as if she no longer recognizes them. "Great. I'll be sure to thank Verrick for the awesome genetics. Right after I stab him in the nuts with his own sword. *Hard.* With a little twisty motion just to *really* make it hurt." She mimics the move with her hands, wrenching her invisible sword sideways, then chopping the air. "Or maybe a slicing motion? Which one do you think would inflict the most pain?"

I laugh. "Not my area of expertise, I'm afraid. That's more a question for J—" His name dies on my lips, sadness and fear wrapping around my heart before I can even say it.

"Jude," Westlyn finishes for me, no more than a whisper.

"I... sorry. I shouldn't have mentioned him. I didn't mean to upset you. I wasn't thinking. I just—"

"No. Don't apologize for this, Draegan. Don't talk about Jude like he's... like he's already gone, because he isn't. Neither is Rook."

"Of course they're not bloody gone. But..." I get to my feet, shoving a hand through my hair. "I'm scared, Westlyn. Okay? I'm scared. Terrified, if you want to know the truth, because I just don't know how we're going to get them back."

"I'm terrified for them too," she says softly. "But some part of me just... I don't know. I trust that we're going to figure this out. And before you say anything, yes, I do realize how naïve that sounds, but that's my story and I'm sticking to it."

I don't know how she manages to get another smile out of me, but she does.

I sit beside her on the bed, sliding an arm around her shoulders. "Not naïve, love. Hopeful. And right now, I'll take all the hope I can get."

She gives me a playful nudge in the ribs. "You have to take mine because you don't have any for yourself."

"Hope, as you know, is *also* not my area of expertise." I lean in and press a chaste kiss to her temple, lingering just a moment. "But it *is* yours, so perhaps you'll lend me a bit. Just until we get through this fresh hell."

We sit in silence for a few moments, but all too soon, she's on her feet again, searching the small space for her clothes.

"What do you think you're doing?" I ask.

"Getting dressed? We need to go after Verrick. He's weak, Draegan. I can feel it. I know he bested us both in that cave, but I honestly think it was because he siphoned off some of my magic. I didn't have my amulet with me—it must've fallen out of my pocket back at the tavern."

"Be that as it may, we can't go after him tonight. It's too dangerous. He nearly killed you in that cave, and I—"

"But he didn't, though. He knew I'd heal." She finally finds the clothes and starts to untie the robe, but I grab her wrists, stopping her. "Drae, seriously. He's not going to kill me. I'm basically the anchor for his curse—he's not going to risk it."

She may be right, but there's no comfort to be found there. Not for me. "That doesn't mean he won't hurt you. Verrick is a master of inflicting pains worse than death."

She narrows her eyes, that brief silver glint flashing in them once more. In a dark, deadly voice I barely recognize, she says, "So. Am. I."

A shiver rolls down my spine, and I take a step back, looking at her with newfound appreciation.

Free of my grasp, she unties the robe. "Are you with me, or are you staying here, warming—what was it? Idle hands by the fire?"

At this, she smirks at me and lets her robe drop to the floor, revealing her bare, beautiful body.

I shake my head, unable to stop the laugh that bubbles out. "You would've made one hell of an army commander, Miss Avery."

"Let's hope it doesn't come to that." She laughs too, but it sputters out quickly. "Seriously, though. We should get going before—"

"No." I retrieve the robe and drape it back over her shoulders. "We're not going *anywhere* in this storm."

As if to bolster my argument, the wind howls against the walls, rattling the windows. Even if it were light outside, we wouldn't be able to see beyond the cabin's front steps.

Westlyn huffs. "Well, we can't just... just sit here and do nothing!"

"We can, and we will. I'm not risking your life again tonight. Understand?"

"That's not your decision." She turns her back to me and marches toward the door, though where she thinks she's going in a thin bathrobe with no shoes is anyone's guess.

She reaches for the door handle, defiant until the very end.

"Do *not* open that door," I command.

With a devious glance over her shoulder, she says, "Or what? You'll spank me, *Daddy*?"

I'm certain she meant it to come out like a taunt, but she failed miserably, the last word ending in a breathless whisper that leaves the air between us hot and crackling.

I take a step toward her, then another, falling back into our game with easy, sadistic pleasure. "If that's what it takes to keep you safe, then yes."

Better this game than facing what lies beyond the walls, I tell myself. *Better this game than facing what lies in the dark depths of my heart...*

"Oh, really?" she huffs out. "Finally ready to make good on all those idle threats?" She turns to face me full on and laughs, but it's high and nervous, her robe trembling around her shoulders.

She didn't bother tying it up again after I draped it over her, and now it flaps open, giving me a tantalizing peak at her nipples, stiff and begging for my tongue.

"There is no punishment I won't inflict," I say darkly, closing the last of the distance between us. "No discipline I won't unleash. When it comes to protecting you from your own worst impulses, little mortal, Daddy will be *more* than happy to teach you a lesson... With his bare hands."

Her breath hitches, her heart rate kicking up, but she doesn't look away. Just squares her shoulders and flashes that maddening, smart-mouthed smirk. "You talk a good game, gargoyle. But you've been threatening to 'discipline' me forever. Frankly, I'm not sure you've got the balls to follow through. Oh, by the way? I'm *immortal*, remember?"

"Be that as it may, little *im*mortal, a lack of balls has never been an issue for me. But I'm pretty sure you know that already." I drop my loincloth and push her back against the door, my cock stone-hard between us.

Another little hitch of breath. A slight widening of the eyes.

I lean in close and drag my nose down along the slope of her neck, across her collarbone, past the now-healed shoulder wound. She leans into the contact, her breath warm against my cheek as I glide up her throat and stop a hair's breadth from her lips.

"The filthy things," I whisper. "The *punishments* I could wreak upon this beautiful, unbroken body..." I skim my claws down the center of her chest, thumbs brushing her nipples. "The fae royals of old would wither and die just to witness it."

A soft whimper is all she can manage, the scent of her desire washing over me in a hot rush that makes my head spin.

"Need to use your words, love?" I kiss a path to her ear, nipping the lobe between my teeth. "Say them, and this ends right now."

She bites her lower lip and shakes her head, and when I finally draw back and meet her gaze again, she flashes that wicked grin I love so, so much and says, "I want it, Daddy. I want you to—"

"Come. *Here*," I command, my mind already spinning with all the filthy possibilities as I drag her back to that bed.

Her mouth snaps shut, and the little immortal obeys, following without another word of protest.

I sit on the bed in front of her, positioning her between my knees.

It's all I can do not to shred the robe with my claws and fucking ravage her where she stands, but that would only prove her point.

She's right; I *have* been making idle threats.

That ends now.

"Take off the robe," I whisper. "Let Daddy see his beautiful little brat again."

She lowers her shoulders, letting the robe fall away once more to reveal her smooth skin. My mouth waters for a taste of her, my hands aching to touch her, to roam over every soft curve and dip, but I force myself to remain still. To catalogue the shapes and shadows with my eyes, one torturously slow inch at a time.

The firelight dances in her eyes, and she reaches for my wings, her lightest touch making me shiver. I could easily lose myself in this pleasure, but... no. Not yet.

I grab her wrist and deliver a dark warning. "You are *not* the one calling the shots tonight, Miss Avery. Now lace your fingers behind your head and do *not* move."

She does as I ask, and I tug her closer, wrapping my hands around her hips and holding her firmly in place as I bring my mouth to her nipple, painting it with the tip of my tongue, then sucking, my claws digging into her soft flesh.

I can feel the tension in her muscles, the slight twitch as she fights against the urge to lower her hands and bury them in my hair, but she doesn't dare give in, and I reward her with a slow, torturous brush of my tail between her thighs.

"Draegan," she whispers, spreading wider for me.

Fuck, she's already so wet. So desperate for it. I can't...
Fuck.

In a flash I pull her down so she's lying on her stomach across my lap, bare skin to bare skin, hot and warm and perfect.

"Stretch your arms up now," I say softly. "Grab the top of the mattress."

Again, she obeys without protest, and I skim my palm down her lower back, caressing her scars with a loving touch before drifting down over the soft curve of her arse, claws teasing the backs of her thighs.

She shivers at my touch, her hips already circling.

"Is this what you want?" I whisper, barely audible over the crackling fire. "Daddy's handprint on your arse, marking you? My mouth claiming you in all the naughty ways you dream about when you're all alone in bed and your monsters slumber in stone on the rooftop above?"

"Y-yes," she breathes. "Please."

"Mmm." A slow, satisfied grin slides across my face. "Such a bad, bad girl."

"I can't help it, Daddy."

Fuck, that word. Her soft skin. The slow grind of her hips against my thighs and the hot rush of her breath and the wild, ragged beat of her untamed heart...

Without warning, I lift a hand. Bring it down hard on that smooth, unmarred flesh.

The crack echoes through the small space, and she cries out in a perfect symphony of pleasure and pain, of shock and wanton need.

I wait for her to use her words, but she merely writhes in my lap, fingers still curled tight around the mattress.

I raise my hand again and bring it down on the other cheek, two smacks in quick succession, one more in the center, and then my mouth is on her skin, tonguing the red-hot welts as I drag my fingers through the wetness between her thighs, stroking her gently, all of it making her shudder.

"I... I'm so close," she pants. "Why is this happening so... so fast? Goddess, I'm going to come. I'm—"

"Not yet, you aren't." I pull her upright and shift her legs so she's straddling me backward, her spine arched, her luscious black-and-silver hair cascading down her back.

Nestled firmly against my cock, the satin skin of her arse is hot and red with my marks, a sight that nearly undoes the last of my control.

Gripping a fistful of her hair, I retract my claws and slide my other hand between her thighs from behind, fucking her with my fingers as my tail winds around to tease her clit, circling with just enough friction to keep her suspended on that knife's edge of pleasure.

She pushes back against my thrusts, taking my fingers deeper, chasing that beautiful, blissful end I'm holding just out of her reach.

"For all your stubborn resistance," I murmur, "you're always so wet and eager for me, love. So damn *needy* for my touch."

"You... make me crazy," she pants.

"And yet..." I draw my fingers out slowly, then push back

in, the wet, hungry sounds of her cunt belying any protest in her words. "It seems Daddy's naughty little brat *likes* getting spanked. Yes?"

"Oh, goddess. Yes. Right there, Daddy. Don't stop. You feel so... yes. Yes!"

"*No.*" I pull back again, dragging out her punishment—a delicious torment for us both. "When I finally let you come tonight, it will be on my tongue. I want to *taste* you as you come undone for me."

A gasp is the only response I get before I lean back on the bed and shift us so she's straddling my face, her arse in the air, her mouth tantalizingly close to my cock.

"What... what are we doing?" she breathes, long hair tickling my thighs.

"Well, if you really must know... *I'm* currently enjoying a *lovely* view of your backside as I consider just how long I'm going to make you wait for my tongue." I unfurl it and flick her clit with the tip, then drag it lazily through her slick heat, giving her an all-too-brief taste before pulling back again. "And you, little immortal..." My tail snakes around her throat and drags her down to my cock, leaving no doubts as to what's in store now. "*You* are going to suck on Daddy's cock until my cum is spilling out of your smart little mouth. Understand?"

A long, desperate moan escapes her lips, the heat of it ghosting across my flesh.

Fuck. I'm seeing stars already.

"Do you *understand*, Miss Avery?" I grind out, digging

the tips of my claws into her thighs just hard enough to make her gasp.

"Y-yes. I mean, yes, Daddy. I understand."

"Good. Now close your eyes, open your mouth, and *swallow* it." I tighten my tail around her throat and she obeys, those soft pink lips slowly parting over the tip, tongue darting out to tease me as she slowly takes me in.

"*No,*" I growl. "Like you're fucking *starved* for it, woman."

With that, I bury my tongue inside her, making her shudder and moan as she takes the rest of my cock in a single, perfect thrust. I feel it hit the back of her throat, feel the hot pulse as she gags around me.

It feels so fucking incredible.

"Tap my leg twice if you want to stop," I say.

Her fingers wrap around my thighs, but to my immense relief, she doesn't tap out.

To my immense relief, she goes down on me even harder, groaning around my aching cock, her tongue undulating just right.

Gripping her thighs, I spread her wider, licking and fucking, hitting that sweet spot inside her with the tip of my tongue until she's bucking against my face, then I'm pulling back right before I let her fall over the edge. She groans with pleasure and frustration both, then scrapes her teeth along my sensitive skin before diving back down again, repaying me with an epic tease of lips and tongue that's got my soul leaving my body.

"*Westlyn*," I growl. "You always make Daddy feel so... so fucking good."

She's damn near choking on me, but every strangled gasp only seems to further spur her on, like a dare she just can't refuse.

I've never been more grateful for the little brat's tenacity in the face of a challenge.

"Don't... don't you *dare* stop," I pant. "That's... perfect. Fuck..."

Those are all the words I can string together before my mind liquifies and I'm back between her thighs again, devouring her hot little cunt with my mouth as she digs her nails into my thighs so hard she draws blood.

The exquisite sting of her scratches mixes with the pleasure unleashed by the velvet strokes of her tongue, making my balls throb with the urgent need to come.

Fucking *hell*, this woman. This touch. This taste. I can't hold on much longer. Neither can she, her body already trembling, her hips bucking against my face as she licks and sucks me into another realm.

I sigh against her hot flesh, and she pushes back once more, again, harder, faster, riding my face with every roll of her hips as she takes me deeper into her perfect little mouth, her hand curling around my balls and squeezing them just right, and then... *oh, fuck*...

Westlyn falls apart first, coming on my tongue with a moan that vibrates straight down to my balls, her body melting as she rides out every last thrust, her lips so perfectly wrapped around my cock that I've got no choice but to follow her right over the edge, completely and utterly.

My muscles seize and tremble and seize again, then finally unspool in a blinding rush of pure pleasure, and I come in her mouth with a shudder and a roar that knocks the snow from the windows and echoes out through the barren forest to remind this forsaken realm that *yes*, we are still fucking here.

Yes, we are still fucking alive.

CHAPTER TWENTY
DRAEGAN

Soft. Warm. Perfect.

Home.

Those are the words that come back to me first, the words I think of when Westlyn turns around in the bed and faces me, her hands sliding up my chest as she straddles me again, knees bracketing my hips.

Every time she tosses her dark head, the ends of her hair brush my skin, making me shiver with divine pleasure.

And when I open my eyes and she finally smiles for me, lips swollen and pink, it's such a thing of beauty it makes my heart ache.

"You," she says, her smile turning wicked, "are down-right dangerous. You know that, right?"

"Dangerous, huh?" I tease, running my claws through her hair and brushing it away from her face, memorizing the feel of each silky strand. "Does this mean my witch has finally had enough? Or does Daddy need to punish you some more?"

She lowers her face close to mine, eyes glinting in the firelight. "Maybe *I* need to punish *you*."

I laugh. "Oh, you think so?"

"*Someone* needs to teach you a lesson. And since I'm the only one here at the moment, logic dictates I—*Draegan!*"

I've got us flipped around in a blink, her body imprisoned beneath mine, wrists trapped in my clawed grip and pinned above her head.

Lips brushing the shell of her ear, I whisper darkly, "I would *very* much like to see you try."

"You might be stronger than me," she protests, "but I've got... other methods."

"Is that so?"

She gives me a smug smile. "*Failsafe* methods."

"Ha! More like tricks. *That's* what you've got. A bag of tricks."

"Sure. Guess it's a good thing you're too clever to fall for them, huh?" She parts her thighs and arches her hips, circling once, twice, the heat of her body radiating across my cock.

Fuck, I'm hard for her again, more than ready to claim her, to bury myself, to lose my damn mind in the feel of her, but after all the obscene, red-hot debauchery we just indulged in, something is suddenly holding me a back.

And all it once, it feels so immense, so insurmountable,

I'm afraid to even name it, for fear the words themselves would crush the very breath from my lungs.

I just claimed her on this very bed like a wild, mindless animal in heat.

I've taken her on my desk. I've taken her against the wall. I've fucked her hot little mouth while the others watched, and I've commanded her pleasure in ways that continue to fill my every fantasy—waking and sleeping both.

But this... I've never taken her this way. Never felt the soft, wet heat of her body envelop me as I stared deep into her eyes, into the place where all the secrets die in the light of a raw, painful truth neither of us can hide.

Not anymore.

And bloody *hell*, the moment feels too close now, too intimate. Too much like the real thing.

The one thing I so badly want... but haven't dared to let myself have.

Haven't dared to hope that it could even be possible.

Because it isn't.

I close my eyes, desperate for a reprieve from her gaze, but it doesn't work. I can feel her watching me. Waiting. Giving me the space to open up to her, as she always does, even after all the terrible things I've done and said.

"Draegan," she whispers, her warm breath caressing my lips, and that's it.

I'm done.

Done running. Done pretending she hasn't completely, utterly, irrevocably changed me.

"Tell me," she whispers, and I release her wrists and roll onto my side, finally meeting her gaze again.

A soft, genuine smile graces her lips. "It's just us, Drae. You and me."

I nod. She's right—it *is* just us. Tucked away in this remote cabin in the Wintermoon wilderness, marooned by a storm, oblivious to the rest of the known world. Here, there's no more room for games and taunts. No more walls or excuses to hide behind.

All we've got left is this immense truth, a confession for which I'm not even sure the words exist.

But I have to try.

I trace the shape of her face with my fingertips.

"All these centuries," I whisper, "I thought Verrick's curse was the cruelest thing I'd ever have to endure. But dark-fae magic doesn't even come *close* to the blade wielded by time itself." I sigh and bury my face against her neck, my hand sliding across her stomach, memorizing the silken feel of her skin. "Time. Damn it, Westlyn. I had so much of it I feared it would never end, and now—in what feels like my final hours—all I want is just a little more. A few more days to hold you. To take care of you. One more hour to tell you all the things I should've told you before, but was too damned scared to even try."

Her breath catches, and I want nothing more than to

capture it in my mouth, to breathe it in deep and hold it inside forever.

But I can't. Not until I get this out.

"The truth is, Westlyn," I continue, "before I met you, my life hadn't meant anything for centuries. And after all those endless years, I finally accepted the fact that it never would—not after everything I'd lost. My sole purpose was freeing my men from the curse, and I wasn't even able to do that. So what did anything matter anymore? But then you came to us, and everything changed. *Everything*."

"Everything changed for me too, Draegan."

"No, you don't understand. I..." I climb off the bed and kneel before her, and she sits up and stares at me expectantly, her eyes bewitching and beseeching both. Reaching for her hands, I say softly, "Even after you arrived, even after you and I got physically close, even after I could feel myself falling under your spell, I... I hurt you, Westlyn. I pushed you away at every turn. I said so many awful things, dimmed the light in your eyes so many times... It's a wonder you've got any patience or kindness left for me. It's a wonder you haven't turned your back on me completely."

She opens her mouth to respond, but I shake my head to silence her, lacing our fingers together, holding her tight.

"The night of the fire," I press on, "when I saw Rook's security footage, something inside me shattered. I couldn't bear to think you were taken from us. That you were imprisoned somewhere, frightened and alone. Yet, I couldn't bear the thought that you were anything *but* frightened and alone, for any other possibility was just too terrifying. Was someone hurting you? Did you perish in the fire? I had no bloody *idea*. I only knew that you weren't *home*, weren't in my arms, and the very last thing you and I shared in your waking hours was another stupid argument because I refused to be honest with you. Refused! As if my smug silence could actually protect me from falling in love with you."

She searches my face, tears slipping down her cheeks.

"I vowed to myself right then and there that when we found you again," I say, "*when*, not if, I wouldn't wait another moment. I would be honest with you. Completely, utterly honest, because the thought that you could be taken from me without knowing how I truly felt... The thought that I might never be able to speak to you again, to hold you, to gaze upon your face and see that look in your eyes when you say my name..." I cup her face, my thumb brushing her tears. "But of course, everything else happened so fast. The attack at the cathedral, the portal to Winter-moon. Rook, and then Jude, and now... Now I fear I'm almost out of time, and I can't—I *won't* let that happen. So this is me, Westlyn Avery. This is me on my knees, confessing all the things I've kept locked in my heart when I should've freely given them to you from the very start."

"Draegan," she whispers. "What are you saying?"

"I'm saying... I'm saying that for all I've obsessed over it, I can't even remember the exact moment I fell in love with you. There were so many of them, I'm not even sure there even *was* a moment, some single event or conversation that tipped me over the edge. When I try to recall it now, I feel them all wrapping around me, burrowing in deep. Then one night I just looked at you, and you smiled at me, and I knew. I knew, despite all my denials." I take one of her hands and place it on my chest, right over my heart, holding her close. "No matter what the outcome is in Wintermoon, know this. You have healed a heart I'd long thought ruined beyond repair. For the first time in more centuries than I can recall, I feel whole when I'm with you. Not because you've erased the past... the grief... but because you granted me the space to feel it. You didn't give up on me, on us, even when I gave you every reason to doubt me. To run for the bloody hills. My heart is fully in your hands now. And though I don't pretend to know how much time I've got left, I promise you, Westlyn Avery. If you'll let me, I'll spend what remains of my life showing you just how much you mean to me. Showing you just how much I love you."

Her eyes flutter closed, and for a long moment, she doesn't speak. Her tears fall freely, her lashes dark with them, cheeks pink, a tremor shivering through her body.

"Please don't cry, love," I whisper. "I can't stand the thought that my words are still hurting you."

"It's not your words," she finally says, opening her eyes to look at me once more. "I've been waiting to hear you say these things to me for so long. And now that you have, there's so much... And you just... And I... *Goddess*, Draegan. I want to trust you. To trust what we have and what you're saying and all the things I feel for you—all the things I've *always* felt for you."

"Then trust it. Trust *this*." I press her hand more firmly against my heart, letting her feel every wild beat.

She nods, but the sadness in her eyes deepens, and my heart beats even more furiously, everything in me desperate to ease her pain.

"What is it, love?" I ask.

She unleashes a pent-up breath and shakes her head, lowering her gaze. "It's... silly. In the grand scheme of things."

"Westlyn." I hook a finger under her chin and lift her face until she's gazing up at me once more. "*Nothing* that puts that devastated look in your eyes could possibly be silly."

At this, the tiniest smile graces her lips, but—like every smile that's come before it here in this forgotten realm—it fades all too quickly.

"All this time," she says softly, "all the things we've done, all that you've just confessed. And you still haven't truly kissed me. Every time I asked you to, you turned me down or walked away."

She's right. I haven't.

Kissing someone is its own sort of confession, and before now, I couldn't bring myself to offer it to her, no matter how desperately I longed for it.

"Because I'm a damned fool," I say. "A fool who likes to

torment himself by denying himself the one thing he wants more than the very air he breathes."

"If I asked you for a kiss now," she says, her voice dropping to a whisper as her thumb ghosts across my lips, "I mean, a *real* kiss... Would you turn me down again?"

"What do you think, my beautiful, insatiable little immortal?"

Genuine fear glazes her eyes, and she lowers her hand from my face. "I think I'm too scared to find out."

Not a taunt or a test this time, but a confession as bare as my own.

A confession for which there's only one response.

"Then perhaps it's best *not* to ask," I whisper, climbing back into the bed with her and brushing my lips across her brow bone, then lower, lower still. "Perhaps it's best to just lie back, close your eyes, and..."

CHAPTER TWENTY-ONE

WESTLYN

The last time I was intimate with Draegan—the night I not-so-affectionately referred to as The Incident—I stormed out of his room in a blaze of frustration and anger, so tired of his games, of his inability to be honest about his feelings, of his constant need to push me away every time we get even remotely close.

Now, hidden away in this remote cabin in the middle of a crazy storm in the middle of an even crazier realm, Draegan has just handed over his heart, obliterating everything that ever stood between us.

Every wall. Every argument. Every secret shame and past regret.

Gone.

And I've never been more terrified in my life.

Being alone with him like this now, naked and vulnerable, my heart thundering, my nerve endings electrified…

Goddess, if he doesn't kiss me soon...

No. I won't survive that kind of rejection. I can't. Not again.

I lie back and close my eyes, just like he told me to. I wait for the span of several heartbeats. More. A minute. An agonizing eternity, and still, he hasn't kissed me.

I feel the solid, comforting weight of him as he rolls on top of me again, the urgent press of his cock settling between my thighs.

I feel his hands in my hair.

I feel the warmth of his skin near my face, lips brushing close, but not close enough.

I feel his breath misting on my throat, my cheek, my mouth.

And then, just when I'm convinced he's going to walk away and shatter my heart in a way so irreparable not even my fae magic can heal it, Draegan Caldwell kisses me.

His lips are gentle at first, a tentative sweep as soft as butterfly wings. Then, a deep moan of pleasure reverberates through his chest, and he crashes against my mouth, hungry, greedy, devouring.

I part my lips for him and deepen the kiss, and his tongue sweeps inside to tangle with mine, his confident strokes plumbing every soft curve, tasting me, claiming me.

My heart feels like it might burst, but it doesn't shatter this time. It expands. It warms. It beats inside me like a furious drum, and I slide my hands into his hair and grip his horns, drawing him closer as he nips and teases and takes, takes, takes.

And all I want is to give him more.

I open my thighs for him, welcoming the feel of his hard, perfect length as he sinks inside me, deep and slow, filling me so completely I can't even remember a time when we *weren't* close like this. When we weren't open and honest and just... in love.

I finally open my eyes and find him looking at me with an intensity that makes my toes curl, but his every movement is tender and sweet and slow. Reverent.

Cupping my face in one of his big, strong hands, he rolls his hips again, the base of his cock stroking my clit as he slides inside me, one perfect inch at a time.

A tear slips free, unbidden, and he kisses it from my cheek.

"What is it, love?" he whispers. "Am I hurting—"

"No, it's nothing like that." I trace his jaw with my fingers, memorizing the feel of it. The shape. "I just... Goddess. Is it wrong to admit that I almost don't want the storm to end?"

An understanding smile touches his lips, and he leans in for another kiss, slow and sweet. Then, "We're here *now*. Right here, right in this moment. Stay in it with me, love. Just like this." He lowers his mouth to mine once more, drawing my lip between his teeth, teasing it before deepening our kiss, shifting the angle of his delicious thrusts to hit that perfect spot inside me, making my toes curl all over again.

"Draegan," I breathe, losing myself in this intense pleasure. "You feel so... so good."

At this, he kisses my throat and moans against my skin, his hips circling faster, the friction against my clit sending shockwaves through my core.

Sex with Draegan has always been off the charts, but this time, it's so much more than just a physical connection. It's trust. It's honor. It's vulnerability and sweetness and a deep, unbreakable sense of security I didn't even realize I'd been longing for with him.

But most of all, it's love.

The love I've felt from him for so long—the love he promised me tonight—finally left unguarded, finally allowed to blossom.

Draegan blazes a hot trail of kisses up my neck, across my jaw, finally claiming my mouth once more. And then, with one final sweep of his tongue and a deep, hot thrust between my thighs, he unravels me.

The orgasm explodes inside me, shattering me, ruining me, setting me on fire. I grip his horns and ride out every hot pulse, every throb of pleasure, my body trembling as Draegan shudders against me and comes inside me, filling me, marking me, owning me.

Loving me.

Exhaustion sweeps over us both, and I yawn and turn onto my side, Draegan's muscled chest a warm, solid comfort against my back.

"Sleep," he says softly, kissing my shoulder and drawing me closer, a wing draped protectively over me.

And there, before the fire in a tiny bed in an old cabin in the woods, I relax into my gargoyle's strong embrace, his arms wrapped tight around me, his lips close to my ear, his final words the softest, sweetest whisper as I finally drift off to sleep.

"You are *everything* to me, Westlyn Avery. And you have my whole heart. You've had it from the very start."

The Wintermoon sun rises on a new day, and I awaken to find Draegan busy in the cooking area, spooning piping hot oatmeal into two bowls and setting them on a tray.

"I'm no Augustine Lamont," he says with a smile as he carries it over to the bed, "but the oats were still fresh, and I managed to find some black tea, too."

He sits beside me and leans in for a deep kiss that almost has me thinking we should skip breakfast altogether.

"What was that for?" I tease.

"Special occasion."

"Which one?"

"The occasion of waking up to find a beautiful naked woman in my arms, bathed in sunlight."

I grin at him. Despite the circumstances of our travels, this feels like the perfect start to the perfect day. "Thank you."

"For the kiss or the tea?" he asks, handing me a mug.

"Both."

We eat breakfast in companionable silence, a freshly made fire crackling in the hearth, but all too soon, reality sets back in, our little adventure coming to its inevitable end.

We need to get back to the inn. We need to shore up our defenses and figure out a plan.

"There's no doubt we need to take Verrick out," Drae says, clearing away the breakfast mess while I get dressed. "I don't want to leave Wintermoon until we accomplish that."

"Agreed."

"But we've got a decision to make." He washes and puts away the dishes, and I push the bed back against the wall and do a quick check to make sure we're not leaving anything behind. "We can go after him now—see if we can track him. Or we can return to the inn and regroup."

"He wants us to follow him now," I say. "He knows we're less powerful when it's just the two of us. And I don't have my amulet, which I think is why he was able to tap into my magic in the cave. When he hit you with that spell? I don't know. Something tells me he wouldn't have been able to do it without me. As soon as he nailed you to the wall, I felt it —like a drain on my energy."

"That could explain why he hasn't mounted a stronger attack against the group. Jude and Rook... His power might just be accelerating the effects of the curse. He didn't attack the witches, though—perhaps he couldn't."

"He *looks* weaker, too. Like this whole thing is taking a toll on him. Another strange thing? Both times when I saw him open a portal—at the inn and again in the cave—his face did this weird flickering thing."

"What do you mean?"

"It was almost like... like he had *other* faces beneath his own and was cycling through them. At first I thought maybe they were just fae glamours, but there was something oddly familiar about some of them. I can't quite put a finger on it—everything happened so fast, so I didn't really get a good look." I stand before the fireplace, taking a final opportunity to warm up before we venture out again. "I have a feeling he's going to show up back at the inn. He wants me, but he also wants the Codex. Maybe he thinks he can tap into its power, or maybe he just doesn't want anyone else to do so. Either way, I'm wondering if maybe he's been pulling the strings on it all along—the strings that eventually led the Archmage to its location in Ireland. We know they've been working together—at least they *were* working together before Verrick betrayed him."

I stare into the flames, still trying to puzzle it out.

"The Codex had a spell powerful enough that it enabled me to form some kind of magical connection with Verrick and bring him to our realm without a traditional fae portal.

Then, some combination of my magic and the Codex brought us here, to Wintermoon. Now, according to Verrick, the alleged Spell of Unmaking won't work on your curse, but that doesn't mean it won't work on other things, and it doesn't mean there aren't other spells that *will* work on the curse."

"You're right." Draegan joins me by the fire, his hands warm and steady on my shoulders. "Whatever the reasons, I'm fairly certain the last thing he wants is for that book to remain in our hands, especially now that you can read it and we've got witches working to help crack its cryptic mysteries."

A log shifts in the fire, sending up a burst of sparks. "You know, I keep thinking about my nightmare the night of the library fire. The woman I saw from the Tarot—from the Judgement card? She kept telling me I had a task to complete. But then she turned into Verrick, and I decided she must've been an illusion. That it was him all along, twisting my dreams into nightmares, slowly worming his way into my head. I don't know how he got to me so easily, but he did. Not just my thoughts, but my intuition, too. All of a sudden, I *wanted* to bring him here. Needed to. Nothing had ever felt so important, so right."

"Verrick is a master of trickery and illusion. The fact that he conjured an image from the Tarot to manipulate you—"

"But that's just it. The more I think about it, the more I

think she *wasn't* an illusion." I turn around and look up into his stormy gray gaze. "I'm pretty sure she was part of *me*, Draegan. Part of my magic. My soul. Bringing Verrick to our realm wasn't the task she set out for me—*that* part was his manipulation. His darkness overpowered her—overpowered me. But when she tried to tell me about my task, I think she was speaking of a larger purpose. Something that led me to connect with the other witches and better learn to use my magic. To somehow... I don't know." I close my eyes and take a deep breath, the words feeling suddenly immense. "To reclaim the prophecy and choose what it means to *me*."

Laney's words from last night echo.

Your task, Westlyn, is to decide what kind of witch you want to be. Not the witch the Archmage and his ilk wanted you to be. Not the one Verrick is attempting to control and manipulate. Not the witch some ancient prophecy has dictated for you, generations before you were even born. Not even the witch you believe your gargoyles want. But the truly powerful, divine witch of your heart and soul...

I share those words with Draegan now.

"And you believe this is the very task your Tarot vision was speaking of as well?" he asks.

"I'm not sure, but it... it feels right." I press a hand to my heart. "In here, it feels right."

He tucks a finger under my chin and dips his head low, pressing a gentle, reassuring kiss to my lips.

"Then it *is* right," he whispers, and the simple declaration of his words, of his kiss, of his gentle touch, of the fierce, unwavering look in his eyes... All of it steadies me, bolstering me for what's to come.

"We need to find our way back to the inn," I say, resolute in the decision now. "I don't suppose you have any idea where in the wretched frozen hell we are?"

"As a matter of fact, I do." He leads me to the window and points to a high peak towering in the distance, its jagged edges clear now that the storm has passed. "If memory serves, that's Shadowcliff Mountain, part of the Blackfeather range that runs along the western edge of Wintermoon. The village is due south of us, maybe about forty miles or so, as the crow flies."

"You mean, as the gargoyle flies?"

"Precisely. As long as we head in that direction and the skies remain clear, we should be able to reach it fairly quickly."

"Okay, then." I blow out a breath. "Let's do this."

As Draegan puts out the fire with the last of our cooking water, I take one more look around our cozy little cabin and smile, sending it a silent prayer of thanks for being our refuge in the storm.

For giving us the opportunity to share our first kiss.

For that alone, it will remain a bright spot in my memory of an otherwise terrible place.

"All set," Draegan says, and I nod, following him out into the bright daylight.

Then, after closing the cabin door behind us and sharing one more delicious kiss, my gargoyle and I are soaring up into the Wintermoon sky, his arms wrapped securely around me, the sun deceptively warm and lovely on our faces.

CHAPTER TWENTY-TWO

ROOK

I feel her before I see her, our bond so impossibly strong now—such an innate part of me—I wonder how I existed for so many centuries without sensing her soul.

Minutes later, she and Draegan burst through the doors of the inn, breathless with both exertion and relief.

Auggie rushes to them, sweeping her into his arms and crushing her against his chest. "You're back, thank the devil."

"Not sure the devil had much to do with it," she says, "but it's good to be back just the same."

"What happened?" he asks, setting her on her feet. "One minute you were here, and then the portal opened up and Verrick just... Fuck, West. We were going out of our minds."

"Just another failed attempt by the dark-fae king to claim what isn't his." Draegan runs a protective hand over

West's head. "He'll be back for more, no doubt, assuming he hasn't already tried."

"All's been quiet here," Auggie says, casting a quick glance at me and Jude. "Too quiet."

"Where are the witches?" West asks. "I've got a few theories I'd like to run by them about Verrick's magic."

"They've been sequestered upstairs with your notes on the Codex," Auggie says. "Trying to see if they could crack the mystery of Verrick's portals. Oh, Laney found this under the sofa. Gave it to me for safekeeping."

He hands West her amulet.

"Thank the goddess." She presses it to her chest, the magic glowing bright at her touch. "Have you—"

"Westlyn! Oh, am I ever glad to see you, child." Tatiana descends the stairs, Laney and Fleur behind her, their arms laden with candles and jars of herbs and the stacks of parchment they've been using to work through West's translations of the Codex. "We've unlocked the Spell of Unmaking. We haven't been able to open the Codex without you, but your notes were immensely helpful."

West nods, but her smile doesn't reach her eyes. "Verrick told us the Spell of Unmaking won't work against the curse—no spell will."

She tells the group about the tether. The so-called loophole. The utter futility of it all.

It was always a long shot, but still. Hearing confirmation that the Spell of Unmaking won't actually set us free...

Fuck. If I could actually move right now, I'd probably punch something.

Fleur sets down her bottles and jars on the closest table and takes a seat, nodding for West and the other witches to join her.

"We came to the same conclusion, unfortunately," Fleur says gently. "The gargoyles' curse isn't just of dark-fae making. Parts of it were forged in hell, then fused together with Wintermoon magic, all woven in with Verrick's cruelty and malice. With his hatred for the men he holds responsible for killing fae soldiers during the war."

"If you tried to use the Spell of Unmaking to break the curse," Laney explains, "it might destroy the fae magic, but it wouldn't touch the demon magic. The whole thing would become completely unstable, very likely resulting in magical side effects even worse than the curse itself."

"What sort of side effects?" West asks, but I already know the answer to that question.

The magic used to forge the curse is so dark, destabilizing it can only result in more darkness. Total insanity, a complete disconnect from reality. An irreversible, magically-induced coma. Eternal damnation in the most terrifying parts of hell. A plethora of other things I can't even think about without feeling sick.

Laney confirms all of this for West, but then her eyes brighten. She reaches across the table and takes West's hands, giving them an encouraging squeeze. "However, we're pretty sure we've discovered a *different* application for the spell."

"Tell me," West gasps.

"Reversing whatever magic locked the gargoyles in stone."

"But.. What?" West is suddenly on her feet, pacing before us. "Isn't that all part of the same curse?"

"Yes and no," Tatiana says. "While turning to stone may be the final outcome of the curse in the long run, the fact that both gargoyles' transformations coincided with an appearance from Verrick suggests that these particular turnings are *not* a result of the curse, but of a direct magical attack."

"And because the attack is dark-fae made," West says, her turquoise eyes glimmering with new hope, "a dark-fae Spell of Unmaking can reverse it. Goddess, that's... that's good news! *Excellent* news!"

The other witches nod, and Draegan and Auggie draw close, a cautious hope filling their eyes as well.

West reaches up to stroke the edge of my stone wing. "I assume you haven't tested it yet?"

"We were short one key ingredient." Tatiana hands Westlyn a kitchen knife. "The spell requires dark-fae blood."

Westlyn and the witches spend the next hour talking through the planned ritual and gathering supplies for the spell—more herbs and dried plants from the stores in the basement, bottles of oils, salt, ash from the hearth, enough candles to light up half the realm. I'm not even sure what else they collect—they come and go up and down stairs and in and out of closets so quickly, it's all a blur.

Draegan is on guard outside, making regular flyovers, and Auggie remains stationed at the bar, strapped with swords and daggers from their supply run, ready for another surprise attack from our illustrious dark-fae king.

We all know it's only a matter of time.

Finally, after moving around furniture and covering the common room floor with candles and salt, the witches are ready to begin.

West comes to stand before me and Jude, her amulet glowing from a thin muslin pouch she's now wearing around her neck.

"The girls and I would like to try something, if you guys are up for it." She watches us closely, brows raised, eagerly awaiting our replies.

I try to send her my thoughts. I'm sure Jude is doing the same.

We're up for anything that gets us out of these prisons and back to fighting by your side, my wild girl.

"Since I'm not hearing any protests," she says with a teasing smile, "we're taking that as a yes."

"It's time, Westlyn." Tatiana gestures for West to join

them on the floor, where they're all seated inside a circle of candles and salt.

The Codex is open on the floor between them, its pages glowing with their now-familiar violet and indigo light. Next to it, a large stone bowl holds a mix of the dried herbs and oils, and at Tatiana's direction, West slices her palm and makes a fist, spilling her blood into the bowl.

Clasping hands, the witches begin a low chant, calling upon and blessing each of the elements—salt and herbs, representing the earth. Ashes and candles, representing fire. West's blood, representing water. Their breath, representing the air.

Soon, their chanting slows, their tone deepening, the words melting into an ancient language I don't speak but I assume is the Spell of Unmaking.

Magic electrifies the air. I can feel it on my stone skin, warm and tingling and heavy.

Dangerous.

But somehow, hopeful.

Please, please let this work.

The chanting doesn't stop, but the witches release West's hands, then close the circle around her.

She places her left palm on the Codex, her right dipping into the bowl containing her blood. A violet flame flickers to life, and she removes her hand, painting a line of blood across her forehead, then stretching her hand toward me and Jude like she's making an offering.

As the witches continue their dark and soothing

murmurs, West closes her eyes and begins a chant of her own.

> *Spell of darkness, spell of stone*
> *Woven through blood and skin and bone*
> *As it is written, by my breath and blade*
> *So shall this magic be fully unmade*

Voice rising steadily above the witches' chants, amulet glowing bright in her pouch, West recites her verse alone, again and again, the magic gathering strength, visibly sparking to life around us.

It swirls in great clouds of black shadow with wild arcs of magic that flicker like an electrical storm.

She keeps chanting, louder and faster, the concurrent chant picking up speed to match, those otherworldly clouds enveloping me and Jude completely, until all I can see—all I can *feel*—is magic. Is *Westlyn's* magic.

The transformation begins in earnest at my feet, my toes slowly warming to life, my calves twitching as the magic races up my thighs, spinning inside my gut until it spirals outward, a rush of heat and electricity zipping around my bloodstream.

I think I hear Auggie calling West's name, but it's a distant sound, muted by the sudden pounding of my heart and the rush of blood to my head.

She's doing it. She's fucking doing it.

Come on, wild girl. Almost there.

"I'm not giving up, Augs," she says, her voice cutting through the din. "We're so close. I can feel it. It's working."

"It's draining you," Auggie says.

"I'm good. I can keep going. Just... just let me have a few more minutes."

Auggie mutters something to Tatiana, but she doesn't stop chanting either, and he must back off because West starts up her spell again, faster and faster, louder, the magic rushing through my wings, down my tail, up to the very tips of my horns, and—

"We've got incoming!" Draegan bursts through the doorway. "Demons!"

"Hold them off!" West shouts. "I'm almost there!"

"Fuck!" Auggie again, followed by the unmistakable sound of glass shattering, wood splintering...

"As it is written," West shouts at the top of her lungs, "by my breath and blade! So shall this magic be fully unmade!"

With a thunderous boom, the magic enveloping us disappears, and all at once, I can breathe. I can feel and hear and see and taste the air around me, the candle smoke, the burning herbs.

I can move.

Jude and I explode out of those stone prisons as though our girl set off bombs inside us.

"It worked!" she leaps to her feet, tears in her eyes, her face pale and drawn, but that smile... that fucking smile makes it all worth it.

But there's no time for the celebratory kiss I long for.

The front door is hanging off the hinges, all the front windows shattered. Outside, the clash of swords and fire and dark magic echo through the desolate town as Drae and Auggie try to hold off the demons.

Jude and I charge through the door, the witches close behind us, all of us bursting out into the blinding sun.

Into pure chaos.

My newly re-started heart sputters as I catch sight of our attackers—two dozen monsters straight out of a nightmare, with translucent, tattered skin, wings made of black fire, claws like curved blades, and rows of needle-thin, razor-sharp teeth. The beasts are twice as large as a gargoyle, lethal beyond any foe we've ever battled.

Demons? No. These aren't the simple-minded mage-demons from the cathedral.

These are hell's most elite forces, led by a single commander.

Zorakkov.

CHAPTER TWENTY-THREE

AUGUSTINE

It's worse than all the battles of the fae wars combined.

Because unlike Verrick's dark-fae armies, *these* soldiers were forged in the very fires of hell, honed by thousands of years of endless torture until they knew no fear, no pain, no mercy.

Nothing but chaos and bloodlust.

Standing in front of the gallows in the town square, guarded by three massive demons, Zorakkov casts his wicked spells. The body he occupies—Hunter's body—is ruined. One eye missing, half his skull caved in, bloody fissures cracking his skin, bones protruding from festering wounds.

But he doesn't need his body, only his mouth. Only those dark spells muttered through split lips, calling his legions to fight.

Our only advantage is that we're faster and more nimble

in the air, but what the demons lack in speed and flexibility they make up for with sheer power, not to mention their ability to strike terror into the heart with a single roar.

Armed with daggers and short swords, Drae and I fend off their attacks in midair with a series of jabs and cuts—about as much as we can manage before we're forced to dart away to avoid a bite or a swipe of their deadly claws. Black blood and gore stains the freshly fallen snow below, but our minor attacks are not enough.

With Zorakkov's spells giving them life, they're nearly impossible to kill. Decapitation is the best option, but so far, we've only managed to cleave off one head.

But then, just when I'm about to start writing our damn eulogies, the ground below lights up with magic, an explosion of red and gold and orange that rivals the Fourth of July Spectacular at the South Street Seaport.

The witches have entered the game, trudging out into the snow with their proverbial guns loaded.

Which can only mean—

"Save some for us, mate." Jude soars into view, Rook right by his side, and if I wasn't holding two blades and covered in guts, I'd tackle-hug them both.

She did it. Our girl fucking did it.

A smile is all the gratitude I've got time to show before Draegan's barreling toward us, a demon on his tail.

Wasting no time, Jude rockets straight for him, and just before they collide in midair, Drae drops out of the way, giving Jude the perfect shot.

He may be unarmed, but that crazy motherfucker is going for the jugular.

Literally.

He's fucking feral, claws slashing rapid-fire at the demon's neck and face, shredding it to the bone.

The demon roars, black flames scorching the air, but Jude's all in now. He's got his whole body wrapped around the creature's half-mangled torso like some kind of psychotic barnacle, his gargoyle wings batting wildly at the demon's arms, claws still slicing and dicing.

Then, kill shot—a move that happens so fast, I barely see it.

One second he's cursing at the demon, and the next, he's tearing out its throat with his teeth, sawing through the back of its neck with his claws until its ugly head drops to the ground, the body spiraling down after it.

"Well, that's one way to do it, you fucking showoff." I grin at him once more, then bank left, dodging another beast.

Draegan swings back around to take on another one, while Rook goes head-to-head with a third. Jude's back in the mix too, and soon we find our rhythm, a wild clash of swords and claws and fangs. Blood and bone. Rage and ruin.

No sign of Verrick—a blessing for which we've only his cowardice to thank. Of course he'd let his enemies tear each other apart first. Makes his job that much easier.

Down below, the witches continue casting their spells, West's signature violet magic weaving in with the other colors. I don't know what kind of mojo those women are packing, but whatever it is, it's working. Between their spells and our physical attacks, we're finally making a fucking dent.

The demons are weakening.

Not surrendering, but giving us just enough breathing room to try to come up with a better strategy.

A few of them break off from the group, sailing toward the barren trees at the edge of town. Rook and Jude are in hot pursuit, leaving me and Drae to deal with the rest—nine or ten to go.

Better odds than when we started, but still not great. Both of us are fucking exhausted, bleeding and gouged and quickly losing steam.

"Zorakkov," Drae shouts, nodding toward the gallows where the demon prince is still chanting. "We need to take him down or we'll be at this all fucking day."

"Go. I got your back."

Drae nods and takes off, spiraling down toward the gallows. Tatiana spots the move from the ground and redirects her attack on the demons guarding Zorakkov, slowly drawing them away.

A quick glance at Rook and Jude confirms they're holding their own, so I run interference for Drae, grappling with another demon looking for a fight.

Blood and sweat sting my eyes. Muscles tremble with exhaustion. But I keep going, just like everyone else.

Just like West.

I can't see her now, but I can feel her—her magic. Her life force.

Somewhere on the snow-covered street below, through all the blood and fire and destruction, my witchling keeps fighting.

She fights for the other witches—women she just met, but with whom she's already formed an unbreakable bond.

She fights for herself, determined not to let anyone else write her destiny.

She fights for the world she wants to see—a world where beauty still exists, in all its incredible forms.

And she fights for us. For the gargoyles whose cold, dead hearts she resurrected from the grave. The gargoyles she loves.

The gargoyles who'd do anything to ensure she lives to see another sunrise.

Drae's on the ground now, desperately trying to get a hit on Zorakkov, but the fucking demon prince has magic to spare. With a burst of dark energy, he knocks back every one of Drae's attacks.

Fuck. If we can't take that asshole off the board, I'm not sure we'll survive this.

Another demon smashes into me, rolling us in the air, his fiery wings singeing my palms as I grapple for purchase. I finally get us righted, then shove away from him, darting around to surprise him from behind. My sword makes quick work of his head, and I take a moment to enjoy the sight of him splattering on the ground, black flames fizzling out in the snow.

Movement near the gallows catches my eye, and I head down closer to investigate.

Drae's still locked in a stalemate with Zorakkov, but behind them, slowly creeping along the back edge of the gallows platform, is another mage.

Brian fucking Avery. Holding a blade in one hand, his lips muttering a spell I can't even guess at.

What the hell are you up to, Avery?

Another flash of movement a few dozen yards off, and I glance down to see West making her way to the scene.

Fuck. She must've spotted Brian.

And now she's going to protect him.

She loves him. She might hate him, but she loves him. And love... Well. That can make us do all sorts of crazy shit.

I bank hard and dive toward the gallows, hoping to head West off at the pass. But another demon's on my ass. I spin around and strike, catching him in the gut. He swipes at me, landing a deep gouge in my arm. A burst of bright orange magic explodes between us, disorienting him.

I spot Laney on the ground and give her a quick nod of thanks, then haul ass to get to West. She's already there, already running after Brian, the look on her face one of pure desperation.

"Dad!" she cries out. "No!"

At the sound of her voice, Drae loses focus, the momentary distraction just enough for Zorakkov to hit him with a blast that knocks him unconscious.

"West, stop!" I land with a hard crash, but she's still too far out of my reach.

"Dad!" she cries out again, but before I can get to her, before I can scoop her up and carry her away from danger, another figure darts out from behind the gallows, tackling West to the ground.

"You're mine, you ungrateful bitch!" her attacker screeches.

That voice. That fucking voice.

Eloise.

Zorakkov turns at that piercing sound, his movements awkward and jerky as he lumbers toward the women now grappling in the snow.

I don't think. I lunge, crashing into him and taking him down, trying to slash, but he's a lot stronger than he looks. He rolls us, pinning me beneath him just as Brian appears before us.

"I'm so sorry," Brian says to West, his eyes full of regret. "In life, I was a terrible father. Perhaps I can finally do right by you in death."

"No," she gasps, still struggling against Eloise's hold as I wrestle with Zorakkov. "Dad, no! Wait!"

But he doesn't wait. A deep slash of his blade across his wrist, and his blood is spilling into the snow. He recites a spell and the blood glows like hot coals.

"Dad," she whispers. One last attempt.

One last goodbye.

"I love you," he says, then smashes his palm into the glowing snow. It surges bright, and suddenly Zorakkov bursts into flames on top of me.

I shove the burning carcass away and jump to my feet, and a dark entity explodes from his mouth like a plume of thick, oily smoke. It spirals and swirls above us, then dives straight into Brian's mouth.

He howls in pain, but reins it in fast, his lips moving in yet another spell as he struggles to maintain control of his body—a battle of wills between his humanity and the demon prince now possessing him.

All around us, the demonic army drops from the sky, their bodies exploding into ash and smoke when they hit the ground.

I haul Eloise off of West and pin her arms behind her back, forcing her to her knees. My witchling runs straight for her father.

He's on his knees too, black blood leaking from his eyes, the glow from his spell finally fading.

"What's happening to you?" West whispers, kneeling before him and reaching for his wounded hand. "What is this magic?"

"It's a containment spell," Tatiana says, joining us with the other witches. Rook and Jude are back too, helping a stunned but unharmed Draegan to his feet.

"Containment for what?" West asks. The heartbreak in her voice nearly guts me.

"Your father summoned Zorakkov from his broken vessel," Tatiana says, "allowing the demon prince to possess him instead. Then, he trapped him there. When your father passes, Zorakkov will be no more."

"Oh, goddess." West closes her eyes, tears streaking her dirt-smudged cheeks.

Brian coughs, black blood spilling from his lips. His eyes flash red, his neck snapping back at an unnatural angle.

And then, with a final wheezing breath, he's gone.

"He saved our lives," I say softly, because that's the simple truth of it.

"What a hero," Eloise sneers. "You know, Westlyn, you've only yourself to blame. If you'd stuck to the plan, this—"

Her words choke off as I wrap a hand around her throat and haul her up off the ground.

"You will *not* speak to her again," I seethe. "Ever."

I toss her to the ground face first, then kick her over onto her back. "If you'd like to use your shadow magic to make an escape, now's the time."

She covers her head, begging me to let her be.

No more mojo, then. Good.

Beside us, West rises from her father's broken body, as silent and graceful as a dancer. When she meets my gaze, her eyes flash with silver.

With vengeance.

With death.

"Are you... are you going to kill me?" Eloise gasps, blinking up at me with wide, terrified eyes.

"No," I say, knowing it's not my place. Then, leaning down with a fanged grin straight out of the Jude Hendrix Playbook for Psychopaths, barely resisting the urge to tear into her fleshy throat, I say softly, "That honor belongs to your stepdaughter."

CHAPTER TWENTY-FOUR

WESTLYN

Shock and adrenaline and magic course through my veins, my whole body buzzing and electric, but I'm grateful for it. I'm fucking grateful for this power, this rage, this grief.

This darkness.

"Y-you don't have to do this, Westlyn," Eloise whimpers. We've got her locked in a pillory in the town square, head and hands sticking out of the holes, her back bent at a painful angle, feet bound together.

The scent of magic hangs in the air—ours. Zorakkov's. Brian's.

"We can... talk," she suggests.

"Talk," I repeat.

The delusional hope shining in her eyes warms my soul, and I suppress a grin.

I can't wait to see it flame out.

Taking my silence as an invitation to continue, she says, "Yes! Talk! Like we used to? Maybe... maybe have some tea, or... do a Tarot reading?"

I let out a dry laugh. "You said my Tarot interpretations were as trite and meaningless as my whining."

Her face falls. "Well, that was... extenuating circumstances. I was under a lot of stress with the wedding planning, and—"

"You're not even a real witch," I continue. "That's what you said to me."

I cup my hand, watching the magic dance across my palm.

Then I arc back and slap her hard across the face, gripping her cheek and sending a shock of pain through her skull.

My fae rune burns bright. I don't have to see it to know it's there. I can feel it searing the back of my neck. Marking me. Claiming me.

The others stand around us, watching me close. If I'm freaking them out, they don't show it.

I'm pretty sure there's no one here who doesn't know what it's like to want vengeance.

"Stop!" my stepmother screams. "I don't want to die! I don't want to die!"

I remove my hand, and she gasps for breath.

"Beg me for your life," I say.

"W-what?"

I grit my teeth. Lift my hand once more, the magic more than happy to dance for me. *"Beg. Me."*

Tears fall freely down her face, each one plopping into the snow.

Eloise meets my gaze. Terror clouds her eyes.

She sucks in a shuddering breath.

And then?

Oh, how the wretched bitch begs.

I hate the sound of her pathetic voice. Her mewling.

But I love the fact that she has no more power over me.

Finally, when I can't take another minute of her insipid whining, I hold up a hand to shut her up.

"Does... does this mean you'll let me go?" she whispers, that faint glimmer of hope returning to her eyes. "Oh, Westlyn! It really is the best outcome. I'm—"

I lean in close and grip her jaw, nails digging into her skin. In a soft whisper only she can hear, I say, "Your pleading is as trite and meaningless as your life. You're not even a real witch."

Then I shove a dagger into her gut.

Her eyes go wide with shock, then rage. With a last, desperate gasp, she says, "I should've smothered you the moment you slithered out from between your whore mother's legs."

And with that, a final spark of dark magic surges from her wound, smashing into my chest, nearly knocking me off my feet.

I regain my balance quickly, and with great pleasure, I jerk the dagger out of her gut and watch the last of the hope—and the life—bleed from her eyes.

Eloise Avery, the woman who murdered my mother, who manipulated the man I call Dad, who paid teenage mages to bully me, who spent her entire adult life plotting to end mine... is finally gone.

And when I step back and reach up to clutch my amulet, I realize that's gone too.

Eloise fucking destroyed it.

I have about three seconds to process the fact that the bitch got in one last cruel dig before the air begins to shimmer, a silver tear rending the space.

"Westlyn!" Draegan shouts, and Jude's eyes go wide, and my witch sisters draw up their hands in preparation for another magical attack, and Rook and Auggie try to push me out of reach...

But it's too late.

Verrick steps through the portal and grabs me, muttering a spell that feels like it's sucking the magic from my very veins.

There's a sound like a sonic boom, the ground rumbling beneath us as a wave of dark power rolls over us.

The witches are blasted into the air, falling back to the ground with sickening thuds. They're either unconscious or dead.

And the gargoyles—their faces twisted in horror and

pain, their hands still outstretched as if they might be able to reach me in time—turn to stone.

Consciousness returns to me slowly, my body frozen and unmoving, the blood sluggish in my veins.

I try to wiggle my toes, but I can't feel them. Can't move my fingers, either, which can't be a good sign. Frostbite? Paralysis? More dark-fae drugs?

I blink rapidly, trying to make sense of my surroundings. I'm still outside in the town square—I can see the stone gargoyles, Eloise's corpse slumped in the pillory, the unmoving bodies of the witches in the snow.

All of them are in clear view, but...

My world is upside down. Literally.

It takes me a few beats to realize why.

I'm strapped to the guillotine, my head dangling backward over the edge.

"Verrick!" I shout. The sound of it rips through the silence, making my skull ache. I try to reach for my magic— for even a whisper of it—but there's nothing.

He stole it from me. And Eloise gave him the perfect opportunity by destroying my amulet—the *one* thing that could've kept him at bay.

If I end up in hell, I'm going to hunt down her ruined soul just so I can murder her all over again.

"Verrick! Show yourself, you fucking coward!"

"Now, now," comes the chilling reply. "There's no need to curse."

"What the fuck do you want?"

"I've already told you what I want. That hasn't changed." He lets out a put-upon sigh, then finally moves into my line of sight.

His clothes are well-appointed again, his hair gleaming, his silver eyes bright.

The gold crown sits firmly atop his head, cruel in its regal, red-jeweled beauty.

Apparently, my magic does wonders for his appearance.

But the dapper dark-fae king, I see now, is not alone.

Behind him is none other than Archmage Lennon Forsythe, looking refreshed and relaxed as ever.

Goddess, is he stealing my mojo too?

"You remember Lennon," Verrick says, as if we're all about to sit down to tea.

"So the bromance is alive once more?" I roll my eyes. "Good. You two deserve each other."

"Sometimes a ruler must make an unholy alliance in order to achieve a greater end." Verrick strokes the hair back from my forehead, his touch making my skin crawl. "When you're queen, you'll learn the benefits of—"

"I will *die* before I become queen of this wretched land!" I snap.

A flick of his wrist, and the blade falls. I barely have time to gasp when it suddenly stops, mere inches from my throat.

"That can be arranged," Verrick says. "Though that's more of a backup plan."

I close my eyes and suck in a deep breath, trying to calm myself. He doesn't really want me dead—he wouldn't bother with this whole charade otherwise.

It's a slim hope, but I'm clinging to it.

"What's the main plan, then?" I ask, trying to sound contrite. "Hopefully it's one where I get to keep my head."

"It's better if I show you." He strokes my hair again, fingertips trailing across my forehead. This time, magic tingles in the wake of his touch, warming me. "If you promise to behave yourself, little moon, I'll return some of the magic I borrowed."

Borrowed. Right.

I bite back a snort.

"I'll behave," I say instead, and with my next breath, my body comes alive as the magic rushes back to me, tingling through my arms and legs, my chest. My heart beats faster, and I can move my fingers and toes. Deep inside, those cold embers spark back to life.

"Now close your eyes and feel what I need from you."

He presses cold fingertips to my temples, and I do as he asks, that blade still alarmingly close to my flesh.

At first there's nothing, but then... a pulse of magic. A connection—that strange bond that ties me to him. I feel the fae rune flare to life on the back of my neck.

His so-called claim.

And then, through the twisted bond that connects us, I feel his desires. His commands.

He wants me to kill my gargoyles. To turn my magic on their stone forms and shatter them where they stand.

The very thought of it has my heart stuttering, my lungs threatening to give out.

"Don't resist," he says calmly. "This is the best way. The only way."

I want to scream, I want to fight, I want to tell him I'll take the blade over this cruel punishment.

But then my magic surges once more, and in my mind, I suddenly hear Tatiana's words from the other night.

Become its vessel... Know that the ultimate source of the magic in your blood comes from life itself—from creation, from destruction, from the air you breathe and the ground you walk upon. It comes from the trees and the sky, from the rivers, from fire. From love. Allow all of that to come to you, to flow through you, and eventually you'll learn to channel it back out through your intentions...

Taking a deep breath, I force my heartbeat to steady. Force myself to remain absolutely calm. To become that vessel, just like she said.

I reach out with all my senses, feeling the bite of the cold air on my cheeks, smelling the magic that still lingers, tasting the tea I had earlier. I listen for the whisper of the wind through the barren trees beyond. I reach for a connection to the witches, relief flooding me when I sense a faint spark of life.

I recall the touch of my gargoyles, the ever-present teasing spark in Jude's eyes, the vulnerability in Drae's when he finally confessed his true feelings, the joy in Auggie's when he loses himself in his art, the light in Rook's when he makes some new discovery.

I think of our nights together at the manor, the lattes and night breakfasts, the wild love we've made, their fierce protectiveness.

Love. It fills me up and twines with my magic, clearing away the clouds and the fear, revealing more truths.

Verrick is only asking me to kill the gargoyles because he can't do it himself.

He'd never make an alliance with a lone human Archmage unless he was absolutely desperate.

And if Verrick wants me to *kill* the gargoyles, it must mean that they're still alive.

Which means there's still a chance.

"It's time, my moon," Verrick says, removing his fingertips from my temples. The magic stays with me, though, and I force myself not to react.

"Now, Westlyn," he says, and takes a step back, clearing the view to my gargoyles.

I don't say a word. Don't move. Don't even breathe.

There has to be a loophole. A way I can take advantage of his weakness. I just need to find it...

A disappointed sigh is all the warning Verrick gives me before he grabs my head again, crushing my skull between his palms like he's trying to break me.

Something inside me shatters—some sort of protective barrier.

My Cerridwen magic, I realize. It was trying to keep me safe. Balanced. But it's soon overpowered by the dark-fae magic—mine, and whatever Verrick's got left of his. He forces it inside me like a physical thing—like another person jammed into my head.

He may not have much active power left—not the kind that could destroy four powerful gargoyles. But he still has the power of manipulation. Still has a claim on *my* magic, however tenuous.

My whole body trembles against his hold, against the force of his dark power as it shoves inside me, chasing away the light, the goodness, the hope.

I close my eyes and grit my teeth against the pain. Visions flicker behind my eyelids. Faces. Verrick's first, then... Goddess. Jacob Pomeroy. Alonso Florentine. The mages who tortured me as a kid—the ones Jude and Auggie helped me kill.

"You reaped their souls for me," Verrick hisses in my ear. "You condemned the monsters of your past to serve me for eternity. All I'm asking now as that you do the same to the monsters of your present."

Reaped their souls?

Oh, goddess. No.

I remember the night we killed the mages. The Tarot reading I'd done right before Drae took me to the meat packing plant. I'd pulled the Tower card, and the moment I touched it, an otherworldly voice whispered through my head.

Upon those screaming hours
Bathed in blood and breath
You will give them light, my moon
And I will give them Death.

My light. My runes. My magic. I gave their souls to Verrick.

"No," I gasp, not wanting to believe I could do something like that, not wanting to believe Verrick's been manipulating me for so long.

But before I can get out another protest, the faces change from the mages I killed to a more recent one.

Eloise.

Then the horrifying demons from Zorakkov's earlier attack—the ones my magic must've helped destroy.

The demons quickly morph into new faces—dark fae I don't recognize. Hundreds of them. Thousands.

The fae of Wintermoon.

"You... you killed them," I grind out, forcing myself to stay conscious through the agonizing pain. "Your... your own people! You killed them!"

"A necessary sacrifice. Their dark souls feed my magic, as do the dark souls of your mages and stepmother. As will the dark souls of your gargoyles. We're connected, my moon. You and I. And soon, all the dark souls we've reaped will feed *your* magic as well."

Turning to the Archmage, he says simply, "Bow."

Lennon obeys, the fucking coward.

Then, without ceremony or preamble, Verrick removes his crown, its rubies glittering like blood against the snowy backdrop, and smashes it onto my head.

CHAPTER TWENTY-FIVE
WESTLYN

"I crown you Queen of Wintermoon," he bellows, holding the crown to my skull. "Daughter of Darkness, Bringer of Peace."

"No!" I scream, refusing to accept Verrick's words, but it's no use.

The crown fuses with me in an instant, an irremovable extension of my body, tendrils of dark magic spiraling out from the gold and burrowing deep into my mind.

Every ounce of Verrick's malice, his evil, his cruelty pours into me, racing through my blood like ice water. My heart is slowing, my breath shallow, everything inside me threatening to burst.

I can't fight this kind of darkness. This pure, unfiltered hate. Even if I was a full-blooded Cerridwen witch instead of just half, there simply isn't enough light magic in the world to counteract this darkness.

"Together, little moon," Verrick says, his voice soothing now, "we will be as unstoppable as an army, more powerful than the demons of hell, more powerful than the dark fae who came before us, than all the witches and mages across time immemorial. The souls of the gargoyles are the final piece."

His words loop through my fracturing mind.

Unstoppable as an army. More powerful than the demons of hell.

Unstoppable...

Holy shit. The demons.

No, not Zorakkov's hellbeasts, but the mage-demon legions from the cathedral.

The ones who swore fealty to me.

From the glowing embers inside me, a dark flame flickers to life.

Maybe there isn't enough light magic in the world to fight this kind of hatred.

So maybe I need to call on the darkness instead. To embrace it.

To stop fighting my nature.

Tatiana sensed the demons' presence here right after we came through the portal. Fleur said they just hadn't materialized because they had nothing to physically tie them to this realm.

But they *exist*. Here. Somewhere.

And I don't need their physical bodies.

I only need their demonic power.

I have to summon them to me.

With my amulet destroyed, the Codex out of reach, and all my allies down for the count, this is my only shot.

Goddess, it's a crazy plan. A legion of demons is the last thing I need to deal with right now.

But like an evil king once said—like ten minutes ago, actually—sometimes a ruler must make an unholy alliance in order to achieve a greater end.

"I'll cast the magic!" I shout now, a surge of renewed hope blasting through the pain in my skull. "Make it stop hurting, and I'll cast the magic."

Verrick flicks his wrist again, and just like that, the pain is gone.

The crown, unfortunately, is not.

I suck in a ragged breath, blinking away the stars dancing before my eyes.

My gargoyles come into focus once more.

Hang on, boys. I'm coming.

"Why are they still *alive*?" Verrick demands.

"I need to say the spell," I bite back. "Sorry, pops. I can't just break into people's heads and wreak havoc. That's not how my magic works. So if we're going to rule the realms together, you'd better start getting used to it."

Annoyance pinches his face, but my declaration seems to mollify him. He takes a step back, motioning for the Archmage to get to his feet.

You're next, you washed-up shadow magic shithead...

"You may begin," Verrick says.

I take a deep breath. Let the words of the spell come to me. Open myself fully to the power of the dark-fae magic coursing through my blood.

The blood that's foretold to bring the world down.

As quickly and stealthily as I can, I reach up and drag my palm across the blade, making a deep gash. I close my fist around it, feeling the blood warm my skin.

Then, I cast my first spell as the Queen of Wintermoon, Daughter of Darkness, Bringer of Peace.

Bringer of hell.

> *Legions of hell, of darkness, of flame*
> *I call on you now to honor the claim*
> *Mine to control, mine to command*
> *Bow to the Moon Blessed, queen of this land*

I don't even get a chance to repeat it before the deadly guillotine splinters around me, the blade dissolving.

Verrick is so shocked, it takes him several long beats to realize I tricked him.

He turns those wicked silver eyes on me, but I'm not afraid of him. Not anymore.

The words of the prophecy appear in my mind, pulsing with every beat of my heart.

> *A child conceived 'neath moon so bright*
> *Born of the union of darkness and light*
> *Blessed is the babe who inherits the crown*

Blessed is the blood that brings the world down

For thousands of years, witches and mages and scholars alike have analyzed that prophecy. The dark fae and demons co-opted it for their own nefarious purposes, twisting it and reshaping it until it suited them—until they truly believed they could bring about their own glorious reign of terror.

But the prophecy was never about them. It was never *for* them.

I'm the fucking Moon Blessed.

And *I* decide what that means.

"You will pay for your treachery!" Verrick booms.

I offer him a cruel, cutting smile. Maybe it's a smile I inherited from him. Maybe it was my mother's, buried in darkness beneath all the good she tried to bring to this world. All the light.

But one cannot exist without the other.

I close my eyes, and the woman from my vision appears —the woman from the Judgment card.

We're back inside her cauldron, flames licking up around the edges, but they don't burn us.

"Your task is upon you now," she says, and I nod, thinking again of Laney's words.

Your task, Westlyn, is to decide what kind of witch you want to be... the truly powerful, divine witch of your heart and soul....

The woman smiles. I smile back.

I know who she is now.

She's my mother, a woman who loved fiercely, stolen too soon.

She's all the Cerridwen witches who came before her.

She's Tatiana and Laney and Fleur, the witches who've become my sisters.

She's me, just like I told Draegan the morning after the storm. The divine witch of my heart and soul.

I'm a Daughter of Cerridwen. But I'm also a Daughter of Wintermoon. Of darkness. I could no more choose between the two than I could choose just one of my gargoyles to love.

"Are you ready to ascend?" the woman asks now, reaching out for my wounded hand.

I take hers without hesitation, my blood warming at the press of her palm. "I am."

She smiles once more, then vanishes, leaving me back in the town square.

I'm standing behind the ruined guillotine, Verrick seething before me.

He lunges for the crown, but I easily dodge his grasp.

He won't touch me now.

He will *never* fucking touch me again.

"Blessed is the babe who inherits the crown," I growl, my voice the voice of all witches. Of all women who've ever felt powerless. "Blessed is the blood that brings the world down!"

I slam my bloody palm to Verrick's chest.

There's a wild burst of violet and silver magic, and he staggers backward, falling to the ground.

All around us, my legions fill the realm, a living, breathing darkness that consumes all the light. Shadow and flame dance before my eyes, and I stretch my arms out, calling them to me, welcoming them.

Mine to control, mine to command.

Their dark fire grows brighter, hungry and desirous.

Mine to control, mine to command.

It consumes the bleak forest beyond the town's edge.

Mine to control, mine to command.

It consumes the abandoned buildings that line the street, the gallows and the pillories in the square.

Mine to control, mine to command.

It consumes the body of my stepmother, the body of the man who raised me as his own and sacrificed himself so that we might have a chance.

Mine to control, mine to command.

It consumes the charred body of Hunter Forsythe, the vessel for a demon prince my dad destroyed.

Mine to control, mine to command.

It consumes the body of the Archmage of Manhattan, a slow torture that blackens and blisters the skin, splitting him open like meat left too long on the grill.

Mine to control, mine to command.

Only the gargoyles and witches remain untouched. Protected.

The dark fire comes to me, and I lift my hands higher,

commanding it to rise, rise, rise for one final task.

And then, with a terrible rage befitting an evil fae king, I turn that fire on Verrick of Wintermoon.

His clothing ignites. His hair incinerates. His face begins to melt from his skull, and yet those silver eyes remain locked on mine with a look of pure shock.

Of horror.

Of endless agony far worse than anything he's inflicted on me.

And then, finally, of pride.

Don't fear, little one. Everything is unfolding exactly as it should be...

His last words whisper through my mind, and a blast of dark energy slams into me, stealing my breath, locking onto my magic with a determination that rivals my own.

The tether to the gargoyles' curse, now mine, just like he said it would be.

His earlier spells unravel, releasing the gargoyles from stone, bringing the witches back to consciousness.

Their orders fulfilled, the demon legions temporarily retreat, and light floods back into the town square, illuminating the full extent of the devastation.

No tree or building or structure remains standing. The snow has melted away, revealing the barren gray rock beneath.

The bodies of Brian Avery, Eloise Avery, Hunter Forsythe, and Lennon Forsythe are gone.

And there, in the spot where Verrick of Wintermoon

burned to ashes—the dark-fae father who entranced my mother and created me just so he could one day destroy me —only a shadow remains.

"I don't know what happens next," I admit, stepping through the ashes of what used to be the inn.

After I told everyone what happened with Verrick and the demonic legions, we'd hoped to find the Codex. But after hours of searching, no sign of it remains.

Tatiana believes it served its final purpose—connecting me with my magic, with my Cerridwen bloodline—and simply ceased to exist.

"You don't need to know everything," the elder vampire-witch says now. "It will come to you as all things do, one day at a time. One moment at a time."

"But I don't know how any of this actually works," I say. "The Codex was one thing, but this?" I touch the crown that still rests on my head, too afraid to try to remove it.

Too afraid to consider what it means if I can't.

Tatiana offers her kind, wizened smile. "Westlyn of Wintermoon, you are the rightful heir to the crown and all the magic that comes with it. Whether you keep it or release it is for you to decide, but decide you must. The crown must remain in Wintermoon, and so must its bearer. It's too dangerous to bring back to the earthly realm."

"Decide," I repeat, and she nods.

Decide what kind of witch you want to be…

I close my eyes, searching myself for the answer. For a sign.

Wintermoon magic comes to me at once, so different from the Cerridwen magic that follows. While my mother's magic is warm and comforting, Verrick's is icy and severe, deadly.

Intoxicating.

After a lifetime of being powerless, of being looked down on and bullied, of being pushed around like a pawn on a chessboard by all the people in my life who were supposed to love and protect me, the magic of the Wintermoon crown feels like an impossible dream.

Verrick once promised me riches beyond my wildest imaginings. Power like nothing I'd ever experienced.

I know now that this is what he meant.

I can already feel it working its charms on me, seducing me, enticing me to stay. To make a life for myself here in Wintermoon, my ancestral homeland. To be its queen.

I would be alone, but I'd be unstoppable. There's nothing I wouldn't be able to accomplish. No desire or whim I couldn't manifest.

I think about my gargoyles. The men who fought to protect me. Who believed in me. Who even now still sift through the ashes in search of a magical book simply because I don't want it to be gone.

I love them. There's no question.

And maybe the curse means they'll leave me far too

soon. Maybe it means I'll end up alone anyway, wishing I'd taken the crown when I had the chance.

I sigh. There was a time when I would've traded in absolutely *everything* for this.

But now?

No. There's no decision to make.

Wintermoon will always be a part of me. It's in my blood, my magic, my memory.

But my place—my *home*—is in the earthly realm. My home is with the men I love, for however much longer fate sees fit to grant me the privilege.

With a sense of utter rightness, I finally reach up and lift the crown.

I feel its dark tendrils trying to hold on, but then it releases me.

Tatiana's wrong. The crown can't stay in Wintermoon, either.

It must be destroyed.

The demon legions are still in Wintermoon, formless as they were before I called upon them. Now, I call upon them for one final mission.

The shadows return at once, swirling before me in a dark vortex, faster and faster until the formless smoke takes the shape of a single demon merged from all the rest, with glowing red eyes and horns that curl around its ruined face.

The demon inclines its head, a hundred voices whispering in my mind as one.

What do you ask of us, Moon Blessed? We are yours to

command.

"Destroy," I reply, placing the crown in his hands.

At his fiery touch, the gold melts away, the rubies dropping to the ground and vanishing in a puff of red smoke.

The last of its cruel tendrils retreat from my mind, and I blow out a sigh of relief.

"Now I command this legion to return to hell," I say firmly, "forever banished to your dark realm, never to answer the call of another summoning. Never to possess another being. Never to rise for another master."

There's no questioning or bargaining. The demon simply turns back into shadow, then mist, then disappears entirely.

In its place, a white light appears, growing larger and larger until it finally takes the shape of a doorway.

I turn to Tatiana and the others, and grin.

All of them look at me with wonder. With the sort of happiness I didn't think we could ever feel in a realm like this.

"Fucking hell," Jude says. "Is that—"

"It's the way home, boys," I confirm, and Tatiana gives me a knowing wink. Laney and Fleur rush me with a group hug.

My gargoyles join in, too.

Then, as bloodied and battered as when we arrived in this forgotten realm, three witches, four gargoyles, and one dark-fae Wintermoon Cerridwen witch from Brooklyn step into the light.

Time.

It moves differently in the fae realms, and what we thought was a mere few days in Wintermoon was actually an entire month back home.

The night after our return, the gargoyles and I are gathered in the study, watching the news coverage on my laptop. The reporter's voice accompanies an aerial shot of the rubble formerly known as Thornwood Cathedral.

"After a weeks-long investigation," the woman says, "authorities have confirmed that the deadly collapse of Thornwood Cathedral in lower Manhattan last month was the work of a dangerous cult with ties to ancient witchcraft and demon worshipping. In total, two hundred and seventeen members of the cult—most of them with known ties to organized crime—committed mass suicide by detonating a series of highly sophisticated explosive devices that caused the structure to collapse, crushing the people who'd barricaded themselves inside. It is not yet known whether hallucinogenic drugs were also a factor. A spokesperson for Blackmoor Capital Group, the historic preservation firm that owns the landmark building, has stated that they will not be pursuing criminal charges. However, three of the cult's most notable members, Lennon Forsythe and his son Hunter, along with Eloise Avery, have been missing since the explosion and are still wanted for questioning. Authorities are asking anyone with information to contact—"

I snap the laptop shut and scoff. "Ties to ancient witchcraft, my ass. If they only knew it was witches who saved the city from a demonic takeover at the helm of a dark-fae madman."

"Speaking of witches who kick all kinds of ass." Auggie grins as Westlyn enters the study, three ravens hopping in a row behind her. "Good evening, witchling and company."

Apparently, Jean-Pierre escaped the portal spell that sent us all to Wintermoon and made his way back here, where he found Lucinda and Huxley tucked away in Draegan's room.

At the time, we thought we'd only be gone a few hours.

Fortunately, the ravens—clever little beasts that they are—escaped, likely with the help of J.P.

But not before they made a delightful mess of Drae's linens. And his carpet. His furniture. His bath. Pretty much no surface was left unscratched or—not to put too fine a point on it, un-shat upon—a thing that brought us all an immeasurable amount of joy.

Even Draegan himself couldn't help but laugh.

He's planning a complete remodel of his bedroom, but hey. At least he finally sees the humor in it.

West insists the birds were more upset about being left out of the fight than about being locked up, but according to her, they've decided to forgive us.

I'm doing my best to win back their favor by sneaking them cookies at regular intervals, just to be on the safe side.

Still, they haven't left her side since we returned. It's like they're afraid she might just disappear again—might end up somewhere dark and terrible where they can't follow. Can't protect her.

I know the feeling.

She hasn't left our side, either. She stayed with us on the rooftop all day—insisted on it. Jude set up a tent and bedding for her, but still. I can't imagine it was too comfortable.

I don't think she slept a wink, anyway.

"I was hoping I could speak with Rook," West says now. "Alone."

The guys are worried about her—we all are—but they leave the room as she asks. The ravens are the only ones permitted to stay.

I join her by the fire, leaning in to steal a quick kiss. "Everything okay?"

"Yes. I mean no. I mean..." She lets out a heavy sigh.

"We haven't had a chance to really talk since we got back, and everything was so chaotic in Wintermoon and there was never a good time and I just... I wanted to apologize, Rook."

She meets my gaze, her eyes full of sorrow and regret.

I cradle her face, brushing her cheeks with my thumbs. "Westlyn. What in all the realms could you possibly have to apologize for?"

"Um... everything?" She laughs, but it quickly turns into a shuddering sob. "Goddess, Rook. There's so much I need to explain. To try to make sense of the craziness and... I just... I'm sorry. I'm so, so sorry for what I did to the library, and—"

"No," I whisper. I can't bear the thought that she's tormenting herself. "It wasn't your fault. Not even close."

"You saw the video. Those were *my* flames, Rook. My magic. I set the books on fire with my bare hands. Fault doesn't get any more clear than that."

"You never intended—"

"No. But I still did it. Does intention matter?"

"In this case? Hell yes, it matters. You were tricked and manipulated by a monster far more powerful than you, than any of us."

Tears fall from her eyes, splashing onto my thumbs. "The library was *everything* to you. Absolutely everything. And now it's—"

"Not everything. Not even close."

"But—"

"*Westlyn.*" Anger simmers inside that she could even *think* such a thing. "Do you have *any* idea what it felt like that night? What I went through?"

She shakes her head, lowering her gaze.

"I smelled the smoke before I could even open my eyes. We all did. In our stone forms, our senses don't sleep, even when our bodies do. By the time the sun set and we could take on our living forms, I knew. I just knew it was the library. Seeing it engulfed, seeing the ashes of all those books floating in the air, knowing all my decades of research and hard work were gone, all that computer equipment, those precious tomes... You know what I thought? What single, terrifying thing utterly *consumed* me?" I tilt her face up, forcing her to meet my gaze again. "Where is she? That's what I thought. I was terrified we'd lost you. I was terrified we'd find your bones in that rubble. I was terrified I'd never hold you again, never kiss you, never hear your laugh, and I wanted to *die*. I hate that they took you, West. Hate what they put you through. But the moment I saw the signal from your watch on my screen, far the fuck away from that fire, I felt nothing but relief."

"But I destroyed—"

"But you were *alive*!" I insist. And fuck... Just saying the words out loud, remembering that night... It all comes back to me in a rush, igniting a fury inside me that burns brighter than any fire could. "Fucking *alive*, woman! All those books, the electronics, the research and the loft... All of that can be replaced. Rebuilt. *You* can't be. So no, I'm not going to stand here and blame you for this. I'm not going to let you blame yourself. I'm not going to ask you why you did it or what came over you or how the fuck that monster got inside your head. I'm just... Hell, woman. I'm just going to kiss you, because you know what, West? *You're* the only piece of this equation that's everything to me. Absolutely everything."

A little gasp is all she manages before I crush her mouth with mine, lips and tongues and teeth clashing. I haul her up off the floor and spin around, pinning her against the nearest wall.

I've only just replaced my glasses, and now those too crash to the ground with a clatter that portends their doom, but I don't care. Add it to the list of things I'll replace later, because right now, all that matters is this.

The feel of her, whole and alive, wild for my touch.

Desperate for it, just like I'm desperate for hers.

Not daring to break our kiss, I shred her shorts and panties with my claws, then free my cock from beneath the loincloth, pulling back just long enough to say, "Okay?"

"Yes," she breathes, and I crash right back into her again, claiming her mouth with my tongue, claiming her divine pussy with my cock.

There's no teasing tonight. No watching through the camera. No dirty talk, no toys. No sharing.

Just us and the fire between us and the taste of her kiss as she moans into my mouth.

She grips my horns, holding on tight as I rail her against

the fucking wall, hard and fast, pouring everything I feel into each deep thrust, as if I need the reminder that she's here, that I'm here, that we fucking survived.

"Rook!" she cries out, and her body tightens around me, sending shockwaves of pleasure straight to my balls. I slam into her one more time as her orgasm fully takes hold, shaking her to the core, and I come with a growl that chases off the ravens and every last lingering fear in my heart.

"Absolutely everything," I whisper, burying my face in her neck and breathing in the scent of her as we slowly come back to earth. "I love you, my wild girl."

CHAPTER TWENTY-SEVEN

AUGUSTINE

The rich scents of espresso, almonds, and chocolate fill the kitchen as the cappuccino machine whirs to life at my expert touch, and my heart warms with indescribable cheer.

Real time aside, we were only gone for a few days by our reckoning. Yet now, two nights after our triumphant return home, it feels like a lifetime has passed since I last enjoyed the simple pleasure of making my woman an almond joy latte in our kitchen.

I revel in every second of it.

"Is that what I think it is?" My witchling yawns adorably as she enters the kitchen with her ravens, all of them padding across the floor on silent footsteps.

Before I even turn around to respond, she's got her arms around me from behind, her cheek resting against my back.

I cover her hands with mine and hold them to my chest, reveling in the warmth of her touch, the feel of her breath between my wings, the solid reminder that we survived. That we earned another day with her. Another minute.

All too soon, she's pulling out of my grasp and ducking under a wing for a closer look at the cappuccino machine. "Soooo, about that latte I smelled from all the way upstairs..."

"What about it, curious little kitten?"

"Any chance it's for me?" She gives me her best puppy-dog eyes, bouncing excitedly. I take a second to scan her from head to toe, from the adorable frizz of her bun, to the too-big red flannel shirt buttoned crookedly down her chest, to those *oh*-so-sexy knee socks skimming the tops of her thighs.

"As if I could ever say no to you, witchling." I lean down and kiss her forehead, then hand over the goods. "I figured you could use a pick-me-up."

With an enthusiastic nod, she takes the offered mug and inhales the almond-scented steam. "Augustine Lamont, you are a god among monsters."

I laugh. "Pretty sure *no* one has ever accused me of that before."

"Well, they're obviously not paying attention, because it's true." She takes the first sip, her eyes sparkling. A sweet moan escapes her lips—a sound whose only purpose in life is to make me instantly hard, and god *damn* does it ever do the job.

Ignoring the aching throb in my balls, I step closer and

tuck a loose lock of hair behind her ear, fresh worry gnawing at my gut.

I know she hasn't slept much, and she's clearly exhausted. Still... As much as I want to put her into a real bed and insist she get some rest, I can't blame her for wanting to stay by our sides. Hell, if we weren't cursed to turn to stone every morning, the boys and I would stay awake too, never letting her out of our sight.

However much time we've got left together before the curse makes its final claim on our souls, we don't want to miss a single minute of it.

West finally lowers the mug and glances up at me, her big blue-green eyes glazed.

White froth coats her upper lip, and I laugh again. Why the fuck is she so damned cute?

"Hold still. You've got a bit of..." I cup her face with my big hand and swipe a thumb across her milk-foam mustache, but stop when I spot a fresh tear rolling down her cheek. "Oh, no. Is the coffee bad? I know I'm a little rusty, but I thought—"

"It's not the coffee, Auggie. The coffee is perfect. *You're* perfect. Everything about this moment is so damn perfect, I wish... I wish I could just live in it forever."

"Then why are you so sad, witchling?"

Her eyes flutter closed, warm breath ghosting across my fingertips. In a broken whisper, she says, "Because from now on, every single moment that passes between us might be the last. The last almond joy latte. The last touch. The last kiss. The last—"

"Westlyn." I thread a hand into her hair and pull her against my chest, my other arm winding around her back, holding her close. "It was always that way—even when we were humans, long before Verrick cursed us. Nothing has changed. That's part of what makes this life so bittersweet. *No one* knows which moment will be their last. All we can do is make the absolute most of the ones we get—whether it's a thousand, or a million, or just a handful of them. *You* taught me that."

She snuggles in closer, another sigh escaping.

"I know, I know." I laugh, my breath stirring the frizzy hair on top of her head. "It sounds like something that belongs on a motivational poster."

"On a coffee mug, at the very least," she agrees.

"Fine, a coffee mug. But that doesn't make it any less true. Before I met you, I just... I let myself forget it. I was so wrapped up in the curse, in my rage over what Verrick did to us, in all the dark and dirty shit we had to do to survive in this city... *Goddess*, West. I truly forgot the simple pleasure of lounging in a hammock in the orchard and sketching the pattern of the leaves in the moonlight. I forgot the feel of bread dough between my fingers and the satisfaction of eating a meal I put together with my own hands. I forgot the indescribable happiness that fills me up when someone I care about eats a dish I cooked for them. I forgot how much I love photographing beautiful people and animals and plants. I forgot how much I love drawing. Hell, I was so caught up in death, I forgot how much I truly love... life. The best and worst parts of it. The boring parts, the excitement, the craziness, just... all of it."

She pulls back and blinks up at me, her face earnest. "How did you find your way back to it?"

Brushing away her tears with my thumbs, I shrug and give her the most honest answer I've got.

The only answer that even matters.

"I fell in love with you. And then it just unlocked everything else. I don't know how to explain it. It's like... like you brought life back from the dead for me—showed me all the colors when I'd been drowning in a sea of gray."

Her eyes glaze with some new emotion, vast and deep and more beautiful than anything I've ever painted or drawn or photographed.

"It's true," I say. "So whether this life is mine for another fifty years or fifty minutes, I'm grateful for it, and I'm not going to waste any more time being angry about what already happened or worrying about what may or may not come. Because I've got you. I've got *you*, my witchling, and I've got my brothers, and we have this beautiful home and an orchard full of apples and a fire crackling in the hearth and that's... Well, it's enough. It's everything."

And finally—*finally*—my witchling smiles. She sets down her latte, then stretches up on her toes and loops her arms around my neck. "I fell in love with you too, you know."

"Oh yeah?" I can't help the answering grin that spreads

across my face. Nudging her nose with mine, I say, "When, exactly?"

"If you really want to know... It was the waffles that did it."

I crack up. "She mocks me, ladies and gents. I confess my undying love, and the woman mocks me. Have you no shame?"

"Are you kidding me right now? I would *never* mock you about something as sacred as home-made vegan waffles with apple-cinnamon compote. Seriously, Augs. You won me over with those bad boys."

"I should've known food was the way to your heart the minute you started lecturing me in my own kitchen."

"*Organic* food," she clarifies.

"Obviously."

She leans up to press a soft kiss to my lips, then says, "So now that we've got our origin story down, what happens next? Goddess, I really, *really* hope night breakfast is on the menu, because I'm starving."

"Night breakfast can certainly be arranged, but if it were up to me..." Flashing a devious grin, I lift her onto the countertop and settle myself between her knees, my hands trailing up her thighs, thumbs brushing the tops of her knee socks. "I'd suggest we start with an appetizer. Maybe something sweet, like..."

I kiss the corner of her mouth, lingering just a heartbeat before moving to the other corner.

She smiles into my kiss, but I'm just getting started.

"After that," I say, "I might move on to something with a little more... *bite* to it." I kiss my way down her throat, grazing her skin with my fangs, drawing a shuddering gasp from her lips.

My claws trail across her collarbone, then down to her flannel, slowly unbuttoning it to reveal her perky, braless breasts.

"The next course should be a bit richer," I whisper, "in an effort to satisfy the sophisticated palate of the most discerning of connoisseurs." I brush my thumbs across her nipples, then lower my mouth to one of the dusky peeks. I flick it with my tongue before closing my lips around it and sucking hard, moaning against her skin as she arches into me.

"That's... oh, *goddess,*" she breathes. "You're... That's perfect. Right there... Just like... *Wait*... The guys? Are they—"

"Out. For a little while longer, at least." I return to her nipple, savoring it for another minute before slowly kissing my way back to her ear. "Draegan had to run down to JFK to deal with some imports he ordered. Jude and Rook went to Kingston for groceries."

"So I've got you to myself?"

"For now."

"In that case..." A grin as wide as the Hudson splits her face. "In keeping with our theme of making the most of every moment, we should probably get to it."

"Get to *what*, exactly?" I slide my hands higher up her

thighs, thumbs brushing beneath her shorts to scrape against the lace of her panties, just over her clit. She's hot and wet for me, every touch unleashing another gasp of pleasure.

"That," she breathes. "Exactly that."

"I think that's a wise course of action, witchling."

"Don't make me wait. I need you inside me, Auggie. Now."

With that delicious demand ringing in my ears, I don't waste time tearing off clothes—hers or mine. I merely free my cock from beneath the loincloth, shove her short-shorts and lace panties to the side, and fucking *claim* her with a thrust so hard and deep, we're both moaning at the intensity of it.

Once I'm fully inside her, I go still for a beat, pulling her upper body close against mine, breathing in the scent of her skin, listening to the steady beats of her heart.

She slides her hands into my hair, glancing up at me with so much adoration in her eyes it nearly undoes me.

"I love you, Augustine," she whispers. "So much."

I open my mouth to reply, but West doesn't let me. She closes the distance between us, her lips crashing into mine in a hungry, devouring kiss I feel all the way to the tip of my tail. I kiss her back, marking her, claiming her, tasting every bit of her, of this moment.

It's hot and sweet and dirty and delicious, everything at once, my hands tangling into her hair, her fingers wrapped tight around my horns, thighs gripping my hips as I fuck her hard and fast on the countertop, one perfect thrust at a time.

The wet, silken heat of her body centers me in a moment so divine, I'd be damned lucky if it *was* my last.

Because hell, what a fucking way to go.

But after every deep stroke comes the next, and the next, and a flurry of hot and gasping breaths in my ear, fists tightening in my hair, hips bucking wildly, coffee-flavored kisses and shuddering wings and black-and-silver waves slipping loose from a bun and curling down over nipples begging to be sucked, and I'm still here.

Alive.

I take one of those perky pink nipples between my lips, rolling the other between claw-tipped fingers, my tail wrapping around to graze her clit as I slide in and out, harder, faster, my beautiful witchling begging for more, my body powerless to do anything but give it to her.

There's one more moment then, a pause in the beautiful chaos when we both stop and our gazes lock and something deep and vast and downright fucking mystical passes between us.

Panting, I brush the fallen hair from her face and smile, whispering against her lips.

"I love you too, witchling. I've loved you since the very start, and I'll continue to love you for every moment we've got left in this life, and every moment in the next. *That's* what you hold on to now. *That's* what you keep in your heart when everything else feels like it's falling apart around you."

She smiles back at me and touches my face with her fingertips, delicate and perfect, everything about her so warm and precious and real it feels like the only thing I've ever really known, and then all at once her body tightens around me and she's arching back and trembling with the force of her release, pulling me right down with her.

I spiral and spin and fall into the depths of oblivion as I come inside her, thrusting once more, twice, a final epic shudder before I lift her off the counter, wrap her up in my wings, close my eyes, and breathe her in.

Just fucking breathe.

CHAPTER TWENTY-EIGHT

AUGUSTINE

I could've stayed inside her forever, holding her close and drowning in her scent, but I'm only granted a few minutes of this bliss before we hear the car pulling up the driveway.

I give her one last soft, lingering kiss, then set her down and help her clean up, smoothing her hair and clothes back into place mere seconds before the boys descend, arms laden with groceries and wine, the mood celebratory.

Draegan is with them, his smile as bright as Jude's and Rook's.

There was a time when that would've been unusual, but being with West... It's changed us all for the better.

"Don't tell me we missed the best meal of the night," Jude says, dropping the bags on the counter to sweep her up in his arms, attacking her face with kisses. "Damn, you taste good, scarecrow."

"You didn't miss anything." She laughs, meeting my eyes over his shoulder and flashing an adorable wink. "We were just... getting started, actually."

"I like the sound of that," Draegan leans in to kiss her lips, probably hoping for more, but she darts away from him in a fit of laughter.

"I'm glad to hear it, *Daddy*." Her eyes blaze with mischief, and with a devious grin, she grabs a pile of aprons from the linen drawer and tosses one at each of us. "Because you're on vegetable peeling duty. Rook, you've got avocados to mash. Jude, I want you slicing fruit. Auggie, you just... do whatever it is the head chef does best."

The three of them glance at each other like they're all waiting for the punchline.

"This little group gathering took a *serious* detour from where I thought we were heading when I first walked in," Jude says. "GPS is *way* offline here."

"Yeah, I feel like we missed a step," Rook says. "Some crucial part of the ménage à gargoyle instruction manual."

"If only you'd shown up a few minutes earlier," I tease. "You could've sampled the tasting menu. Alas—"

"Boys!" Westlyn shoos us all off. "Get to work! This family meal isn't going to make itself, and your girl is fucking *starving*."

Cracking up, they all don their aprons. I grab one too, tying it tight and reaching for my favorite filet knife.

And then, under the adorably demanding orders of our adorably sexy witch, we get to work.

Too many cooks in the kitchen may spoil the soup, but right now, they're damn sure making the moment all the sweeter.

It's the first time we've all cooked a meal together, ever, and my kitchen is stuffed to bursting with wings and tails and elbows and a riot of ingredients spread out on every flat surface.

Knives clack against chopping blocks, whisks scrape the sides of bowls, vegetables sizzle in a pan laden with far too much oil, and other than esteemed head chef Augustine Lamont, it's *definitely* amateur hour in here.

But tonight? I wouldn't have it any other way.

I pour us all another round of drinks, passing them out while the others continue working diligently. Cooking is second nature to me, so easy I could almost do it with my eyes closed, but tonight I force myself to really take in the scene. To memorize every detail, freezing it in my mind like the perfect series of photographs, framed and hung on permanent display in my memory.

Rook, poring over my entire cookbook collection and making notes about substitutions to try, regaling us with random facts about the origins of certain spices and regional cooking techniques.

Jude, wild-eyed and quick with an innuendo, one hand cutting up apples with a meat cleaver—peak Jude Hendrix

—while the other can't help but find its way to Westlyn's backside every time she passes him.

Draegan, once crippled by guilt and preferring to spend his nights locked away at the office or in his rooms, finally learning to open his heart to love and family, laughing at Jude's antics and stealing kisses from Westlyn just as often as our crazy brother.

And Westlyn herself. Our witchling. Our fae queen. Powerful and beautiful. Our heart. Our home. Playfully swatting at Jude's wandering hands. Sharing heated glances with Draegan. Asking Rook a million questions about international dishes and all the travels that brought him the knowledge. Grinning at me as I feed her samples of bubbling sauces and spicy toppings and fresh fruit until everything is sautéed, simmered, and crisped to perfection.

And then, after hours of work, it's finally time.

"Let's eat, heathens," I announce, and the crowd cheers, all of us eager to indulge in the fruits of our shared labor.

We get out the real silver and the good dishes, some fancy bone china from the seventeenth century Draegan had been keeping on display in a cabinet I'm pretty sure no one has ever opened before. Rook fills a set of ornate crystal goblets with water and more wine and home-brewed hard apple cider for everyone.

"To family," Draegan says as we take our seats, his eyes shining with the utterance of a simple word that encompasses so much, and we all lift a glass and echo the toast. "To family."

Then, we dig in.

Our meal has no unifying cuisine, no rhyme or reason. Vegan bruschetta. Apple-berry pancakes served with cinnamon maple syrup poured from a terrine Jude crafted out of a man's skull. A taco buffet with three different kinds of beans, heirloom tomato salsa, and Rook's hand-smashed guacamole. Stuffed acorn squash. Pumpkin sage soup with wilted spinach. Sautéed mushroom caps and shallots. Apple cake with chocolate-coconut filling.

We eat and drink until our stomachs hurt.

We laugh until our ribs hurt, too.

And there, over our mix-'n-match buffet at the massive oak table in the formal dining room of Blackmoor Manor, we talk.

We talk about our best memories, about all the beautiful things we've seen and experienced in this world. About the people we loved and lost along the way.

We talk about our dreams for the future as if we've got forever to build it, and hell. Maybe we do. Right now, surrounded by good food and even better company, it certainly feels like it.

It's the best night we've ever had together. The most real thing I've ever experienced.

It's life, with all the blank spaces removed, only the beautiful parts remaining.

And through every bite, through every peal of laughter, through every story told and retold, all I keep thinking is...

After everything we've overcome to get here, how could

anything that feels so perfect, so right, so fucking *incredible* be smashed to bits by a curse without a cure?

CHAPTER TWENTY-NINE

WESTLYN

As we gather in the study for post-pigout cocktails, the crackling fire replaces the boisterous conversation from the dinner table, and the mood inevitably shifts.

After the amazing meal we just shared, I know none of us means for it to happen. It just does.

Because no matter how much laughter we fill up the manor with, no matter how many wild stories we tell, no matter how many dreams we share... Deep down, everyone in this room knows the bitter truth.

Our time together *does* have an expiration date. And the sweeter our nights of revelry and joy, the heavier and more painful our inescapable truth becomes.

Curled up on the leather sofa with Jude, I lean back against his outstretched arm and close my eyes, fighting back tears.

Against the craziest odds, we defeated our enemies. We destroyed a vicious fae tyrant who'd murdered his own people for a shot at power. We vanquished a prince of hell, a demon army, and an evil coven of shadow mages who would've gladly ushered in an age of terror on earth.

And after all that, we made it back home alive with our new witch allies.

By all rights, tonight should be the happiest of my life—the happiest of all our lives.

Yet now, in the peaceful aftermath of all we've accomplished, all I feel is dread.

I don't want any credit for what we did. I don't want fame or glory or riches, or some magical crown bestowed upon me like a hero in some ancient fairy tale. Hell, I don't even want a dinky little trophy to display on my bookshelf with a plaque that says #1 Witch.

I just want a *chance*. A fucking chance to save the men I love from eternal damnation. A chance for us to build a life together—a life filled with laughter and love and delicious meals and wild sex and walks through the orchard and late-night fires and stiff drinks and apple muffins and road trips and just... *Goddess*. All of it. I want all of it. All those crazy, boring, exciting, amazing, terrifying, beautiful things that make life on this crazy planet so damn magical.

But with every breath I take, that chance slips further out of reach.

"What's got you so quiet all of a sudden, scarecrow?"

Jude brushes a kiss to my temple, his voice soft and full of concern. "What are you thinking about?"

I suspect he already knows the answer. We're all thinking about it. Feeling it.

The ticking clock looms large.

Snuggling in close, I rest my cheek against his chest and close my eyes.

"Time," I whisper. The one word that comes closest to encapsulating it.

When we were waiting out the storm in Wintermoon, Draegan told me that time itself was the cruelest monster he'd ever endured. That after his long immortal life, all he wanted now was just a little bit more of it.

But he couldn't have it—the curse made sure of that.

Never have I understood his words more deeply than I do tonight.

Because if I had just a little bit more time, I could keep working with Tatiana, Laney, and Fleur on a spell—maybe not the Spell of Unmaking, but a different one. An as-yet undiscovered one.

If I had just a little bit more time, maybe Rook and I could uncover something in the occult or seminary databases that would unlock whatever part of my magic I'd need to cast it properly.

If I had just a little bit more time, I could somehow —*somehow*—go back through all the lore, the legends, the prophecy, my mother's diaries, Verrick's mysterious half-truths, and finally connect all the dots on out how to break this terrible curse—a curse he tied to his immortal bloodline to ensure it *couldn't* be broken.

Not unless our line ended.

He's gone now, but I remain, ensuring my gargoyles... cannot.

A shudder ripples through my body, and Jude pulls a blanket over me, his wing curling protectively around my shoulders.

No one speaks.

The fire crackles softly in the hearth, and it's not long before I finally drift off, the calming presence of my silent sentries making me feel safe, the steady beat of Jude's heart against my cheek lulling me into a fuzzy half-sleep.

But even there, dreams don't find me. My mind is still turning over every leaf, still rearranging all the puzzle pieces to see if *this* time, with just the right twist and turn, I can make it fit.

Dark curses.

Tethered.

Immortal bloodlines.

Broken by one whose love is true.

Tethered to an immortal bloodline.

Unbreakable.

Tether.

Cursed.

Immortal blood.

Tether...

Wait... tether?

My eyes fly open, and I gasp as the realization smashes into me.

"Holy shit, that's it!" I leap from Jude's embrace, the blanket falling to the floor, adrenaline making my heart dance behind my ribcage. "Guys, that's it! It's the tether! The tether is the key!"

They're all staring at me with wide, confused eyes.

"Bad dream, darling?" Jude reaches for me, trying to pull me back into his lap. "You know I'd be more than happy to help you relax again."

"I'm not dreaming. I'm wide awake. I'm so wide awake I'm buzzing." A laugh bursts out of me, making me bounce on my toes. "The curse. I think I know how to obliterate that fucking curse!"

"What?" Jude's on his feet now too, Rook and Auggie following suit.

"Tell us," Rook says eagerly, pushing his glasses up his nose.

Auggie watches me expectantly. Even Draegan, as still as a statue on one of the chairs, allows an uncharacteristic flicker of hope to shine in his eyes.

It's only there for a second, but I saw it.

And I can't *wait* to put it back there. Permanently.

Grabbing Jude's hands, I say, "We've been looking at it all wrong. Verrick said the curse tether can't be broken while it's tied to our bloodline—not unless our bloodline is broken first. But he also said I'm immortal like him, which means I won't die of natural causes and our bloodline will remain—"

"You won't die at *all*," Jude says, tightening his grip on my hands, "because we're not going to let anyone fucking near you again, and—"

"Jude, listen to me. You can't make that promise anymore. I know you want to, but you just can't. We all know the curse is going to claim your souls before I die. You can feel it, can't you?"

"But you helped us in Wintermoon," Auggie says. "You reversed—"

"I was able to reverse the spell that turned you into stone, but that was based on a singular action that Verrick took in my presence. The curse is different. It's demonic magic, tethered to my bloodline, cast before I was even born. I have no power to reverse it the way I did Verrick's attack."

"What are you saying?" Jude asks.

"I'm saying if we do *nothing*, the curse will run its course, you'll all turn to stone, your souls will never find peace, and I'm going to outlive you all."

"Damn straight you are," he says. "Doesn't matter if you're the key to ending this thing or the key to ending the whole damn world. We're not going to end *you* just so we can—"

"That's the thing, though. We don't *have* to end me." I

release Jude's hands and turn to Draegan, my heart thudding with this new realization. "We've been so focused on what Verrick said about the immortal bloodline part, because we assumed he meant I'd have to die in order to break the curse. But do you remember what he *actually* said, before we got lost in the details?"

Draegan nods, that faint flicker of hope glimmering again as he recalls the words Verrick taunted us with in Wintermoon. "The only way to break the curse is to break the tether, and the only way to break the tether is to break the bloodline it's tied to."

"Exactly!" I nod, my smile widening. "Then he told us it was tethered to *his* bloodline, which meant it would pass to me the moment he died, and we never moved beyond that. Especially when his death proved he wasn't lying. The tether *did* pass to me."

After the pain of the initial transfer, I got used to the constant drain on my power, but I can still feel it, even now. Like some otherworldly presence sucking away a little more of my magic every day. A little more of my soul.

"I'm... still not following," Auggie says. "What does this all mean?"

"The only way to break the curse is to break the tether," I repeat. "And the only way to break the tether is to break the *bloodline it's tied to*. So guys, all we need to do is—"

"Tether the curse to a different bloodline," Drae says excitedly, the dots finally connecting for him too. "A *mortal* bloodline that can then be broken by killing the mortal, thereby cutting off the power source and destroying the curse."

Auggie's eyes widen. "Can that be done?"

"Only one way to find out," I say.

Jude cradles my face in his claw-tipped hands, his gaze sweeping up from my lips to my eyes. When he speaks again, his voice holds a note of wonder.

"Your serious," he says softly. "You want to murder a mortal in order to set us free."

I close my eyes, thinking back to the conversation Auggie and I had about what makes a person good or bad.

From the moment I learned I had dark-fae blood, I was terrified of becoming evil.

When I discovered that my dark-fae blood came from Verrick of Wintermoon, I was terrified of becoming *him*.

Now, after everything we've been through, after everything we've fought for, I know I'm not my bloodline. Not my father. Not the so-called legacy he tried to pin on me.

But I will *not* hesitate to trade the life of a cold-blooded asshole to save the men I love. So if that's the thing that ultimately makes me evil? Well.

Welcome to the fucking dark side.

Because I will *not* stand by and let them fade into oblivion if I've still got a chance to do something about it.

"Find me someone who's spent his life getting off on hurting those weaker than him," I say, "and I will gladly get the job done."

"I'm not sure it's quite that simple," Auggie says. "I

mean, yeah, we have dossiers on lots of people in this city that fit the bill. But choosing one to execute is—"

"Actually, I may be able to offer a solution." Draegan tosses back the last of his drink and rises from the chair. "We've a suitable guest down in the workshop. Unconscious, for now. I've been pondering various methods of... disposal."

"You sly dog." Jude laughs. "Does our unannounced guest have anything to do with your trip to JFK?"

Drae nods. "Imported the bastard all the way from Argentina. You wouldn't *believe* the paperwork."

By "paperwork," I'm pretty sure he means the cash required to bribe the customs agent to alert him the moment Detective Reedsy got off the plane, but I'm not going to press for details.

Smirking at him, I say, "I thought we didn't keep secrets in this house."

"It's not a secret, love. Just a bit of rubbish that needs taking out. No need for you to soil your precious hands touching that sack of utter filth."

"Draegan Caldwell," I scold. "After everything your *guest* put us through, I'd be more than happy to soil my hands turning him into a bloody pulp they won't even be able to identify with dental records."

"And there's my little psycho, back after a brief hiatus." Jude cracks up, then sweeps me into his arms with a devastating kiss I feel all the way down to my toes. "I fucking *love* you, darling."

"Well that's good to know, because I fucking love you, too. All of you." I pull out of his embrace, a wicked grin stretching across my lips as my new plan finally takes shape. "Okay, boys. Enough with the chivalry. Time to head down to the workshop and commit a violent felony, family style."

CHAPTER THIRTY

JUDE

Detective Grant Reedsy kneels on the floor of my workshop, wrists bound behind his back with the strap of his department-issued holster.

Terror is a sweet, delicious perfume in the air, and I can't help myself.

I'm downright *brimming* with anticipation.

"Admit it," I say, walking a slow circle around him as I swing my trusty crowbar. "You missed us, Detective."

He glares up at me, but the effect is somewhat lessened on account of the fact that one of his eyes is swollen shut—Draegan's doing this time, not mine.

"Sorry, did you want to say something?" I ask.

Bastard doesn't say anything, of course—hasn't managed a single peep since we all trundled down the stairs earlier, hollering and whooping, ushering in the world's loudest wake-up call.

"Shy tonight, huh?" I purse my lips. "You poor thing. Totally understandable. You've never seen us in our true forms, and that can be pretty scary for a first-timer." I flash him a grin full of fangs and menace, wings rippling behind me. "Something tells me you weren't betting on seeing our girl again either, so that's gotta be a shock to the system too, right?"

Oh, the glaring. Oh, the anger. Oh, the unfairness of it all.

Ha! What a fucking joke.

"I get it, the whole suffering-in-silence bit," I say. "It's a lot to take in. *We're* a lot to take in. But there comes a time in every man's life where he just has to start accepting reality. So... cue the gameshow announcer... Detective Grant Reedsy, welcome to *yours*!" I sweep my hand across the small space, indicating the group standing around him. "Four crazy gargoyles and one badass witch, not a bloody clue which one of us will have the ultimate pleasure of separating your head from your body, but hey. A bit of mystery keeps the romance alive, doesn't it?"

There's a series of loud squawks from above, and I glance up at the highest shelf and wave to our live studio audience.

Nestled in among the bleached bones of more enemies than I care to count, Lucinda, Huxley, and Jean-Pierre watch over the proceedings with great interest, though to be fair, they're probably wondering which one of us brought snacks.

"Now, in most cases," I continue, nudging Reedsy's chest with my crowbar, "I'm the Chief Executive Dismemberer around here, and trust me when I say it would be my great honor to smear you from existence tonight. It'd be a great honor for you, too, come to think of it. I'm considering retiring after this—got me a girl now. Yep, you're looking at a regular family man right here. Going domestic, as they say."

"What's... what's stopping you from retiring now?" he blubbers, the first words out of his big, dumb mouth.

"Oh, I don't know." I let out a dramatic sigh, stroking the crowbar as I wax poetic. "Perhaps it's because you've made it your life's mission to dog me and my brothers over crimes we didn't actually commit. Then again, maybe it's because I don't like your haircut or your beady little eyes. Or maybe it's—oh, wait! I remember now!" I get in his face with a snarl, a fucking animal barely leashed, all the jokes and pleasantries evaporating. "You and your mage friends tried to *destroy* the woman I love. So you can skip town all you want, cross the fucking continent on foot for all I care, but I always knew I'd have you right back here one day, and here you fucking are. Why? Because *no* one walks away from hurting my girl, you worthless piece of shit."

I bring the crowbar down on his shoulder, knocking it right out of the socket.

He wails. Moans. Wails again.

Drool runs down his chin. "I... I was just... f-f-following—"

"Following orders, yeah, I know. And now you get to follow the rest of the shadow magic bastards straight to hell. Should be pretty easy for you to find the way, too—just listen for the tormented screams. Oh! And I hear there's a whole batch of new demons down there, *real* pissed off and looking for a bit of fresh meat."

"P-p-please," he stammers.

"Say goodnight, Detective Dickhole." I lift the crowbar, more than ready to feel the unmistakable crack of a bashed-in skull.

But a soft touch on my arm steadies my swing.

"Um, Jude?" Westlyn says.

I glance down at her, and my sweet girl rewards me with a flash of that lovely smile of hers.

"Yes, darling?"

"It's not that I don't appreciate your special brand of... well... *you*," she says. "But we need Reedsy *alive* for this part. Just until we transfer the tether to the curse."

"*Curse?*" Reedsy exclaims, at the same time I say, "*Alive?*"

Draegan rolls his eyes. "Jude, we talked about this. Remember?"

"Did we? Oh. Right! Of course. My apologies." I lower the crowbar and give him a gentle tap on the dislocated shoulder instead, making him yelp. "Just softening him up a bit. Um... Westlyn? Just curious. This 'alive' business... How long will that part take, exactly? Not that I'm rushing your curse work. Just asking for... planning purposes."

"*Curse?*" Reedsy says again, but everyone seems content to ignore our sacrificial lamb.

"Depends on how quickly the spell kicks in, I guess." Westlyn shrugs, her nose crinkling. "It's my first dark-fae curse re-tethering."

"Well, you're gonna be *great* at it," I say with an encouraging smile. "No doubt."

"Yeah?"

"Absolutely."

She beams. I beam back. It's all *very* adorable, and I can't wait to get this unpleasant head-bashing business done so I can take her up to my bedroom, shred the clothes from her body, unfurl my tongue, and—

"Fucking *Jude*," Auggie grumbles, breaking into our little Hallmark moment and putting my balls back on ice. "Let's get on with it, shall we?"

West laughs, her touch warm on my arm once more. "The minute I'm done with him, Jude, he's yours for the taking. Blood, bones, and all. Hell, if you behave yourself, I'll even let you strike the killing blow."

"Damn, I fuckin' *love* you, scarecrow." I press a hand to my heart and grin. Then, turning that megawatt smile back on our drooling, sputtering guest, "See what I mean, Detective? When you find a woman like her, you do *not* let her get away. Anyway, where were we? Ah, yes. I believe I was about to embed something sharp and rusty deep into your—"

"Jude? Sweetness?" Westlyn gives me another smile.

"Oh! The curse. Alive. Right." I smack my forehead and

laugh. "He's all yours, darling. Do your scary, dark-fae worst."

"Thank you."

I flash her the thumbs-up. "You've got this."

"I know."

"I'll be right over here if you need—"

"Jude!" She cracks up and rolls her pretty eyes, and I vow to spend the rest of whatever life I've got left finding ways to put that *exact* look on her face every fucking night.

So hopeful. So happy.

So sure that this is the key to our future.

Watching her now, seeing that sparkle in her eyes, it's easy to believe anything's possible.

Even something as wild and crazy as finding the loophole to shatter an ancient dark fae curse.

Even something as wild and crazy as four ancient gargoyles of Britain finding their happily-ever-after with a kind, sweet, naughty, raven-loving, dark-fae Wintermoon Cerridwen witch from Brooklyn.

Hey. Stranger things have happened.

So for now, I take a deep breath, toss aside the crowbar, and raise my hands in surrender, nodding for Westlyn to do her thing.

She turns off the lights. There's a brief moment of complete darkness, but then she begins to glow with her magic, illuminating the workshop in soft indigo light.

She gestures for us to stand at equal intervals around the prisoner, one of us at each of the cardinal directions. We obey, watching in silence as she lights four black candles and places them on the ground in front of each of us, then draws a small blade across her fingertip, squeezing a few drops of blood onto each candle.

The flames turn silver, unwavering.

Turning to Reedsy, she says, "Give me your hand."

"No way, you c-c-crazy—"

I'm about to smash my fist into his jaw, but Westlyn beats me to the punch, pun intended. Girl clocks him with a killer left-hook that knocks him out cold, then grabs his hand and slices open his palm, collecting the blood in a small white bowl.

No, not a bowl, I realize. A kneecap. *Randall's* kneecap —the bloke who harassed her in the park the first night we met.

I can't help the grin that stretches across my face. Really warms the heart to see her using my gifts in such a creative way.

She catches my eye and winks.

I wink back.

Have I mentioned I love this woman?

When she's got enough of Reedsy's blood, she pours a few drops onto each candle. It mingles with hers, sizzling before turning completely black. The flames glow brighter.

"Join hands," she tells us, standing before an unconscious Reedsy as we clasp hands and close the circle around them.

Then, taking a deep, steadying breath, she closes her

eyes and begins walking backward inside our circle, reciting the spell as she goes.

> *Magic of Wintermoon, magic of hell*
> *Unbind this curse as I cast this spell*
> *My blood is now pure, untethered from thee*
> *I bind you anew, so mote it be*

She repeats it three times, making three complete rotations around the circle.

The moment she stops, the candle flames surge once, then flicker out, as does her magic, plunging us all into darkness.

"It's done," she whispers.

"Did it work?" Rook asks.

"We have no way of knowing what the sign will be," West replies. "We just have to wait until—"

A strangled gasp cuts her off, and Reedsy rises up on his knees, black blood leaking from his nose and mouth, silver light bursting out of his eyes.

"I think that's probably the sign," West says. Then, to me, "It's time, Jude."

I nod once, then move to my worktable, selecting a sharp blade instead of the crowbar, no longer in the mood for a prolonged send-off.

I step behind him and grab a fistful of his hair. If he realizes what's going on, he doesn't show it, blood and light still leaking from him like a man possessed. I jerk his head back hard and bring the dagger to his throat.

This is it. The moment of truth that will either condemn us to eternal hell... or set us free.

With one last glance at my girl, I smile, all for her.

Then I drag that blade across his throat and sever his fucking carotid.

More blood gushes, all of it black as tar. Reedsy gurgles and gasps one last time, then sags.

I release his hair, and the body slumps forward, all that black blood pooling on the cement floor.

But I'm only looking at Westlyn now.

At the silver runes glowing bright on every inch of her skin, her hair crackling with magic. She closes her eyes and the runes begin to spin and shift, gathering into one larger rune just below the hollow of her throat. I don't know what it translates to, but it's dark magic. Evil. I can *feel* it in my fucking marrow, like everything inside me is suddenly filling with ice.

Then, the symbol collapses on itself, nothing more than a pinpoint of silver light.

Westlyn gasps, and it explodes out of her, light and shadow, flame and smoke.

Reedsy's corpse jerks at my feet, and I glance down to see the rune glowing bright on the back of his neck. It burns into his skin like a brand, then vanishes.

Reedsy's corpse turns entirely black.

Silence descends on us.

We all hold our breath.

But nothing happens.

Nothing *bloody* happens.

I can still feel the curse in my blood. Still feel that ticking clock in my heart.

It didn't work. It didn't fucking work, and now all I want is for Reedsy to rise up from the dead just so I can kill him all over again.

I never should have hoped, because that's the fucking thing about it. Spend your whole immortal life without hope, and you don't think twice about another ho-hum disappointment. But let it seep into the cracks of your heart for even a *moment*, and when it all goes to shit after that, the crushing disappointment explodes like a nuclear warhead.

Something inside me shatters. The last fragile thing holding me all together. That's it. Fucking gone.

I drop to my knees with a roar that damn near shakes the foundation of the manor.

After everything. After every terrible thing, this—this one *fucking* thing should've been ours.

Pain like nothing I've ever felt shreds my heart, liquifying it.

I wonder if this is what Reedsy felt in his final moments, because I know, deep down, that these terrible seconds can only be *my* final moments.

But then...

The softest brush of lips against my ear. The scent of apples and magic. The touch of her fingers grazing my wing.

"Jude," my little scarecrow whispers. "Open your eyes. *Please* open your eyes."

Damn it. She knows I would never deny her. Not a fucking thing. And if she's hurting, and I've still got the power to ease her pain...

I hold my breath and brace for the worst, slowly cracking open one eye, then the other.

But when I finally find the courage to meet her turquoise gaze, it's not the sadness of an impossible goodbye I see reflected back at me.

It's not even hope anymore. It's past that. It's...

It's joy. Pure, unfiltered joy.

I get to my feet and cup her face, and she smiles at me and presses her palm to my heart.

"What do you feel?" she whispers.

"I feel... It's..." I cover her hand with mine and suck in a deep breath, and then, out of fucking *nowhere*, it's like someone just kicked down the iron-bolted door inside me, letting in the light for the first time in fifteen hundred bloody years.

It fills me up—every cell, every space, every dark hollow. I swear I can smell the salt of the ocean, feel the sunlight on my skin, warm and bright and perfect. I can taste the sweetest chocolate and hear all my favorite songs and Westlyn's laughter and the softest breeze through the orchard trees.

All the good things in life, muted for so long by the burden of the curse, now impossibly vibrant.

I can breathe. I can truly breathe. And in that moment, I know.

"It's... gone," I gasp, and my little scarecrow nods.

I finally glance around at my brothers, my best mates, and I see the same happiness and wonder shining in their eyes, too.

"There's one final part," Westlyn says, gesturing for us to join hands once more, and I recall what she told us about the other bit—that if the curse was broken by one whose love is true, we'd be granted the choice of whether to remain on the earthly realm as immortal gargoyles... or pass on as the men we once were.

"There's no need for magic," I say softly. "We can just tell you what we want."

She shakes her head, tears glazing her eyes. "It's not the kind of choice you can make with your head, Jude. It has to be the truest desire of your heart—a desire you may not even consciously recognize."

"So you're saying there's a chance we could just... just turn back into mortal men and die?"

Her smile is soft, her voice barely a whisper. "Only if that's your heart's true desire."

"You would risk it?" I ask. "Knowing we might leave you?"

"It's not my choice to make, Jude. I don't want to lose you. I don't want to say goodbye... I *won't* say it—not like that." She reaches up to touch my face, smiling through her tears. "Our time together has been a gift. One I never thought I'd be blessed with. For that, I'll always be grateful. I'll always love you. But in the end, the decision is yours. I vow to honor the wishes of your heart, even if it breaks mine."

Once again, I'm overwhelmed by her capacity for love. By her willingness to do this for us, knowing she might be left alone...

But no. She *won't* be. I don't even know why we're having this conversation. I *know* my heart's desire—it's her. That simple. So she can do all the magic she wants, all day every day, and I'm still going to be here when she's done.

One look at the boys, and I know we're all on the same fucking page.

"So I guess this is it," she says, and I can tell she's trying to shore up her courage. "Before we do this, I just wanted to say, I—"

"No goodbyes, love," Draegan says softly. "Remember? No goodbyes."

She nods at him and dashes away the last of her tears. Then, with a firm squaring of her shoulders, she gestures for us to join hands once more.

"I'll say the spell," she says, "but for this one, you guys need to repeat it too. Three times, just like before. Ready?"

We all nod, and she recites the spell slowly, making sure we've all got it.

Then, holding tight to each other, closing our eyes, the gargoyles and I speak the words that will reveal the true desires of our hearts and determine—one way or the other—whether we'll open our eyes to find our girl smiling back at us, or...

Never open our eyes again.

Magic below, within, and above
We stand here before you, in honor and love
Souls unburdened, truths unbidden
Secrets uncovered, desires unhidden
Our circle complete, our bonds never ending
Reveal our fates as our hearts have intended

At the final recitation, magic gathers around us like a soft breeze, caressing my hair, rippling through my wings, tingling across my gargoyle skin.

Then I feel it on *human* skin, *human* hair, as if I'm already transforming. It's back to my wings in a flash, then bare human feet, then sliding along my tail, testing me. Searching.

It's warm and pleasant, and I feel myself relaxing, everything inside me unwinding, a deep knowing settling over me.

It's going to be okay. Whatever happens, it's going to be okay...

A contented sigh floats from my lips.

Then, just as quickly as it touched us, the magic is gone. I wait for an explosion of light, or a scream, or a fucking harpist welcoming us to the afterlife, but no. There's only silence.

And more silence.

I hold my breath, waiting, not wanting to be the first one to open my eyes.

But then...

"I *knew* it," Westlyn says, and I'm damn near ready to burst.

I finally open my eyes to see that wicked little grin, her arms crossed smugly across her chest, her laughter better than any damn harpist in all the realms.

"Monsters," she declares. "Every one of you."

I feel my wings unfurl, my fangs descending, and I look at my brothers and watch the same transformation taking place.

A burst of laughter explodes out of me. Out of all of us.

She did it. She fucking did it.

After fifteen hundred years of living in fear and darkness, the men of shadow and stone are free.

The curse is gone.

We're still here.

And we're gargoyles, right down to the very last tail, the very last wing, the very last horn.

But best of all?

We're hers.

CHAPTER THIRTY-TWO

DRAEGAN

Two Weeks Later...

In the top-floor office of the Blackmoor Capital building, with steaming hot lattes from Stella's in hand, Westlyn and I sit in front of the massive windows and watch the sunrise set Manhattan ablaze.

In the weeks since our curse was destroyed, I've seen over a dozen of them now. As many sunsets, too, and I never tire of them. Precious gifts I never expected, but have embraced nevertheless.

It seems that the desires of our hearts also included freedom from the limitations of our gargoyle forms, allowing us to turn to stone at will, enjoying the sunshine on our faces for the first time in fifteen hundred long years.

I'm seated in my leather executive chair, Westlyn curled up in my lap, no words exchanged between us. This has become our morning ritual—a predawn flight to the city, followed by this silent show of light and beauty.

In its quiet perfection, we're still saying our goodbyes.

Westlyn, to Brian Avery, the man she'll always call Dad. The man she'll always love, despite his mistakes and her complicated feelings. To her mother, whose loving embrace she never got to feel. To the childhood she was never allowed to live.

Me, to Moira and Anastasia, the wife and daughter I couldn't save and never before mourned. To the guilt and grief that festered inside me for so long. To the men who fought bravely by my side during the original dark-fae wars, their souls finally set free by the shattering of our curse, the stone gargoyles of Manhattan remaining as memorials to their great sacrifice.

Jude and Rook and Augustine have said their goodbyes as well. To the friends and family we lost. To the innocence and hopes and dreams that ended the day Verrick of Wintermoon declared war on our homeland.

To the men of Britain we once were.

Some time ago, I told Westlyn that those men died the moment Verrick cursed us, and that was absolutely true. After that fateful night, we lived in a sort of half-life, never fully waking from our nightmares. Never fully living.

And then a crazy, black-and-silver-haired, raven-loving witch crashed into our lives.

She fell in love with us as monsters, never questioning it. Never lamenting the fact that we weren't truly human.

She saw us for who we were, and she loved us anyway.

She loved us as monsters who sometimes posed as men.

She loved us as monsters who schemed and blackmailed and murdered to achieve their ends.

She loved us as monsters, and when she cast her spell upon us that night in Jude's workshop, standing in the blood of the last man to die at our hands, it was monsters whom the magic revealed as our heart's true desires.

And she loved us still.

So perhaps now we can find a way to love ourselves, too.

I never thought it would be possible. But when she touches me, when her laughter echoes through the manor, when she kisses me, when she whispers my name, I feel like *all* things are possible.

Light, when before there was only darkness.

Hope, when before there was only dread.

And love. A thing so vast and beautiful, even to name it feels like sacrilege. Yet name it I do, because for so long, I couldn't form those words. Couldn't even fathom them. And now, the shape of them reminds me what it means to be alive.

Of all the gifts she brought into my life, the capacity to love with all my heart, regardless of the risk, is perhaps the most precious.

And I intend to earn that gift every single moment.

"I love you, Westlyn Avery," I say now, breaking the morning silence. "Eternally."

She turns around in my lap and straddles me, her smile

as bright as the sun as she threads her hands into my hair and kisses me.

She tastes like almonds and chocolate, so sweet and warm, and it's not long before I'm hard for her.

She kisses a hot path along my jaw, and whispers in my ear, "Take off my clothes, Daddy. I'm too hot."

Bloody fucking hell.

Under normal circumstances, I'd have her naked and bent over my desk by now—another of my new favorite pastimes that's quickly becoming tradition.

But today, I promised my brothers I'd hold off on the ravishings until we were all reunited. They've got big plans, and as much as I'd love to give in to her naughty little taunts, I will not break my vow.

I rise from the chair and set her on her feet, but she sits down again, giving me a pout that has me thinking *very* dark thoughts about that lush little mouth...

Pull it together, Caldwell.

"Come," I say firmly, holding out a hand.

"I'm trying," she huffs. "But you're being *very* uncooperative."

"Not for much longer, I promise." I laugh and lean in for a kiss, soft and quick, lest she get any more ideas. Then, not giving her another say in the matter, I haul her out of the chair, throw her over my shoulder and head for the door. "We've got a surprise waiting for you at home."

CHAPTER THIRTY-THREE

WESTLYN

"Surprise!"

With an epic blast of party horns and wolf-whistles, three gargoyles leap out from behind the furniture in the study just as Draegan and I enter.

"Happy Birthday!" they shout, then they all launch into the song, Draegan too, and I'm just standing there laughing my ass off, because *girl?*

The sight of three massive, winged, horned, tailed, and totally ripped gargoyles wearing nothing but loincloths and tiny paper party hats is *definitely* one to behold.

Tears well in my eyes as I take in the scene. Not just the adorable party hats, but multi-colored streamers hanging from the ceiling, and a big silver "Happy Birthday!" banner tacked across the mantle. A huge glitter cannon is set up in the corner, shooting off at regular intervals to shower the room in pink and purple sparkles.

Hopping around on the mantle, looking like they have no idea what the hell's going on, but they're glad to be part of it anyway, Lucinda, Huxley, and Jean-Pierre flap their wings and caw—their version of Happy Birthday.

"You guys did all this for me?" I gasp, emotion tightening my throat.

Jude gathers me into his arms and plants a kiss on my cheek. "Didn't think we'd forget your birthday, darling. Did you?"

"No, but... it kind of got lost with the weird Wintermoon passage of time thing."

"Precisely," Draegan says. "And now that we're home and everything's back to rights, it's time for a proper celebration."

Auggie sets a plastic tiara on my head, then leads me to the sofa, where he sits me down as the others proceed to bury me in presents.

I've never had a birthday party before, let alone a surprise party. I've never gotten presents before. It's completely overwhelming in the best possible way, and it's all I can do not to tear into the wrappings like a wild animal.

Forcing myself to go slow, I unwrap every precious gift, each one so completely perfect it's like they've known me for decades.

There's a set of vegan cookbooks, enough goodies from Sephora to open my own cosmetics store, two new Tarot decks, and a whole bunch of scandalous leather outfits I can't wait to try on.

Rook got me a new smartwatch and a few collectors edition books on Celtic witchcraft. Auggie surprised me with a framed sketch—the one he drew of me and Rook at the inn in Wintermoon. I didn't even realize he'd saved it. And it wouldn't be a present from Jude if it didn't involve the bones of my enemies—this time in the form of bookends carved into witches riding broomsticks. I'm pretty sure they're Reedsy's bones, and I don't ask *which* bones, but it doesn't matter.

The craftsmanship is downright exquisite.

"Do you like them, darling?" he asks now. "I thought they'd be perfect for the new library."

"They *are* perfect." I beam, excitement bubbling inside. We've already started planning the rebuild, and it's going to be absolutely stunning. "I feel like a princess. Seriously, you guys are amazing. Thank you so much!"

"Not a princess," Drae says. "A queen. *Our* queen."

He takes my hands and pulls me up, leading me to a quiet corner of the room while the other guys take my gifts upstairs and clean up the wrapping paper explosion.

Dipping his head low, he says softly, "Of all the gifts I thought to give you today, nothing could compare to the gifts you've given me. But I wanted you to have something —a reminder of the bond we share. What it means to me."

He takes my hand, placing something smooth and cool inside it.

I glance down to see a palm-sized stone shaped like a heart, similar to the one his daughter Anastasia gave him all those years ago.

But this one is carved with different initials—D.C.

Draegan Caldwell.

My eyes fill with tears, and my fingers wrap around the stone, holding it tight.

After everything we've been through together, after everything he shared with me about his past and his family...

For him to give me a gift like this is... *Goddess*, I don't even know how to thank him. It's not just a stone heart. It's a symbol of *his* heart—every part of it, from the past that shaped him into the man he is now to the future that shapes the man he's still in the process of becoming.

I don't have the words, so I don't use them. I merely stretch up on my toes and kiss him, telling him everything I need to say, just like that.

"There's one last gift," Rook says after they've all returned to the study. Behind his new glasses, his honeyed eyes glint with mischief.

"Seriously?" I laugh. "You guys are totally spoiling me!"

"Always." He winks. "But there's a catch with this one. You have to be in your birthday suit to receive it."

I crack up. "How long have you been planning that pun?"

"Long enough."

"It's so terrible, it's kind of awesome."

"Either way," he teases, "you're not getting the last present unless you comply."

"Oh, if you insist." I unbutton my shirt and slide it off my shoulders, my pants and undergarments quickly following, because of *course* the party was going to end this way.

With *this* bunch, everything ends this way.

"But if *I* have to be naked at my birthday party," I say, "so do the guests."

"I'm more than okay with that." Jude strips off his loincloth, and the others follow suit.

Once content to merely watch, Rook's gotten much more bold since our trip to Wintermoon, and now he sits on the sofa and crooks a finger, gesturing for me to join him.

"Turn around and sit on my lap," he says. "Then close your eyes and spread your legs for me."

I do as he asks, leaning my back against his chest and spreading my legs wide.

His hand slides over my thigh, then dips in front, fingers grazing my clit as he slips two inside me, then three, slowly pumping me until I'm rocking my hips, desperate for more, deeper, harder.

"So wet for your gargoyles," he murmurs. "So eager."

"Always," I breathe.

"Every naughty girl deserves a new toy for her birthday." He slides his fingers out, shifting beneath me as he retrieves something from behind him.

Seconds later, an unmistakable buzzing sound fills the air, and then... oh, *goddess*... He's pushing something inside me, stroking me, hitting me *just* right.

"Custom made just for you," he growls, nipping my earlobe. "Does it feel good, wild West?"

"It's... *fuck*. It feels so... so good. You always... Yes. *Right* there."

The new vibrator is even more powerful than the one we lost in the library fire, even more perfect, and the way he's fucking me with it...

Damn it. He knows my body so, so well.

His other hand slides up to cup my breast, tugging my nipple with perfect pressure as he angles the vibrator to hit... *Oh, fuck*... that spot...

My eyes fly open and I gasp as a jolt of red-hot pleasure shoots through my core.

"Don't stop," I beg, clutching his arm. "*Please* don't stop. I'm already so close."

"Don't you *dare* come yet," Draegan says, coming to stand between my spread thighs as Rook slows the speed of the vibrator, easing me off that blissful edge, just a little. "Daddy wants to get on his knees and worship you first."

Rook slides the vibrator out and moves it behind me instead, slowly teasing my back entrance as Draegan kneels before me.

He grips my thighs and spreads me even wider, his claws scraping my skin, his tongue slowly unfurling. He brings his mouth to my breast, swirling his tongue around my nipple before he sucks it hard between his lips, the scrape of his fangs making me gasp.

"Daddy," I whisper. "I need... more. Don't stop."

"Oh, I have no intention of stopping, love," he says, kissing his way down my belly, lower, lower still. "Not until you come on my tongue."

He kisses my clit, teasing it with wicked strokes of his tongue, hot and perfect and maddening, and then he's thrusting it inside me, fucking me slowly while Rook slides the vibrator deeper into my ass, filling me, setting every nerve ablaze.

"Bloody fucking hell." Jude kneels on the sofa beside us. "I could watch that blush darken your cheeks for days, scarecrow."

"I... I don't think I could last that long," I pant.

"Oh, I beg to differ." Auggie comes to stand on my other side at the end of the couch, his cock bobbing before me. "You've got more stamina than the four of us combined."

Draegan moans between my thighs and goes in harder, deeper, faster, like he's taking Auggie's comment as a personal challenge, licking and sucking, devouring me with his filthy mouth as Rook continues to fuck my backside with the toy.

I try to grip Drae's horns, desperate to hold on for dear

life, but Jude grabs my wrist, stopping me.

"I don't think so, darling," he whispers, bringing my hand to his smooth, perfect cock. "If you need something to hold on to, there are much better options."

I let out a whimper of pleasure and wrap my fingers around him, then reach for Auggie, bringing his cock to my mouth.

Stroking Jude with a tight fist, I lick the tip of Auggie's cock, unleashing a full-bodied shiver that makes me feel even more powerful than my witch-fae magic.

Rook turns up the speed on the vibrator, and Draegan tightens his grip on my thighs and moans against my flesh, both of them fucking me harder, faster, my back arching, my hips rocking as Jude thrusts into my fist and Auggie shudders against my lips.

"Are you ready to come for your gargoyles?" Rook whispers, his voice raspy in my ear, his rock-hard cock pressed against my backside. "You're so close. I can feel your body *begging* for release."

I moan around Auggie's cock, sucking him harder, tightening my grip on Jude and stroking him faster... *Goddess*, I don't want this filthy pleasure to end, but Rook's right. I *am* close.

Right on the edge of madness.

"Come for us, wild girl," Rook commands, and the absolute authority in his voice sends me spinning and spiraling and falling right over that edge.

I come with a shuddering moan, setting off a chain reaction that has Auggie spilling down my throat, Jude coming hot in my hand.

I barely have time to come down from the epic orgasm when Rook pulls the vibrator out, replacing it with his cock, easing himself inside my ass as Drae gets to his feet and claims me with a fierce, possessive kiss.

He fists his cock, dragging it through my wetness before sliding inside me.

It's not long before a second wave builds, Draegan and Rook both thrusting inside me, slow and deep, Draegan devouring my mouth while Rook kisses my shoulder, my neck, and Jude and Auggie watch with wild, blazing eyes.

Draegan brings his tail around, sliding it between us, rubbing slow circles over my clit as he continues to own my pussy, Rook rocking against my backside, harder and faster, deeper, more, everything, and then...

"Yes! Fuck... *yes*!" I cry out as the second wave of pleasure crests and crashes over me, my gargoyles growling as they both come inside me, marking me, claiming me, giving me the best damn birthday a girl could ever ask for.

And I know from the wicked gleam in their eyes that my gargoyles are nowhere *near* finished with me yet.

Sticky with glitter and deliciously exhausted after spending the last few hours getting thoroughly ravished on every usable surface the study has to offer, I finally disentangle myself from the pile of gargoyles before the fire and get to my feet.

"What time is it?" I ask, stretching as I glance down at my new watch. "Oh, shit! How is it already after seven? I need to get in the shower. I'm late!"

"Late?" Jude props himself up on his elbows, giving me a slow, lazy grin. "We're just getting started, darling."

"Come back, witchling." Auggie slides his tail up between my legs, but I swat him away with a laugh.

"No. No more touching. No more doing that thing with your tail and... oh, fuck..." He's at it again, and now Drae is getting in on it too, his tail sliding in from behind, joining with Auggie's in a perfect dance that has my legs trembling again in seconds, and if I don't walk away right this instant...

I pull away and dash toward the exit. "Sorry, gargoyles. As much as I'd love to spend another five hours getting *completely* wrecked by you, I've got witch business to attend to."

"Witch business?" Auggie narrows his eyes. "Is that where you lock yourself in your room, get naked, light some incense, and—"

"Don't be daft," Jude says. "Witch business is where she gets naked with a bunch of other witches and everyone thanks the universe for blessing them with such perfectly suckable—"

"Your knowledge of the craft is downright *encyclopedic*, boys." I roll my eyes and laugh. "But in this case, witch business is where I meet with the girls to discuss plans for the academy. Next fall will be here before you know it!"

After all the craziness of Wintermoon, Tatiana, Laney, Fleur and I vowed to stay in touch. They've been helping me study my magic and practice the craft, and becoming damn good friends in the process.

Not long after our return, I discovered that my dad was telling the truth about the money he'd socked away for me in offshore accounts. When I first heard from his lawyer, I almost refused the windfall.

But then I thought about the last moments I had with him. His sacrifice. And I realized I could use that money for something Brian so desperately wanted, but never got the chance to accomplish.

Protecting young witches and other supernaturals who don't have anyone else to look out for them.

So, I decided I'd put it toward opening a school where witches and fae without family support—or those without families, period—can come to study their magic. To make friends. To build a community where they're celebrated for who they are, regardless of how much power they can demonstrate. Regardless of how many cauldrons full of blue goo they accidentally explode.

I want to build a place where kids can be loved *because* of who they are, not in spite of it.

When I told Tatiana and the others about my ideas, they begged to be involved. And now, just like we were in Wintermoon, we're all in this together.

The gargoyles are so proud of me—Blackmoor Capital is helping with the financing too. And I feel like Brian—the perfectly imperfect dad I never really got to know—would be proud of me too.

But most of all, *I'm* proud.

I've come a long way since that night in the bell tower when I was so, so ready to give up.

"So not only do we have to share you with each other," Draegan says now, "but now we've got witches to contend with too?"

"And ravens," Rook says, tipping his head back as Lucinda circles overhead.

"Also the taco truck guy down in Kingston?" I add. "But to be fair, that's mostly because of the tacos."

Auggie huffs. "Is that supposed to make me feel better? My tacos are unparalleled."

I grin. "Take heart, boys. You're the only ones who get to see me naked, right? And that alone is worth the price of admission, especially because... Oh, wait. On second thought, that's not... *Shoot*. That's not entirely true."

"Excuse me?" Jude asks, incredulous.

I shrug. "The girls and I sometimes practice skyclad."

"Skyclad?" he asks. "What the fuck kind of dark magic is that?"

"It just means naked. We do it outside. It helps us connect with nature, especially when there's a full moon."

He sits up fully now, his brow furrowed. "So you're telling me that you and a bunch of witches sit around drinking tea and telling fortunes and practicing all that mojo... all without clothes?"

"Sometimes, yeah. But not in the snow or anything. Oh! Unless we're at Laney's, because she has a hot tub." I laugh. "Goddess, Jude. Don't be weird."

"I'm not being weird, darling. I'm just wondering how the fuck someone becomes a witch, and when I can sign up for the class."

"Same," Auggie says. "I can bring snacks."

"Simmer down, monsters," I tease. "I'm sure you can think of plenty of ways to entertain yourselves while I'm gone."

"Doubtful," Rook says.

"Draegan? You're the disciplinarian of the operation. Help me out here."

"Sorry, love." He laughs. "You're on your own."

"Well, we're not practicing skyclad tonight," I say. "So you can stop fretting. And the moment we're done with the meeting, I'm coming *right* back home."

"To us," Jude says firmly.

"Where you belong," Draegan says. Then, in a soft, vulnerable whisper that cracks my heart wide open, "Promise me, love."

There was a time when I made promises because I thought my obedience was the only way to ensure my parents wouldn't abandon me. I made promises because I thought it would bring me friends. I made promises by giving away little pieces of myself until there was almost nothing left to keep for me.

But everything is different now.

I'm different now.

I look around at the study, at the manor, at the bare branches of the apple orchard outside. I look at my ravens. I look at the fire crackling in the hearth.

And I look at each of my gargoyles.

Home.

"Yes, my sweet gargoyles," I say. "I promise. Tonight, tomorrow, and for the rest of our immortal lives together, I will *always* come home to you."

Awwww! Is it really over? I can't believe it!

I had so much fun writing about these naughty gargoyles and their fierce little fae-witch, and I am so grateful that you came on the journey with me!

Jude fans, if you haven't already done so, you can sign up for my newsletter and receive A Gargoyle Obsessed, a free story that takes place the night Jude first meets his sweet little scarecrow in the park. This story is available in both ebook and audiobook formats (narrated by Shane East!) and can't be found anywhere else—it's an exclusive gift just for my subscribers.

Visit SarahPiperBooks.com/jude to claim your copy.

Love gargoyles and witches? Never fear! I've got another series for you!

This one features a bunch of dark and twisty monsters—including a strong, silent gargoyle shifter—who are more than ready to be tamed by their fiery witch!

The Witch's Monsters kicks off with a bang in book one, Blood and Midnight.

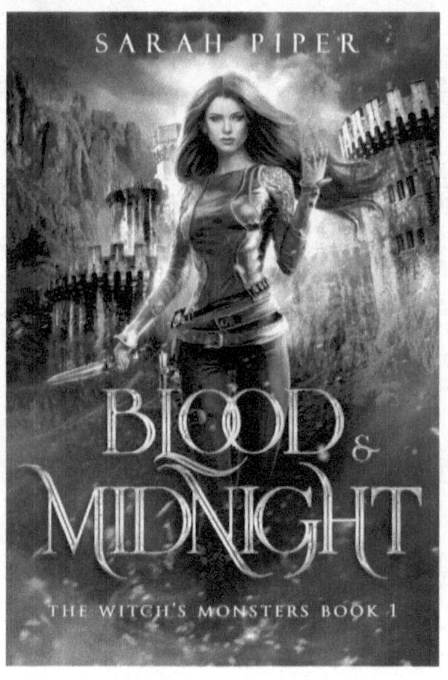

Three sexy-but-psycho monsters. One fiery, determined witch. And a high-stakes heist about to go *very* wrong...

I've made some pretty questionable choices in the name of my witchcraft—dabbling in necromancy, double-crossing vampires—but summoning the dark goddess? *That* was just plain stupid.

Now I'm in her debt, and goddesses don't exactly do payment plans. She wants the blood of the dark fae warlord of Midnight, a realm of exiles where the sun never rises and torture is a competitive sport. It's a death trap only three men have ever escaped—my newly appointed escorts.

Jax, a terrifying demon whose icy touch leaves me trembling in more ways than one. Hudson, a hulking, fiercely loyal shifter hiding secrets so painful he barely speaks. And Elian, a cocky fae prick with eyes like molten silver and a heart full of vengeance—a heart that once belonged to me.

I'll do anything to settle my debts and get back home, even if it means teaming up with my infuriating ex and the other sinfully hot psychos for the most dangerous blood heist in history.

But when it comes to the cruel fae warlord, not even my monsters can protect me...

Especially when we discover why the dark goddess *really* sent us to Midnight.

Read on for an excerpt, and grab your copy of Blood and Midnight now!

SNEAK PEEK: BLOOD AND MIDNIGHT

PROLOGUE

HALEY

There's an old adage about the difference between falling in love with a hero and falling in love with a villain. Go for the latter, it says, because a hero would ultimately sacrifice you to save the world, but a villain? He'd burn down the world just to save *you*.

Sounds pretty epic, right? And let's be honest—who doesn't love a bad boy?

The thing about villains, though... Ultimately, they're just the heroes of their own stories. Still fighting for a cause. Still trying to prove something to the world.

Trust me, I've fallen for both. And those assholes? They broke my heart every damn time.

So now I've got a new saying:

Screw the heroes and villains.

I want the *monsters*.

Dark. Vicious. Depraved. The men who slide into your

heart like a surgical blade, so sharp you don't even feel it until you're on your knees, trembling and soaked in blood.

A monster won't try to woo you with roses and chocolates, with sweet promises whispered across satin pillowcases. He'll kick down a fucking door to get to you, though. Snap a man's neck just for leering. One threat against you, and he'll tear out the guy's throat with his teeth, then kiss you with a mouth full of blood, no apologies.

A monster's got nothing to prove and nothing left to lose.

And in bed?

Damn.

He'll *own* you, pushing until he finds the very edge of your limits, then smashing right through them. And oh, how you'll *beg* him for it—beg him to break you, again and again and again. To absolutely ruin you for anything less than a life of obsession and fire.

And while the hero slays his dragons and the villain burns down the world for the woman he loves, the monster will simply hand you the matches and gasoline, step aside, and smile as you burn it down yourself.

Because all along, the monster always knew you could.

He just had to make sure you knew it too.

CHAPTER ONE

HALEY

The blood on my boots was still wet when I stepped inside.

My weapons needed a good cleaning too, but the novitiate asked me to leave the daggers and stakes at the entrance, and I obliged.

The Temple of the Dark Moon, she reminded me, was a holy place.

Right.

Appropriately chastised, I nodded and followed the swish of her long black robes across the threshold, my eyes widening as the interior came into view.

The temple had probably been beautiful once, but now it lay in ruins. Half the ceiling had caved in, and broken pillars of onyx and moonstone flanked the inner sanctuary, several of them reduced to rubble. Deep, angry gouges scored the masonry as if some feral god-beast had been locked up inside.

Everything smelled like rot and death.

What the hell happened here?

Hoping whatever it was had already been dealt with, I lowered my eyes and quickened the pace.

"Yours?" the novitiate asked from beneath her dark hood, and I knew she meant the blood I'd tracked across the chipped marble floor. I wondered if she'd be the one mopping it up later or if that would be my job now—one of the many menial tasks the Goddess surely had in store for me.

"No." I scraped the toe of my boot along the floor and left another smear, which was about all the acknowledgment the previous owner of the blood deserved. "Listen, I'm sorry about the mess, but I was summoned here kind of last-minute and I didn't really have time to... I mean... Should I bathe before I meet her?" I dragged the back of my hand across my forehead, skin gritty with dirt and sweat and probably more blood. "Maybe do a purifying juice cleanse or... something?"

With a serene smile, the novitiate lowered her hood and said, "The Goddess Melantha does not require purity of body. Only purity of intent."

She looked younger than I expected—only a teenager—and she wasn't a witch. Just a regular human girl. I wondered what she'd done to end up a servant in the realm of the Dark Goddess, a place you couldn't even access without being summoned by the deity herself, then portaled in by her magick. Ruined or not, this temple was more than just a holy place—it existed in a liminal space all its own, nothing but stars and darkness as far as the eye could see.

Didn't the girl have parents? Friends? *Someone* missing her on the other side?

A sharp pain lanced my heart, but I breathed through it. I had no idea how long the girl had been here, but this was merely day one for me, and I had a long road ahead. I needed to stay grounded. Committed.

"How will she know my intentions are pure?" I asked. "Is there a test?"

"Fear not, Daughter of Darkwinter. I'm certain Her Holiness will be quite impressed with your offering."

Ignoring the Darkwinter bit, I forced a smile and scratched the back of my neck, sneaking a covert whiff of my armpit.

Let's hope her Holiness is impressed with Eau de Urban Warfare, because that's about all I'm offering at the moment...

"Come. She's expecting you." Still wearing a look of pure serenity, she continued on through a doorway at the back of the temple sanctuary, gesturing for me to follow.

The antechamber was small and intimate, much less imposing than the main temple. The warm glow of hundreds of candles flickered across plain mud walls and a low ceiling, the ground nothing but bare earth. My boots sank into it with every step, and as the scents of candle wax and dirt washed over me, I let out a sigh of relief.

This room, at least, had remained untouched by whatever monster had gone batshit crazy in the sanctuary.

My eyes adjusted to the candlelight, my gaze drifting to the stone altar in the center of the room—a large slab covered in fresh flowers and bowls of fruit, ringed by votive candles in red glass orbs.

Offerings, I assumed. For the...

Oh, shit.

I gasped as I finally spotted the boy, no more than ten or eleven, lying in repose on the altar. His skin was milk-white, the robe they'd dressed him in much too large, as if it was borrowed in haste from someone much older.

Someone much closer to death than this child should've been.

"How did he pass?" I whispered.

"He didn't." The novitiate frowned. "Melantha's son is very much alive."

"Her *son*?" I couldn't hide my shock. The Dark Goddess was tens of thousands of years old—probably older. Lots of witches prayed to her, worshipped her, wrote volumes about her history and magick. I'd never once heard of a child. "How long has he been like this?"

"Six months." She sighed, running her fingers through the sweep of dark hair across his forehead. "He was cursed by a dark fae warlord called Keradoc. A vicious monster who punishes children for the sins of their parents."

An icy shiver ran down my spine. Dark fae were power-ful, but Melantha was a dark *goddess. The* dark goddess. How could a fae warlord have gotten anywhere *near* her child?

And what sin could she have committed to provoke such terrible retribution?

"He's alive," the novitiate continued, "but his soul is trapped in moonglass." She retrieved a small wooden chest from the offerings at his side, opening it to reveal a glass-like sphere as delicate as a soap bubble. At her gentle touch, it glowed with a bright, pearlescent sheen. "It's made from pure moonlight, cast with dark fae magick that's been banned for thousands of years."

"Because it's a prison," I said, disgust churning inside. It wasn't the first time I'd encountered moonglass. According to legend, the very first fae created it by deceiving the moon into lending the fae her light, then forging the magickal globes to trap the souls of their enemies. Eventually, they'd release those souls into the most hostile fae realms, sentencing them to an eternity of torment. "How did this happen?"

She met my eyes, but her serene smile was gone, replaced now with a look of grim determination. "What matters, Daughter of Darkwinter, is that you alone can free him."

"Me? But... how?"

"Breaking the curse requires the blood of the one who cast it."

"Keradoc. Of course." I blew out a breath, the tightness in my muscles loosening as the pieces clicked into place. I was a blood witch—a damned good one at that. Melantha needed me to do some sort of spell to help the child. "So, when do we start?"

"You will travel to his realm as soon as possible," she replied. "Once you've extracted the blood, you'll return to the Temple of the Dark Moon to perform the spell with Melantha, breaking the curse and—"

"Wait. Did you just..." I blinked at her, my mind racing to keep up. "You don't have his blood? Then how can I do the spell?"

"As I said, once you return to the Temple—"

"Her Holiness expects me to hunt this guy down? Some psychotic warlord from a realm I've never been to?"

She arched an eyebrow, as if in warning. "Her Holiness granted you untold strength and power in your time of need, for which you so eagerly pledged your service."

Tension simmered in the air as she glared at me, making my skin hot and itchy.

"I know. It's just..." I took a breath, trying to regroup. Who *was* this girl, anyway? Where were the other novitiates? Melantha's soldiers? "Forgive me, but when Her Holiness summoned me, I was under the impression I'd be meeting with her elite guard."

"Elite? Hardly." A bitter laugh rang out through the small chamber. "No honor among them. No fortitude. I'm sorry, but the Guard of the Dark Moon is no more."

A prickle of unease tingled at the back of my mind. What the hell did "no more" mean?

Fired? Furloughed? Executed?

Crushed to death by falling pillars?

None of this made any sense.

I paced before the altar, my sudden movement snuffing out a few of the votives. "The guards are gone, so now it's on *me* to assassinate some creepy warlord?"

"Not assassinate, no. If Keradoc dies before we perform the spell, the blood will be useless." She grabbed a taper candle and touched it to one of the votives, reigniting the flame. "You must retrieve the blood without harming him —without so much as *alerting* him—or all will be for naught."

"Are you serious? You just said he's a warlord!"

"And you're a formidable blood witch, are you not? One with access to spells and magick you're only just beginning to tap into."

"I'm good at what I do, sure. But dark fae warlords? I'm not... Look, you seem... knowledgeable. Clearly, you're fond of the boy." I smiled, fighting to keep the desperation from my voice. "Maybe you should go instead? I'll stay here and keep an eye on things until you get back." I took the taper from her hand and lit the remaining votives. "See? Already getting the hang of it."

She pinched one of the flames between her thumb and forefinger, the frustration in her eyes finally boiling over. "One candle remains unlit to honor the darkness that exists in all of us, without which we can never know the light."

"Right." I raised my hands in surrender. "I should've known that, but I didn't. That's what I'm trying to tell you.

I'm not the witch for the job. I'll do anything else she asks of me, but—"

"*This* is the quest the Goddess has set out for you," she snapped. The girl was unraveling, her eyes blazing, her voice nearly trembling. "Are you reneging on your sacred vow?"

"No, of course not. I just think we should look at all the options. I'm sure if we put our heads together, we can—"

"How *dare* you question the will of the Goddess!" she bellowed, the force of it making the ground rumble. Her eyes turned a fiery red, two hot embers smoldering in a shadow-dark face. Flames crackled suddenly at her feet, the inferno rising higher and higher until she was completely engulfed.

The mud walls cracked and bubbled around us, and I watched in mute horror as her robes burned away to reveal a body as black as the night sky, pale white serpents slithering around her thighs and torso. Her limbs elongated before my eyes, twisting like those of an ancient tree, hands and feet curling into monstrous talons. Two massive black wings burst from her back and smashed through the walls of the antechamber, each feather dripping with blood.

The altar remained untouched, the boy undisturbed.

I stumbled backward, my heart slamming against my ribs.

The novitiate.

All along, it was her. Melantha.

And this was her true form. Dark and magnificent. Hideous and terrifying.

I dropped to my knees, half-tripping, half awed, and bowed my head. "Forgive me, Your Holiness. I was wrong to question you."

Sharp claws pierced the underside of my chin, forcing me to look up and meet her fearsome gaze. I blinked through the pain, ignoring the warm blood trickling down my neck.

"Daughter of Darkwinter," she said, her voice echoing across the night like a death knell. "If you value the lives of the sisters you fought so bravely to protect in Blackmoon Bay, you *will* achieve this task. By blood and by blade, as you have promised."

By blood and by blade.

The words of my spell echoed as clearly as they had the night I'd first spoken them.

> *Blood of hell, blood of night*
> *I call on the darkness to show us the light*
> *May evil and malice and violence intended*
> *Return to its hosts uprooted, upended*
> *Dark Goddess I bend, Dark Goddess I bow*
> *Hear my petition, and thusly I vow*
> *My service is yours, by blood and by blade*
> *Until my last breath shall deem it unmade.*

That night, my allies and I—my sisters among them— had been trapped in a prison compound hidden in the Olympic National Forest. We'd managed to free the prisoners—dozens of witches and other supernaturals captured by human hunters and the corrupt fae they were working for—but soon our enemies surrounded us, outgunning us four to one. They were hybrids—nearly unstoppable beasts with the combined powers of vampires, shifters, and genetically altered super-monsters we couldn't even identify.

Even with our own formidable team of supernatural heavy-hitters, there was no way we could've survived their relentless attack.

In a last, desperate move, I petitioned Melantha for the strength and magick to turn the tides. She answered my call at once, and thanks to her, we earned our victory—first retaking the compound, then finishing the job last night at the Battle of Blackmoon Bay.

The battle for our lives and our home. For everything we held dear.

I glanced down at my boots, the last of the blood soaking into the dirt, along with any hope I had of avoiding this disastrous mission.

If I refused her, everything I was able to accomplish through the spell would be undone. The city of Blackmoon Bay would fall. My sisters—the family I'd only just discovered—would die. And everything we'd fought so hard to save would just...

It would end.

A surge of renewed strength shot through my limbs, my blood simmering with magick. *My* magick.

"My service is yours," I said now, repeating the vow I'd

made that night. "By blood and by blade. Until my last breath shall deem it unmade."

"Rise, Daughter of Darkwinter."

I got to my feet and met her gaze once more, hoping like hell we were done with the Big Goddess Energy show. I'd seen enough of her scary magnificence to fill my nightmares for the next decade, thanks.

Her dark wings fluttered in the breeze, and the same rot and ruin I'd smelled in the sanctuary assaulted my senses. I tried not to recoil.

"Are you prepared to accept this task?" she asked. "To see it through by any means necessary?"

"I am," I said firmly. I was in it to win it now, no going back. With what I hoped was a confident smile, I asked, "What must I do?"

Melantha extended her arms. One claw held my weapons. The other clutched a glass vial about the size of a tube of lipstick.

After re-securing my stakes and blades, I took the vial and peered inside. Magick swirled beneath the glass, red smoke shot through with threads of black and gold. It was oddly mesmerizing.

"Keradoc dwells in the dark fae realm of Midnight," she said. "This portal spell will take you there, but you won't survive it alone. There's a man in your home realm—also fae—one rumored to have escaped Midnight alive. You must ask for his assistance."

My heart stalled. All the confidence I'd conjured up

evaporated in an instant.

The ground spun out from beneath my feet, and I fell back to my knees, my lungs struggling to suck in air.

Deep inside, beneath all the magick and fire, behind all the parts of myself I'd sharpened into weapons and hardened into shields, a tiny box lay hidden, bolted with iron chains and encased in cement. That box held my darkest, most private pain. All the ghosts that had the power to eat through my very soul.

I'd sealed them away years ago, vowing to never open that box again, no matter how often it called to me. And though it still rattled inside on occasion, for the most part, I'd kept it on strict lockdown.

Until now.

The dark fae realm of Midnight... One rumored to have escaped... Ask for his assistance...

Her words were the bolt-cutters on those iron chains, unleashing all the pain I'd so diligently buried. It seeped into my heart, burning it like hot acid, taunting me from across the long years as if no time had passed at all.

Midnight. The most treacherous realm in the universe, controlled by the darkest of the dark fae. A place where the sun never rose and so much blood had been spilled upon its war-torn lands, the lakes and rivers ran red. Melantha was right—there was no way I'd survive it alone.

And the fae who had?

There was no way I'd survive *him*, either.

Not again.

"I will return you to the mortal plane," the Goddess continued, as if I wasn't falling apart before her eyes. "To the city of—"

"New Orleans," I whispered, and she nodded, sealing my fate.

A tear slipped down my cheek.

New Orleans. The one place I swore I'd never, ever go. A place that terrified me even more than Midnight.

No, not because of the ghosts that haunted the city's many cemeteries and historic landmarks.

Because of the ghosts that haunted my heart. The ones she'd just set loose.

"And this... this *fae*," I said, still unable to speak his name out loud, even after all these years. "If he refuses to help me?"

Her black lips twisted into a cruel grin, her wings spreading to their full, terrifying span. The ground rumbled beneath her feet, but instead of flames, skulls rose from the dirt, a dead army blooming at her command.

Behind me, a portal opened, ready to ferry me to New Orleans.

To him.

"Convince him, Darkwinter," Melantha hissed. "Or the ones you claim to love will suffer the consequences of your failure."

I nodded and took a deep breath.

Fought off an onslaught of memories—strong hands sliding into my hair. Eyes the color of molten silver.

Promises whispered, promises broken. The salty taste of tears and the dull ache of wounds that never fully healed.

I took a step backward, then another.

Closed my eyes.

And tumbled, ass over teakettle, into my own private hell.

CHAPTER TWO

HALEY

Two years. That's how long I'd spent convincing myself this place didn't exist. Convincing myself that Elian's return from captivity in Midnight and the subsequent launching of a whole new life in New Orleans—one that *didn't* include me—was just a rumor.

Now, standing before the entrance to his exclusive French Quarter club, I could no longer deny the truth.

Saints and Sinners, the sign read. To humans, it was just another abandoned cathedral with blown-out windows and crumbling spires, complete with a hulking gargoyle perched above the main archway. But for those of us who could see past the illusion of the fae glamour, a set of glowing silver doors awaited—an invitation I still couldn't bring myself to answer.

There were no bouncers or velvet ropes, no demands for the secret password. Just the ancient gargoyle and the doors and a small plaque reminding me this was hallowed ground, so could I please check my weapons at the armory inside the narthex?

I practically snorted. *Fat fucking chance.*

This was no Temple of the Dark Moon. Just because Elian's den of supernatural sin was housed in an old church, that didn't make it hallowed ground any more than it made him a priest.

No one showed up in a place like this looking for redemption, anyway. They showed up looking for an escape. Or in my case—to beg.

Damn it. The thought of even *facing* that prick again—let alone asking him for help—tied me up in knots. But what choice did I have? My sisters' lives depended on me seeing this all the way through, and Elian truly was my best shot at surviving the horrors of Midnight. Probably my *only* shot.

So, decked out in a new lace dress the color of the stars and thigh-high leather boots I'd picked out just to make him suffer, strapped from hip to ankle with weapons that would finish the job if the outfit failed, I pushed open the doors and stepped inside. And immediately fell under its spell.

Everything about the place was designed to hypnotize, from the rich, blood-red walls to the restored stained-glass windows that pulsed with magick. Suspended in gilded cages from the ceiling, painted fae couples performed dances so erotic, I was already wishing for a cold shower. Semi-private candlelit alcoves lined both sides of the former cathedral, and the pews had been removed from the nave, the flooring replaced with black marble that glittered with tiny silver points. It looked as if the club's many revelers were dancing across the night sky.

I was relieved not to spot Elian among them. Despite the fever-inducing performances of the fae dancers, five years' worth of resentment and abandonment issues still simmered inside, and one look into his entrancing silver eyes would set it all ablaze.

Not a fire I wanted to face while sober.

Chin raised, shoulders squared, I beelined for the bar and slid into an empty barstool at the end, trying to spot any potential threats. Hunters were always my first concern, but we'd taken a pretty big bite out of their organization during the Battle at Blackmoon Bay. Those who remained loyal to their fucked-up cause would likely be licking their wounds for a good long while.

Here at Saints and Sinners, vampires and fae made up the majority of the clientele, all of them rich, well-dressed, and predatory. The fae were even more refined than the bloodsuckers, their otherworldly beauty as mesmerizing as it was dangerous.

The bartender, though... He didn't fit the profile. Demon. Rough around the edges. A head of messy, jet-black hair and a mouth so sultry it was almost a crime to look at. He wore a white dress shirt and dark slacks but no tie, his sleeves rolled up to reveal muscular forearms mapped with scars.

My own scars practically tingled in response.

As he finished up with one of his vampire customers, I studied him. Another sexy scar ran the full length of his face, slicing through his eyebrow and ending in the dark stubble along his jaw. A black patch covered the injured eye.

When he finally made his way over to me, he nodded and set a coaster on the bar, but didn't smile or say hello. Just waited, arms crossed over his broad chest, one blue eye glowering at me like he was daring me to ask about the missing one.

What I *really* wanted to ask was what time he got off work and how soon he'd like to get started on becoming my next ex-boyfriend, but...

"Drinking or leaving, new girl?" he asked, smooth and cold as ice. "You're holding up the line."

I took a deep breath, trying to re-focus on the mission.

Midnight.

Begging.

Elian.

"Drinking. Definitely drinking. I'll have... I don't know." I offered a flirty smile. "Whatever you think I'll like."

He leaned in close, his demonic scent enveloping me. It reminded me of the smoke that lingered in your hair when you spent too much time by the fire, a hint of lemon simmering beneath it, and holy *hell* did I want to jump across the bar and—

"I need a bit more to go on," he said, then shot me an

icy grin to match his voice. "If it's not too much trouble for you."

"Fine. Let's do something with a kick, but nothing boring or predictable. That rules out whisky, vodka, and tequila. I'm not a huge fan of bubbles either, and I don't like anything too milky. Sweet's good, but not *too* sweet, and a little fruit is fine, but nothing *super* fruity, unless it's—"

"Sorry I asked." Without waiting for me to finish, he wiped his hands on the towel draped over his shoulder, selected a martini glass from the rack overhead, and turned toward the multi-colored bottles lined up behind him.

Before I could offer any more helpful pointers, a wave of vertigo hit, alerting me to the presence of a vampire. One getting way too close and personal.

"Did it hurt?" A husky voice breathed in my ear.

I turned to meet his gaze, resting bitch face locked and loaded. "Excuse me?"

"When you fell from Heaven?" He spread his arms and grinned as if I might find the whole package so charming I'd leap into his embrace, wrap my thighs around him, and ride him all the way home.

"Not as much as it did when they cut off my horns and tail," I said. "Anyway, I'm all set here, so... Have a good night."

"Can I at least buy you a drink, beautiful?"

"No, thank you. I'm not interested."

His face fell, then twisted into a scowl. "You don't have to be such a bitch."

"Actually, I do. Because otherwise bloodsuckers like you assume a smile or a kind word is a full-on invitation to Pussytown, and I promise you, friend. *That's* an exclusive ticket."

"Check the guest list again." He reached over and touched my hair, bringing a lock to his lips before dropping his hand to my thigh and giving it a possessive squeeze. "Pretty sure I'm on it."

Pretty sure you're going to regret touching me, but ooh-kay...

"Well, since you're so persistent," I cooed, "maybe I *should* check." With a faux-seductive smile, I slid my fingers into the top of my boot, seeking that cold, comforting piece of wood I never left home without.

One minute, the hawthorn stake was minding its own business in the boot holster. The next, it was jammed into the back of the fucker's hand.

Such was the beauty of my sharp and pointy friend.

He jerked back with a howl, the hawthorn poison already paralyzing his fingers. I yanked the stake free, spun it in my palm, and shoved it against his crotch, stopping just short of inflicting a more serious injury.

"Touch me again, bloodsucker," I hissed, "and your hand won't be the only thing going limp."

"Go... go fuck yourself, bitch."

"I'd return the sentiment, but I'm pretty sure that hand won't be up for the job any time soon." I laughed. "Get it? Hand? Job?"

He bared his fangs, then stumbled away like a wounded, dejected bird.

"First drink is on me," the bartender said. "That was the best thing I've seen in months."

I reached forward and yanked the towel off his shoulder, then wiped the blood from my stake. "Thanks for the assist, demon."

"You had it handled. Be grateful I don't toss your ass out for smuggling in that stake."

"This teeny tiny little thing?" I finished cleaning it off, then slipped it back into the holster. "It's not like it was going to kill him."

Wooden stakes could poison the fuckers—hawthorn was especially good at interfering with their healing abilities, and a well-placed stake to the chest would knock them out for hours—but still, that was just a temporary fix. Killing vampires required decapitation or burning, and I wasn't about to ruin my new outfit with all *that* mess.

"In any case, best not to draw too much attention." The bartender set down the martini glass, now brimming with pale amber liquid. A single mint leaf floated on top.

"What is it?"

The barest hint of a smile quirked his lips. "It's called a Fallen Angel."

It was the smile that saved him. *Asshole.*

Hiding my return grin behind the rim of the glass, I took a sip, then another.

Damn, that Fallen Angel concoction was good—good

enough to savor over a long conversation laced with innuendo. A conversation that on any other night might've led to a kiss and maybe even an orgasm or two.

But tonight?

I tipped back the glass and chugged it all down. Then, before I could talk myself out of it, I said, "I'm looking for Elian."

CHAPTER THREE

HALEY

I blew out a breath, seriously impressed with my ability to say the bastard's name without crying and/or breaking something.

Progress!

The sexy bartender, however, was *not* impressed. Quite the opposite, actually.

"Elian," he said flatly, folding his arms over his chest again, and I swear the temperature dropped ten degrees.

It didn't feel like jealousy. Aside from a little teasing, he wasn't exactly putting out any "let's take this back to my place" vibes. So why did he clam up when I asked about Elian?

"Is he in tonight?" I pressed.

The guy sized me up with his singularly intense blue eye, which apparently found me lacking. When his gaze finally made its way back to mine, he scowled as if I'd just threatened *his* dick with the stake. "Who the *fuck* wants to know?"

"Pro-tip, buddy. Usually, when a person straight-up tells you they're looking for someone? Dead giveaway right there."

Glaring. He had it down to a science. The eye, the ticking jaw muscle, the flex of those pin-me-down forearms. I tried to glare right back at him, but when it came to squaring off with intimidating, hot-as-hell demons, I was out of practice. "You *do* realize the size of your tip is inversely proportional to your bullshit, right?"

"What do you want with... *Elian?*" His lip curled when he said the name—a reaction I understood all too well.

"I need to speak with him. It's private and it's important. So if you could just fix me another drink for the road and point me in the right direction, I'll gladly—"

"Are you a dancer?"

A dancer? Was this demon for real?

I reached for my stake again. It wouldn't take much. I could probably put it through his good eye before another insult had time to fall out of that sexy mouth.

The thought calmed me almost as much as the booze.

"I'm more of a stabby, pokey kinda girl," I said. "With a little magick thrown in for fun."

"Well, we're all set on security detail and spell casters, so unless you can work that stabby, pokey bit into a cage dance, we're not hiring."

"You think I'm here about a job?"

"Not sure I care enough to give it much more thought, honestly." He grinned, but I could tell he didn't mean it. Something about all this had gotten under his skin. Something about Elian.

I opened my mouth to push him on it, but before I could utter another word, he flicked his hand to shoo me away, already turning to the next customer.

"Enjoy your evening, *angel*," he said over his shoulder.

Enjoy my *evening*? It'd taken me two years and the threats of a scary-ass goddess to work up the nerve to set foot in this city, a killer outfit to walk through those silver doors, and a good dose of booze just to say Elian's name without a string of curses attached. And this demon thought I was *done*? I was on a hot streak—no way was I bowing out now.

I waited until he finished up with his other customers, then tapped my empty glass. "Still needing that second drink, friend."

He watched me for a beat, then muttered something inaudible before clearing away the empty glass and reaching for another. "Shall I start a tab, then?"

"I'm not staying long enough for that." I opened up the black hole otherwise known as my purse, emptying its contents onto the bar as I searched for my money.

Cell phone, lipstick, lip gloss, a vial of shifter blood. Hand sanitizer, emergency tampons, emergency black tourmaline, breath mints.

Three vampire fangs, black eyeliner, a stun potion left-over from the Blackmoon Bay fight, Melantha's portal spell, a hair tie, and...

Aha! Sweet, shiny credit card of questionable remaining balance. After today's shopping spree in the Big Easy, I wasn't too sure how much farther it would get me, but hey. Hope sprang eternal.

"Let's give this one a whirl." I held out the card, but the demon didn't take it.

His gaze was on the glass vial from the goddess, utterly transfixed. The blood-red smoke roiled inside, its black and gold threads shimmering.

He glanced up at me again, and I braced for another argument. A brush-off. Anything but what flashed through that stone-cold eye.

Recognition.

The demon *knew* that particular magick. Which meant... *Holy shit.* Had he been to Midnight too? Was that how he knew Elian?

He reached across the bar and covered the vial with his hand, his voice turning dark. "Put it out of sight. Now."

I did as he asked, too stunned to do anything else.

"Wait here," he said in that same deadly tone. "Do *not* leave this bar."

"Okay, but what about my—" *Damn.* He was already gone. "Drink," I said with a sigh. I was just about to hop behind the bar and make something myself when the vertigo hit me again, this wave so strong it nearly knocked me off my barstool. I fisted my stake and palmed the stun potion, slowly turning to face the newcomers—three of them this time.

My wounded bird was flanked by two of his friends, each one more despicable than the last. Whatever supernatural genetics made most vampires hot as fuck and impossible to resist? Clearly skipped this lot.

A quick scan of my surroundings and my heart sunk. No sign of the demon, and the other patrons in the vicinity were too wrapped up in their own flirtations and petty skirmishes to pay any attention to mine. *Shit*.

"Sorry, boys," I said as the vampires crowded in close. "You really *aren't* on the guest list."

"It's not pussy we're after tonight, witch," my original stalker said, ever the romantic. His hand hung limp at his side, the skin black and blistering. "We're here for—"

I shoved the stake into his chest, taking him down for the count, then hurled the stun potion at the second vamp's feet. It exploded in a bright yellow starburst, freezing him on contact, but the third one wasn't close enough to the blast to feel its effects. I tried to reach for one of my daggers, but he was too fast, too strong, and too smart.

He was on me in a heartbeat, hauling me out of the stool and locking me in a vise grip, my back against his chest.

"Got any more tricks, witch?" he growled in my ear.

I struggled against his hold, but it was no use. My arms were pinned at my sides, my feet no longer touching the ground, and I had maybe a minute before the stun potion wore off on the other vamp. "Let me go and I'll show you all *sorts* of magick."

"I don't think so, pretty girl." With a sick groan of pleasure, he clamped down hard on my neck, fangs piercing the skin. Before I could even cry out, he'd drained enough blood to make my world spin.

I fought to remain conscious, to reach the dagger in my boot, to do something other than let this asshole finish me off. The temporarily stunned vamp was already on his feet again, stumbling toward me with rage in his eyes, fangs bared, mouth practically foaming for a taste...

Someone slammed into us from behind, breaking me out of my captor's relentless hold and knocking me to the ground as another man—the bartender, I realized—staked my two attackers in quick succession.

Guess I'm not the only one good with the stabby, pokey bit...

I caught his gaze and managed a quick smile of thanks, then turned my attention to the guy who'd knocked me down.

The *fae* who'd knocked me down. Half-vampire too, I realized, dressed in a three-piece black Nehru suit that perfectly hugged his leanly muscled frame.

My mind spun. *How was this possible?*

He was partially on top of me from the fall, one hand cradling the back of my head, lips muttering my name like a prayer. His long hair brushed across my face, a fall of silver waves and intricate braids I itched to run my fingers through.

Only the strongest magick could erase time, and there was no magick more powerful than scent for yanking you right back into the past. It washed over me like a dark curse —the particular mix of bergamot and rain that could only belong to him.

Butterflies danced through my insides, my heartbeat quickening. When I finally found the courage to meet his eyes, my breath hitched, and not just because his weight was half-crushing my lungs.

Five years ago, he walked out of my life without so much as a goodbye... and crushed my fucking heart.

"Elian," I whispered. Accidentally. *Shit.*

His molten silver gaze swept down to my lips, then back to my eyes. A cocky grin curved his mouth, tugging slightly higher on the left.

It did things to me, that crooked grin. Always had. Bad things. Stupid things. And before I knew it, I was grinning right back at him.

Elian brushed his thumb across my lower lip, eyes sparkling, his touch making me shiver. "Still dreaming of me, little sparrow?"

"I am," I admitted.

Then, just to prove it, I did something I'd been *dreaming* about every day for the last five years.

I punched that sexy, silver-eyed fae-hole right in the mouth.

Ready for more of Haley and her smokin' hot monsters? Grab your copy of Blood and Midnight now!

LOOKING FOR AUDIOBOOKS?

A New Way to Get Your Audio Fix...

Audiobook lovers, you can now buy audiobooks directly from my author store at **SarahPiperBooks.com/shop** for early access and huge savings!

The books will still be available on other retailers like Audible and Apple, but buying direct means you can:

• **Save big.** Author store prices are 30-60% off retail prices.

• **Be the first to listen.** New releases will typically be available for direct buy for advanced release 1-2 weeks before they hit other retailers.

• **Directly support your favorite authors and narrators.** Your support means the world to me, and helps ensure I can continue to partner with the best narrators in the industry to bring these stories to life!

Visit SarahPiperBooks.com/shop to get started!

Sarah Piper is a witchy, Tarot-card-slinging paranormal romance and urban fantasy author. Through her signature brew of dark magic, heart-pounding suspense, and steamy romance, Sarah promises a sexy, supernatural escape into a world where the magic is real, the monsters are sinfully hot, and the witches always get their magically-ever-afters.

Readers have dubbed her work "super sexy," "imaginative and original," "off-the-walls good," and "delightfully wicked in the best ways," a quote Sarah hopes will appear on her tombstone.

Originally from New York, Sarah now makes her home in northern Colorado with her husband (though that changes frequently) (the location, not the husband), where she spends her days sleeping like a vampire and her nights writing books, casting spells, gazing at the moon, playing with her ever-expanding collection of Tarot cards, binge-watching Supernatural (Team Dean!), and obsessing over the best way to brew a cup of tea.

You can find her online at SarahPiperBooks.com, on TikTok at @sarahpiperbooks, and in her Facebook readers group at Sarah Piper's Sassy Witches! If you're sassy, or if you need a little *more* sass in your life, or if you need more Dean Winchester gifs in your life (who doesn't?), come hang out!